REDEEMING TRACE

BOOKS BY TOM SCHRECK

The Duffy Dombrowski Mysteries
On the Ropes
TKO
Out Cold
The Vegas Knockout
The Ten Count

Getting Dunn
Redeeming Chase

Join "Duffy's Fight Club" for free short thrillers, an audio book, Tom's magazine work, a video on judging boxing, Tom's appearance on "Copy Cat Killers" and Rocky the blood hound singing "My Way." TomSchreck.com.

TOM SCHRECK

REDEEMING TRACE

Down & Out Books
3959 Van Dyke Road, Suite 265
Lutz, FL 33558
DownAndOutBooks.com

Cover design by Pixelstudio

ISBN: 1-64396-312-0
ISBN-13: 978-1-64396-312-9

For Reed Farrel Coleman.
Thanks for the calls.
The Elvis collection is all yours…

PROLOGUE

They felt odd in the black, ninja-style suits. It seemed over-the-top and silly, almost nerdy, superhero cosplay. Still, it was their trademark, what they wore, and effectively concealed their identities. That was crucial; if it came out who they were, it would be a disaster.

Allied Security Systems was a logical target. They specialized in high-tech security systems, but their most profitable product was the "Virtual Fence." It was all part of the government's plan to secure the border. The Virtual Wall was slated to include actual fencing, vehicle barriers, radar, satellite phones, computer-equipped border control devices, underground sensors, and 100-foot camera towers. The towers were outfitted with high-powered cameras that could detect anyone trying to cross the virtual wall for 10 miles. Whenever activity occurred by the virtual wall, information was transmitted to the Border Patrol Office, who would notify agents in the field.

Allied specialized in the ultra-hi-tech radar, sensors, and cameras at the heart of the system. Anti-immigration politicians touted it as the answer to all the political jockeying and a viable solution to keeping the immigrants out. Allied was a perfect first target, and it would not only incapacitate this government's initiative for a long while, but it would also send the desired message that the group wanted. Right now, the message was more important than anything else.

There were six of them in the white Econoline van, each with clearly defined duties, timelines, and contingency plans. All were armed with suppressed M4s and 9mms for sidearms, a redundancy that would probably not be necessary if things went as planned. The Colt M4 was quieter than the AK 47, making more of a "Pop, Pop." They knew to limit their firing to one or two surgical shots. The 47 would shake the entire area and call a lot of unnecessary attention, especially if they let loose with an undisciplined volley. The plan's execution had been practiced, rehearsed, and visualized to minimize anything that would slow it down or interfere with its success. The first two would neutralize the Allied guards at the security gate. This was an essential first step and would cause the entire operation to fail if not completed correctly. It may have been much to do about nothing, but today's private security guards varied in their skill and commitments. An industry like Allied could have hired real ex-military, even ex-special forces and, if that were the case, then the opposing forces' skills would be closely matched. It was what made all of this a risk.

When they pulled up, the Allied security proved a not-worthy challenge. A single guard emerged from the hut before any of them left the van. He was overweight and barely alert, and the short burst from the automatic weapon left him in a bloody heap on the threshold. A second guard followed at the building entrance, this one with a firearm that was probably a 9mm. He met a similar fate, and the team was in.

The first two team members stepped over the guard and scouted the hallways for threats, while the other four followed, carrying the equipment. The equipment, specifically chosen for its efficiency and size, was packed neatly in duffel bags. The strategic packing enabled them to access the items in order and eliminated any confusion that might result in the heat of the moment or under the stress of adversity.

With three carrying weapons and three carrying the duffel bags, the team headed through the hallways following the building layout they had committed to memory. The alarms were almost deafening, but they had anticipated that, and it did not slow them. When they came around the second corner, three employees were in the hallway arguing. The three men looked like typical middle management types with their horned rimmed glasses, khakis, and Allied yellow golf shirts. Instinctively, two of them jumped back as the team ran by, but one of them, a big athletic guy, grabbed at one of the team members carrying a duffel. It lasted about three seconds until he was shot by the lead gunner in the back of the head.

Everything was still on a schedule, and the plans could not be delayed. The team reached the double security doors that sealed the manufacturing plant entrance, and a quick burst from the M4 blew the doors open. From there, there was a flurry of activity, unzipping the duffels, arming the explosives, and placing them around the plant. They knew where the charges should go, and they were preset to adhere to the exact right equipment to bring down the entire Allied operation for the maximum amount of time. In less than three minutes, everything was in place, the bags were zipped, and they were headed back out the front door.

They knew from a study of the plant's emergency preparedness plans that the rest of the employees would have left the building by now and gathered at the company picnic pavilion. The local police would be on their way, but they also knew from studying Allied's drill reports that it took the police between six and eight and half minutes for them to arrive. That gave them four and a half minutes. They were ahead of schedule.

It was time to leave. They would set off the charges remotely from the van so a cascading chain would level the plant and destroy the production capabilities. The cascading explosions were designed to allow them to drive away safely while still having the power to maximize destruction. The human casualties were a necessary part of the plan, not a goal, but they knew that they would garner attention for better or worse.

The first seven team members ran through the front doors at full speed. The last member had a final task before they left the grounds. He pulled out the preformed wooden stencil and placed it at the entryway sidewalk's center. He uncapped the black spray paint and took no more than five seconds to color it in. He then joined the rest of the group in the Econoline.

The Allied Security Systems sidewalk was now branded with black spray paint with a clenched fist and a single word in all-caps.

ANTIFA.

CHAPTER ONE

"Eddie, a woman got beheaded," I said.

"Yup, lost her head. A damn shame," Eddie Hutchins said and sipped his coffee. He was overdoing it. He always overdid it. He let out a coffee commercial "Ahhh..."

I didn't say anything. I just kept quiet. It is called a therapeutic silence, and it is supposed to give the client time to think, reflect and feel. I was doing it at this precise moment because Eddie baffled me. I didn't know what to say to him, and it happened every week during his required check-in. Eddie liked this game; he liked how he could take control back.

He took another sip of coffee. He brought it in his University of Southern California mug—I think on purpose because he knew I went to Notre Dame. I wasn't a huge football guy but I kind of resented him flaunting a rival because he thought it would annoy me. I made eye contact with him. Go Irish! And all of that.

He nodded, gave me a pleasant smile, and took another sip of coffee. His smile was to let me know he could hang out and deal with the awkwardness indefinitely.

"Eddie, science tells us that when agents are exposed to repeated viewings of disturbing acts, it is important to process what emotions come up. We've been contracted with the CIA to provide this service. Since we've been checking in, you've studied an eight-year-old girl getting raped, a grandmother getting shot at point-blank range, and the beheading of a journalist."

I did my best not to let any frustration enter my voice. I don't think it worked.

"You don't have anything to share with me?" I asked but tried not to plead.

He was a big guy. Probably 6'2" with a dark African American complexion. His hairline was receding a bit, and the temples had some gray, despite being in his early forties. He had the build of a good division three linebacker who stopped working out fifteen years ago. His speckled mustache gave him some character, and he smelled a little bit of Old Spice.

He crossed his legs and slumped a little bit, probably to let me know he was super comfortable. His defiance was subtle. Out and out defiance could get written up and reported. Eddie knew not to go that far.

"Dr. Trace," I had asked him repeatedly to call me Trace. This was his way of giving me distance. "These things that happened didn't happen to me. They happened to the poor people in the videos. I know the difference."

I paused a beat.

"You're human. You're flesh and blood. What feelings come up for you?" I asked, drawing on his minute self-disclosure.

He shrugged. He raised his eyebrows.

"I watch it. I analyze what they want me to look for. I write it down, and I complete my report. At the end of the day, I hit golf balls," he said. "Now *there's* something that pisses me off. I got a damn slice that I can't correct."

He did an exaggerated head shake like a lousy sit-com character. He sipped his coffee.

This time I exhaled. For the last two months, every week had been a similar variation on this theme. The check-ins were required, and of the sixteen I had on my caseload Eddie was the worst in terms of frustration. Part of it was macho bullshit, and part of it was being out of touch emotionally, but the fact remained that he was a good agent who did excellent analyses of terrorist acts. It was necessary, and he was an asset to the program. He just wasn't into touchy-feely stuff, I guessed. The problem was it is difficult to predict who is going to develop mental health issues and who isn't. Some guys can act like Eddie for their whole careers, and their biggest worry is their slice off the tee. Others lose mental health and then lose effectiveness as an agent.

I was also a human, and I can only take so much of Eddie's game. It got annoying and, though dealing with resistance is part of a therapist's job, it isn't a fun part for me. Some days I just had to let it go.

"Eddie, I want you to try something," I said.

"Sure, Doctor Trace."

"Close your eyes for a moment. Take a moment to focus on your breathing." I was apprehensive about doing a mindfulness exercise with him. I just kind of wanted to get out of there.

Eddie closed his eyes.

"Now, I want you to observe your thoughts. Just notice what comes into your head. Don't try to understand them. Don't argue with your mind. Just let the thoughts appear and then let them go their own way. It is like they exist independent of you," I said. I tried not to overdo the calming voice.

Eddie gave me an "uh-hmm."

"Just let your thoughts flow like leaves on a stream. Let them come or go just like the leaves on a stream."

"Leaves on a stream..." Eddie said. He was making fun of me through his compliance.

"Notice how thoughts, images, and emotions come and go. Sometimes they get more intense, sometimes they stay the same, and sometimes they go away. Let yourself know this is what happens and that you don't ever have to struggle with them. Just let them do what they do. Your thoughts and emotions are not you,"

"Um-hmm," Eddie mumbled.

I continued despite feeling foolish.

"Know that you can always say. 'I notice I have a feeling, or I notice I have a thought...' and in that way, you can distance yourself from it."

Eddie nodded.

I waited a half of a minute. It was excruciating knowing he was laughing at me internally.

"Just let yourself observe whatever comes into your mind for a moment or two..." I kept quiet to let him experience it. I waited three minutes according to my phone. It was an eternity.

"Open your eyes, Eddie." Eddie did as asked.

"What was that like?"

"I kept seeing my damn slice!" Eddie chuckled. He got a kick out of that.

I rolled my eyes.

"I know this isn't your thing Eddie, but know that if things get to you, you can practice exercises like this. It doesn't make disturbing thoughts go away, but it gives you distance from them." I was looking him in the eye.

"Distance..." He said it with mock solemnity.

I sighed.

"Alright, Eddie," I said. "That's enough for this week."

Eddie smiled on one side of his mouth. He got up a little too fast, careful enough not to roll his eyes or laugh. He took his empty coffee cup with him. He gave an exhale letting me know he thought, "Glad that's over."

As he got to the door, I called to him.

"Eddie?"

He turned and lifted his eyebrows as a response. He was a bit surprised.

"47 and 36," I said.

He looked confused.

"Huh?"

"Actually 47, 36, and 5."

Eddie furrowed his brow.

"What are you talking about, Dr. Trace?"

"Notre Dame has a 47-36 record over the Trojans...with five ties," I said and repressed a grin.

He broke an authentic smile and nodded.

"See 'ya, Dr. Trace," he said.

CHAPTER TWO

It was already five minutes after eleven, which made me late for the research and discovery committee meeting. Late is late, but I wouldn't have sweated it too much, except I was the lead presenter today on a six-month summary of our sub-committee's work. My boss, Dr. Lin Williams, disapproved of tardiness, and she'd let me know it with a look. She had been my doctoral mentor, and she surprised the hell out of me when she hired both me and my fiancé, Maria Taylor, after we got licensed. I had spent my two and half years under her tutelage and was convinced she hated me.

She liked Maria, who was also on the sub-committee, and Maria thought Dr. Williams was the be-all of psychology and womanhood. Maria was out of town at a symposium, presenting her findings on this research data to a group of academic (not CIA) psychologists. Dr. Williams was her hero not just because she was a powerful woman but also because of some of the things she had to overcome, being both a woman and of African American and Cambodian descent. Dr. Williams favored Maria over me, but that wasn't hard to understand. Maria made fewer mistakes, was more precise with data, and, let's face it, they were the same sex. Maria wouldn't have been late for her presentation, either.

Dr. Williams, or technically the firm she owned, LW Psychometrics, was awarded the contracting bid to support agents and research domestic terror groups, specifically their members' psychological makeup. We were thrilled to have jobs when she hired us to stay on, though I was less than thrilled to have to continue to deal with her demandingness.

I was a little out of breath when I entered the room, and I did a quick scan to see who was in attendance. Dr. Williams was in the first seat, left of the podium. Dr. Purcell, the CIA psychologist in charge of the project and our liaison, was next to her, and then six members of his staff. Purcell was a tall 60-ish shrink with a high hairline, thin nose, and weak jawline. He was from Ohio State, knew his stuff, and, though not overly friendly, was at least cordial.

Special Supervisor Michaelson, who oversaw the behavioral division, was also there and, though he didn't look at his watch, his tight mouth told me he didn't have to. Michaelson was short and heavy, with an absence of muscle tone. He kept his readers on his nose and looked over them, giving his non-verbals an even more condescending feel. He had dirty blond hair that needed a trim, and the back of his neck needed a shave. He was wearing a suit today, and I could pick a little bit of a mothball scent coming from his direction.

"Good morning everyone," I said, trying to exude some confidence. "My agent session ran late. I apologize for being late."

Other than Dr. Williams, the attendees nodded without much disdain. Dr. Williams gave me what Maria and I simply called "The Look." It was her way of letting us know, without saying a word, that we failed to live up to her expectations.

I decided to move on and get to the meat of my presentation.

"This morning, I will summarize the findings of the Domestic Antifa Organizations study group. Our goal is to define this group and present a framework for understanding its causes, why it acts, and the situations in which they are most likely to perpetrate violence," I said.

My opening far from dazzled them, and more than a few in the room glanced at cell phones.

"It is important to realize that Antifa is not a single organization. It is the name of a movement or an ideology within which there are many organizations, big and small, tightly organized and loosely formed. The movement goes back as far as the 1930's Italy when citizens rose up against Mussolini." I said.

This wasn't news to anyone in the room. It was an introduction, and I felt like I was beginning to lose my audience. It was the type of opening that was perfectly acceptable in the academic world but came off as bluster in the real world of intelligence and law enforcement. I took a breath and tried to distance myself from my anxiety.

"Many of today's groups cannot trace their roots to the 1930s. Rather they owe much of their origins to the anti-fascist punk rock groups that came into existence in the late '70s, though some can trace their beginnings to more formal Euro groups. Their philosophy is founded on the fact that non-violent protest is often limited in its effectiveness and, for example, if German citizens fought the Nazis in the street when they were forming, Nazism might have been thwarted." I said.

I had that creeping internal feeling that I was losing my audience. At the beginning of a lecture, I often got it and knew that I had to push through it. It would eventually go away, and my confidence would grow. I employed more mindfulness and tried just to observe the thoughts and emotions.

"Dr. Curran?" Dr. Michaelson interrupted. He exhaled a bit of disapproval. "I believe we are aware of how Antifa formed. Please take us to today. For instance, do we have any insight into why they chose Allied as a terrorist target? Is it simply because of the manufacturing of the virtual fence? Why did they decide now to up the ante, and will they continue?"

The insecurity would go away unless, of course, someone said something like that. This wasn't the theme nor the topic of my presentation. It made me tighten up a bit. It was getting harder just to observe my thoughts and emotions. I was starting to fuse with them, which meant, irrationally, feeling them. I said a quick prayer.

"Dr. Michaelson, those topics, though timely, aren't germane to this presentation," Dr. Purcell said calmly and without any hint that he fumed underneath.

Dr. Williams persisted with The Look.

I was only five minutes in. I knew I was introducing the basics, but it was essential to the framework of my conclusions. I guess I was learning about the difference between the academic world and the spy world.

"Sorry, Dr. Curran, for my digression. Please continue," Michaelson with just a hint of sarcasm.

I decided to shorten my introduction, and I shuffled my papers to move toward my findings. "The most prominent domestic Antifa groups include the Black Bloc Brothers, The Rose City Rebellion, The Redneck Overthrow, and The Any Means Necessary Brotherhood."

With that, they all began to rifle through the reports in front of them, taking my tonal change as the crux of the information. The fact that they did the paper shuffle when I did the paper shuffle gave me some confidence that I had them with me to some degree.

God, I hated being so neurotic.

"Of course, we are all aware of the recent rise in political extremism in both Europe and the US. It has resulted in an increase in research on groups such as the aforementioned Antifa organizations."

Using "aforementioned" always made me feel confident.

"In the past, the use of statistically valid surveys of group members has been difficult because of a reluctance to participate and a general distrust for the reasons for the research. Our current research is based on data gleaned from more than 10,000 statements made on Twitter and other social media outlets comparing their text-based psychological constructs with those of more moderate participants."

I was starting to loosen up. They were referencing the notes I had put together as I spoke.

"Left-wing extremists like those in Antifa groups score higher in anxiety than their right-wing extremist counterparts. Our beliefs serve a psychological function in all of us, and there is, of course, a connection between those beliefs and our political orientation. In particular, Twitter messages reveal underlying attributes reflected in word usage because of their length. Their angry rhetoric may point to underlying anxiety within the members about the safety of society and themselves."

Michaelson interrupted.

"Does this also suggest that Antifa members are not only anxious but also angry?"

"Yes, doctor. Other research I am getting to also assesses the predictability of violence in their movement." I was hitting my stride.

"Left-wing extremists score lower on certainty and higher on anxiety than right-wing extremists, perhaps suggesting that they lack confidence in protectors like the government and police. Antifa members score lower on ingroup loyalty and higher on the sense and importance of fairness. This might suggest that they may question authority and their fellow members. Whereas right-wing extremists tend to be more obedient and less concerned about overall fairness."

I paused for effect.

"It is important to note that the group tests highest in their ability to deal with disapproval from others. In other words, when they believe something is not fair, it will raise their anxiety, and then they are willing to act when they believe the cause is right despite disapproval from society."

"Meaning?" Michaelson asked.

"They are emboldened by their cause, fueled by anxiety and driven by what they think is fair." It came off with confidence, and I was pleased. "Today's Antifa shares commonalities with the early groups that opposed fascism, but they have important differences. They have gravitated away from merely protesting strict fascism to protesting what they see as policies and the individuals espousing them as leading toward fascism. What was once alt-right in many people's eyes is seen as a 'pre-fascism.' Members believe that must be stopped."

That left the group quiet just for a moment, and I let the drama of it hang.

"That could mean just conservative republicans," Michaelson said. "That sounds intolerant and potentially dangerous. Tell us the makeup of the members."

I was glad he was interested, but I sensed he was hijacking my presentation. Still, I felt compelled to follow him.

"The groups are predominantly made up of the college-educated or those who attended some college. They are often oppositional in their thoughts and philosophy. Many see themselves as the heirs to those who came before them who protested Vietnam and walked with Martin Luther King," I paused. "There is a large percentage, though, who understand less about their causes and simply gravitate to a non-conformist group and take pride living on the fringe."

"Trace, tell us, as best as you can estimate, what percentage of the groups are serious about the philosophy of their cause and are thoughtful in what they do and what percentage are more like disaffected youth looking to simply rebel and raise hell," Dr. Williams said.

"It varies from group to group. The organizers and those who are loosely in charge of the groups are often passionately educated about their pursuits. Many of the rank and file are as well," I paused. "I believe the danger comes from the mass of the membership who are simpler in how they process the information and see issues in black and white with very little gray."

"That's always the issue," Michaelson said.

It wasn't an affirmation. It was more his way of saying I was coming up with the same old shit they already knew.

"The most salient point the preliminary research points toward is that the philosophical direction of Antifa groups is morphing toward rebellion against not just what is fascist or even considered neo-fascist, but what is considered far-right and, I believe, even merely conservative," I paused to let it sink in. "That means that we may expect more acts with a greater degree of disregard for justification. In their eyes, the 'enemy' can be disposed of without moral regard. It can be seen as a break for their history."

"In other words, there are likely to be more actions with a greater degree of violence," Michaelson said.

"Yes, sir," I said.

"How does this bode for how the agency is prepared?" Michaelson said. His question was beyond the scope of our research. It was beyond what we were hired to do. I decided to let it hang there to see if any of the others in the room wanted to field the question.

Dr. Purcell broke the silence.

"The contractors aren't in a position to comment on that, Dr. Michaelson," he said with an absence of emotion. "They've been contracted to do background on the anti-fascist groups, not form strategy to intervene with them."

It brought an awkward silence. Purcell was taking on the bully in our defense. I was pleased to hear it come from him. It would've felt defensive if I answered with the same words or if Dr. Williams did.

"Well, that being the case, what we've learned is that Antifa, despite its noble beginnings, has morphed into a bunch of young, probably disaffected semi half-assed anarchists who get off on having mini riots over stuff that makes them pout," Michaelson said now being far more overt with his disdain.

I wasn't sure how to address it. I paused, and Purcell spoke up again.

"Yes, despite your sarcasm, that's what the research has told us. I would like to add that the research was sound, and your feelings notwithstanding, useful to our planning for Antifa groups," Purcell said. A hint of anger, but not much more, had entered his tone.

Michaelson looked down, and half smiled to himself, seemingly pleased that he got a reaction. He was the type of guy who got off a little on getting to someone.

"Dr. Curran, please continue," Michaelson said.

I did. I outlined some data about the different groups' membership, regional differences, funding, and goals. There were some questions and discussions, particularly about the origins of funding. We didn't have a comprehensive workup on that but went over the idea that part of what made the groups so agile is that they didn't require much funding.

I highlighted the Antifa demonstration at Boston University from 1991, in which an event that started as a protest against troops being sent to Iraq turned ugly. Tear gas was shot into the crowd by the police SWAT team, the Antifa group answered by throwing rocks and lighting a patrol car on fire. The police were under fire, and when three cops went to restrain a protester, her head hit the pavement violently and she died from the trauma. It incited riots that would last for a week before calming.

"The Boston University incident occurred because of a conflux of incidents, some of which could've been prevented. "The protesters were loud and obnoxious, but they were not violent until the tear gas. The tear gas provoked them, and a faction within the larger group reacted," I paused, a little bit for effect and also because I was afraid of dumping too much information at once.

"Are you saying the police weren't justified?" Michaelson said.

"Not all. Of course they were justified. There was a group that wasn't dispersing, and there was plenty to be concerned about. I'm simply running through the dynamics. The tear gas was the antecedent of the protest turning violent," I said.

Michaelson sat back and folded his arms as if to say, "Bullshit."

I continued.

"The question for procedure with this group is when and where to intervene and are interventions, like in this case, tear gas, worth the risk in the overall scheme of the event."

"Then what's the alternative?" Michaelson said.

"Waiting them out. Staying put, not acting reflexively but in a strategic way that takes into consideration the final outcomes. It is a bit of a paradigm shift, and it will come as counterintuitive to many."

"And this paradigm shift...what do we do, wait until police and agents are assaulted?"

Michaelson said.

"I offer that we examine the most salient predictors of violence. Many of these groups emphasize that they will not act unless provoked and take pride in that axiom. Tear gas gives them the out."

I was happy my presentation followed a logical progression. I don't know if the audience bought it, but it was based on a sound hypothesis and its logical, research-based extension. That was my job. That's what I gave them.

Of course, Dr. Williams would have her opinions. I just had to wait until she called me into her inner sanctum. In the meantime, I had to busy myself with notes and reports from Eddie's session and some others on my caseload. I didn't like documenting that Eddie was somewhat resistant and not taking things seriously, but that was the truth and resistance part of the counseling process. Still, it felt like I was writing down that I couldn't do my job. Sometimes I wondered if I'd ever shake the self-doubt and insecurity. It was tiring living a real-life example of the "Imposter Complex."

My desk phone buzzed.

"She'll see you now," Aisha, our admin assistant, said without tipping me to Williams's mood or feeling about my presentation. I looked at my watch, and it was already four, so this was going to close out my day. I preferred meeting with her first thing to get it out of the way, and while I was psychologically fresh to deal with her personality.

"You did a good job on presenting the findings today," she said to start. "Please don't come in late. It puts the company in a bad light."

"Yes, I'm sorry. My session with Eddie dragged on a bit."

"You can control the timing of the session, and you should work with your clients so they know they have 50 minutes. It conditions them to get work done within the time frame."

"Yes, of course."

"Strive to be more confident in your presentation. I don't like when Michaelson has ammunition to degrade our mission." She pursed her lips like it was difficult for her to think about losing out to Michaelson. I think she was overstating it, but there was no point in arguing it. She was driven to appear flawless. I was more of the mindset that I would never be flawless so I didn't burden myself with trying to be.

"Yes, I understand," I said.

" You don't need to go into as much background with your presentations either. Get to the point faster and more succinctly."

That didn't seem fair.

"I thought the background was pertinent and necessary to give shape to the research."

"I didn't." She let that curt response hang.

I waited a few beats to see if something else was coming. There wasn't.

"I understand," I said, capitulating.

"All in all, it was a good presentation. Thank you," she said by way of dismissing.

She did the management sandwich—praised me-criticized me-praised me. Obviously, the praise part was difficult, but she undoubtedly took a seminar on managing underlings like me. She felt she had to use it.

I was just happy to get out of her office.

CHAPTER THREE

It was time to get out of my cinder block confines and burn off the day's stress.

That meant a quick trip to the condo and then to the Cleveland Street Boxing Gym in the DC gut. I've never boxed in gentlemen's gyms or white-collar "fitness" gyms that have popped up since boxing became something akin to Pilates or yoga. Boxing was my anecdote that brought me back to sanity, and it had been since I was an acne-scarred kid. When I was an insecure teenager, long before I became an insecure adult, boxing taught me how to fight. Sure, it taught me to fight physically, but it also taught me how to fight psychologically. This occurred not because I could suddenly kick some ass. Instead, it came about from getting my ass kicked and getting up after being knocked down, coming back the next day, and looking the same guy in the eye. Honestly, learning to kick a little ass helped too.

The Cleveland Street Gym reminded me of the Albany Parks Department Gym back home. Smelly, gray, and devoid of chrome, purple machines, and saunas, whirlpools, or tanning huts. It had to be a real gym, not a new wave facsimile, and there had to be fighting happening. I always loved it when someone told me they "boxed" and yet had never been in the ring with someone who was punching back.

I planned to do a quick change, grab my gear, and head right back out of the condo. Condo life didn't agree with me. It was antiseptic, clean, and the closets were big. Essentially, it was everything Marie wanted. It was close to the office, the grocery store, and the malls, and there was no walk to shovel or grass to mow. My preference would've been a quirky city place with some years on it, with asymmetrical rooms and windows and the beat of city theater around. At least, that's what I thought I wanted. City theater beats can be a pain in the ass too.

Marie and I spent a lot of time together. Research, the doctorates, and now the working at the same place, although in slightly different capacities. She did more research and fewer sessions. I did more clinical work and some research. This morning's presentation summarized the findings in broad strokes, and I did a bit better in front of people than she did. She was better at crunching the numbers and the statistical crap that was an essential component of psychological studies. I could do it, but it didn't come to me as easily. It was why she was at a symposium of PhDs who would scrutinize her findings in a more academic way than the guys at the agency would.

Spending so much time together was both good and bad. Good, because we loved each other, and she was great to be around. Not so good because each other's constant presence kind of took away the passion one might feel waiting to see the other. In some ways, it accelerated the arc of a relationship because we had already spent about ten years of couple time together. Great for deepening the relationship on an intimate level but not so great at keeping it fresh and new. My guess was coupledom always gravitated towards companionship, but on the cusp of my thirties, I sometimes felt that there should be more rip-roaring passionate times. Maybe that's what everyone thinks.

With Marie out of town, I had no reason to do all my usuals; hurry home, run an errand for her, and stop at the grocery store to get stuff for dinner. We've been living together for two years now, and though I never felt like a hen-pecked boyfriend or anything, spending a night out with the guys for no other purpose but to spend time with them always made me feel a bit guilty. I took some time with the feelings, took a breath, and admitted to myself that it was just a feeling and not the gospel truth. Still, I felt like I was betraying her when she was home.

Tonight, with her away at the symposium, I was guilt-free. That meant the gym, a few rounds of sparring followed by a few or maybe a few more than a few rounds of drinks afterward. Over the last year, I've made kind of an unorthodox friendship with an agent named Ray Brice. Unorthodox because agents usually avoided egghead types like me or at least professionals they assumed were egghead types. Ray and I met at the Cleveland Street Gym, and it wasn't until we did three hard rounds and traded some good shots that we found out we worked at the same place, though because I was a contractor, not technically the same employer.

Sure, he gave me shit about the doctorate and whatnot, and I goofed on his spy status, but he couldn't deny that I stood toe to toe to him when we got in the ring together. Good-natured sparring but hard sparring and the best I've had since I moved here. It isn't easy to find a partner to work with. You got to match up size and strength-wise and most importantly, you've got to match up temperament-wise as well.

"Good evening, doctor," Ray said when I arrived. He was wrapping his hands. "You prepared for an embarrassing and dominating beating this evening?"

"Yeah, yeah, yeah. Keep selling wolf tickets. Gonna make you cash them in ya know," I said.

"I love it when you get all up in the 'hood like that. Remind me of my upbringing." Ray was biracial with a few freckles on his cheeks like that guy who played on the Celtics back in the day.

"Yeah, yeah, yeah..." It was my go-to line when I couldn't think of anything clever.

"How'd you get a permission slip for tonight? School night and all..."

"She's out of town at a symposium. I'm a free man!" I said

with mock exuberance.

"She out there proving to the world how we should all just give our Antifa brothers a cookie and a hug?" He rolled his eyes. He knew the research we did, and I often checked with him to get the agent-level opinion of what we came up with. Ray wasn't a right-wing nut, but he was in law enforcement and he had to deal with obnoxious people, so life had made him, shall we say, a tad cynical.

"You know Raymond, if you were just a little kinder, maybe this disaffected youth wouldn't be so hostile. You just need to get woke," I said.

"Put your headgear on. I'm about to woke your ass up!"

We waited for the round to end and the two teenagers training for the Golden Gloves to finish up. Jimmy, the owner and lead coach, waved us in.

"Okay, my government men. Do your thing."

We touched gloves and went to work. For all the outside of the ring bluster, once we got started, it was proper boxing sparring. Hard, just about all out, but about the skill and art of it, without the goal of hurt. Don't get me wrong, it hurt plenty when you took one, even if we worked with 16-ounce gloves on.

Midway through our second round, I was feeling it, and I knew I had to protect myself. Ray was in a little better cardio condition than I was, and he could last better than I could. At that point, skill meant little. If you're too tired to hold your hands up, it doesn't matter how slick you are.

I was gassed in the third, but I made it through. We both landed our shots, and I had that nice throbbing in my face that let me know I got as well as gave. Man, I loved this shit, and it was great to have a partner to work with.

We both cooled down with a couple of non-contact rounds. I shadowboxed and stretched, and Ray did some light stuff on the bag then worked some technique on the double end ball in front of the mirror. The double end was a volleyball-sized ball tethered to the ceiling and the floor that went back and forth like crazy when you struck it. Ray was one of the few guys in any gym I was ever in who could work it without embarrassing himself.

After showers, we went to Slick's around the corner from the gym. Slick's was a hundred-year-old bar, long, dark and narrow with beat-up barstools and high backs. It had the smell of fryolator grease and spilled beer. Black and white photographs signed by Sonny Jurgensen, Larry Taylor, and Frank Robinson, as well as other sports legends, adorned the walls. The old school jukebox played a great selection of old R & B and soul with some classic rock. Slim, who was actually Slim Jr., was behind the bar. A fifty-something Black guy with a shaved head, dark black skin with some scar tissue around the eyes and ears and the face and hands of an old fighter. Slim had 15 pro fights before a retinal problem drove him out of the game.

Slim nodded and drew two drafts without asking. Ray was strictly a Bud man and I had the Sierra Nevada IPA, Slim's solitary concession to the hipster craft beer.

"You eatin' tonight?" Slim asked with his usual economy of words. He was the perfect bartender; slightly morose, quiet unless you wanted to talk, and experienced in the ring and in life. A word of bullshit never crossed his lips, at least not that I could ever tell.

"I'll have the bacon cheeseburger and fries," Ray said.

"Geez, you're a heart attack waiting to happen," I said.

"Spare me," Ray said, keeping his eyes fixed on SportsCenter. They were talking about how poor the NFC East was this year.

"Turkey club, Russian. Chips." Slim nodded and went to the kitchen's swinging door to let Anthony, the cook, know.

Other than Moses, the short, fat Black guy who was in here sipping beer every single time I've been in here and two middle-aged guys talking about their wives at the other end of the bar, we were the only ones here.

"I wish I could hook off my jab with consistency. I guess if I have to think about it, it is coming too slow," Ray said, almost rhetorically.

"I'd like to be able to defend without moving out of range. Very hard to slip and counter in real life. Can do it on the mitts and in front of a mirror, and it looks cool as hell, but, in action, not even close." I sipped the IPA. Nothing was better than the first sip after sparring.

"Yeah, well, it's what is keeping us from the world title, I guess," Ray said.

We both let SportsCenter fill in the conversational gaps. Ray had become a good enough friend that there wasn't any social discomfort in our exchanges. It's funny being a psychologist. I'm guessing if you asked Ray, he'd just say. "Yeah, Trace is cool."

After SportsCenter let us know how LeBron's stats matched up against Jordan's for the millionth time, Ray started a new conversational theme.

"So what psycho mumbo-jumbo you working on these days?"

"I appreciate your appreciation for my expertise. Two things mostly. Looking at Antifa and counseling fucked up agents like yourself."

"Shiiiiiiit. What have you determined about Antifa? They're not a bunch of half-faggot rich cowardly kids who live in their parents' basements listening to grunge rock?

"Whoa, could you possibly add any more politically incorrect, xenophobic hate speech in one sentence? To say nothing of the fact that Grunge Rock went away in the '90s."

Ray waved a hand at me dismissively.

"Fuck all that shit," he said almost under his breath. "For real, what conclusions have you come to?"

"Honestly, probably what you'd suspect. In a nutshell, mostly educated disenfranchised and probably bored upper-middle-class men who are angry at how society is."

He rolled his eyes.

"You know any *franchised* middle-class men who are happy as a clam? Why do these guys get to throw Molotov cocktails at Civil War statues to exorcise their angst? Sound to me like a bunch of whiney motherfuckers."

"Yeah, except they do stand up against fascism. They've got that going for them."

"Maybe at one time they did. Maybe when they fuck with some true hate monger leader or throw rocks at some dictator's stormtroopers, they're fighting fascism. You tell me what it is when those asshats in Portland were burning down police stations?"

"That's what we're trying to get at it. How did it go from righteous fascist fighting to fighting all authority? Is the BLM movement a logical offshoot for Antifa, or is it taking them someplace they didn't enter before?"

"How many Black Antifa members have you seen?

"Hard to say, but I get your point."

Ray gave me a disgusted look.

"Most of this BLM shit is just that, shit. There's no doubt racism, but so many of these so-called victims are bad guys. They certainly ain't Rosa Parks, shit, they ain't even Emmett Till," Ray said. It was stuff a white man couldn't say and what many Black men wouldn't say in public.

"Anyway, we're trying to put some science to the question of whether or not they gravitated into being a true terrorist organization. Are they moving toward a unified group with true anarchy on their minds? Have they become a danger to the nation?"

"I think we have a short answer to that with what just happened at Allied.

"Yeah, but is that a one-off anomaly or is it where they are going?" Thankfully, Slim slid the red plastic baskets with our dinner in front of us along with a rolled-up paper napkin with the silverware tucked in it.

"And what's with that boss of yours? I mean, how many races can a person have? Is she looking for some sort of rainbow coalition thing?" Ray said. He took a bite of his sandwich and then a massive gulp of beer.

"Can you possibly get more politically incorrect? Jesus..." I said.

"Look, man, I'm one of the downtrodden. I can say what I want. You oppressors have to give me a pass."

"Oh, in that case...she's half Cambodian, half Black. Father was a serviceman. Mother was in a village. Her parents never married, and she spent her childhood over there and came here at eleven. She has a drive like nothing I've ever seen."

"They call that a tiger mom or some shit, don't they?" Ray said and bit down on a fry.

"I think that's Chinese moms but pretty much the same thing, I guess. You know, I recently found out that she applied to the agency seven years ago and lost out to Michaelson for that job."

"Probably explains some of her hostility to the dude."

"Maybe. I think it is more about her just being driven."

After a couple of bites, I changed the subject.

"What are you working on these days?"

"Most of the day, I'm reviewing intercepted email, what the press likes to call chatter. Most of it is translated Arabic nonsense. Two or three motherfuckers going on and on about nothing, occasionally hating on America, but more often exchanging their favorite porn sites and arguing over soccer scores. It is boring as hell," Ray said.

"They ever send you to the counseling like I do?" I asked.

"Nah, it is offered. I've never utilized it."

"Would you?"

He thought for a moment. I could see him turning it over in his mind.

"I'm not against it. I don't think folks who do are weak or any of that old-school bullshit. I imagine it can be useful."

"Studies show that PTSD is prevented by being able to debrief from the events as close as possible from when they occurred. To let them out before they began to form onto obsessions."

"Yeah, well, maybe. If you come from the state of mind that this is what we do, this is our chosen profession, and bad shit is gonna happen, then it becomes a matter of kinda sayin' to yourself, 'That was some sick shit that I just saw. This is what I do.' I don't know if that makes any sense." He was trying to be genuine.

"I guess what we do is help people with that same process when they get jammed up, and what they experienced becomes something more."

"Yeah," he hesitated. "But Trace, ultimately, aren't we alone in our own heads dealin' with our own shit?"

I didn't respond right away. He was right, of course.

Sometimes the years I spent studying seemed a bit foolish.

CHAPTER FOUR

Ray and I finished up our beers, bumped fists, congratulated each other on good ring work, and headed our separate ways home. It was a twenty-minute ride, and now that it was heading toward eight o'clock, I decided to give Marie another call. She had enough time to finish her conference work and get dinner. I called her cell, but it went right to voicemail. Probably at dinner or getting drinks after a long day of poster sessions and tedious panel discussions. She was also terrible at remembering to charge her phone, a frustrating trait that comes up daily.

The condo was, of course, as I left it, which is to say the sweats I slept in were on the floor next to the unmade bed, my used coffee mug from this morning was on the breakfast bar, and my socks and shoes were still next to the couch. I was headed in the direction of the sofa, and I was about to add another day's worth of footgear to the pile while I cracked another beer and watched some college football. I got as far as having the remote in my hand when my phone rang.

Not Marie but Mom.

"Hi Honey," she started the same way she always did. "You okay?"

Starting every conversation by checking to see if someone's okay kind of speaks to the fact that mom's a bit of a worrier. Maybe a bit more than a bit.

"Hey Mom, doing great. How are you and the big guy?"

"He's good. He went to the tavern today and even worked behind the stick for an hour," Dad owned one of Albany's oldest bars and was a legendary character in my hometown. His heart hasn't been great, and he's not supposed to exert himself too much, eat fatty foods or drink Irish whiskey, but you know how that goes. No point in scolding either him or Mom.

"Sounds great. Jack? Molly?" I did the mandatory roll call of my sibs. Jack's the older angry lawyer brother, and Molly is the younger, funnier, parties-too-much 4th-grade teacher.

"They're all great."

"Rocky too?" Rocky was Dad's third bloodhound, all from the same line. About 150lbs of slobbering greatness. I missed him terribly.

"He's a mess, but that's nothing new. He ate the mail today but it was only AARP stuff."

"How's your knee?" Mom never complained about her arthritis.

"Oh, you know it's there. How's Marie?"

"She's in St. Louis, remember? This is the week she goes to the conference."

"That's right. Did you get dinner?" Mom thinks I'm four years old and incapable of self-care.

"Of course, I had dinner, Mom," I said. "I'm a big boy now."

"Here, talk to your father," she said abruptly and handed the phone to my old man for what would be a brief conversation.

"Hey Pally, did you arrest Sadam Hussein today?" He laughed and was quite pleased with himself as he always was when he was having fun at my expense.

"No, we're focusing our attention on bar owners who fail to declare income. It is a joint project with the IRS." I said. Touché.

"Ahh, Jesus wept. You send your Old Man up and the entire West Side of Albany will come looking for ya." He got more Irish the more the kidding escalated.

"They'd be drunk and get lost trying to find me," I said.

"'Tis true, 'tis true. Here talk to your mother," he handed the phone back to my mom as fast as she had given it to him. Born in Ireland but raised in Albany from age three, the old man carried dual citizenship, which added to his bar lore.

"Okay Tracy, make sure you got to church and say your prayers. I pray for you every day," she said. She wasn't just saying it. I know she did.

"I love you, Mom. I'm praying for you guys too," I said, and we hung up. The calls were frequent, probably three or more times a week, but they were short. Mom was just checking to make sure no catastrophe had befallen me and that I wasn't malnourished. Dad left that job for Mom, and other than his nightly spy joke, he didn't have much to say. He was very proud of my Notre Dame education and my doctorate.

I caught myself smiling. I missed my folks, and I felt anxiety because of the fact that they're aging, and it scared me. I did pray, and tonight that would be on my list, along with some gratitude for them and my friend Ray. I also prayerfully thought about Marie and how God wanted us to spend our lives, and what I could work harder on at work and on myself as a person.

Not long after that, I went to bed. While I drifted toward sleep, I found myself practicing watching my thoughts without changing them or criticizing them. I just let them come and took note when I got back into myself, which seemed to be a couple of times a minute. Someday Zen would come, and I'd be perfectly distant from the incumbrance of thought and emotion. Maybe drinking less beer would help that journey.

But Zen wasn't going to come any time soon. I tried Marie again and left a voice mail telling her I loved her and joked that she better not be hooking up with some guy who did statistics better than me. That wouldn't be hard to find, considering the analytics were my weakest part of my psychology game. I figured Marie was out of her room and her phone died and I'd hear from her in the morning.

The buzz from the beers was fading, and I found myself

starring at the ceiling. It was the worst time for me and when I got most insecure. Many of the things I worried about cleared my consciousness by ten the next morning but came back when I was trying to sleep. Insecurities about my competence in just about every area of my life work, relationships, love, social, you name it, and I felt inadequate a good part of the time. Getting in the ring helped that. Just like when I was a teenager, it gave me something concrete to focus on and literally fight back fears. I couldn't imagine not having it in my life in some form.

Tomorrow was another day. Dr. Williams would kick up a fresh new batch of insecurities in me, and I'd do what I could to get by.

CHAPTER FIVE

I got to work the next day fifteen minutes early, exactly how Dr. Williams liked it. She didn't come right out and say that she wanted me in early, but she didn't look at her watch when I came in at 7:45. If it were precisely eight, she'd look at her watch and ever so slightly purse her lips. Besides, it was easy today without having to jostle with Marie over sink time.

A printed memo was perfectly centered on my desk, waiting for me. It was from Dr. Williams and it was entitled: Review of Antifa Demographics Presentation. I didn't realize there was to be such a formal report card, and I felt it in my gut. I read it faster than I should because I wanted to see how bad it got. A couple of sentences caught my eye during my initial pass.

"It is important to be on time for a presentation. Lateness is not only unprofessional, but it also speaks poorly of the company..."

"It is important to convey organization and to speak with an authoritative voice..."

And...

"Most of these deficiencies can be corrected with a greater attention to detail and discipline."

I felt rage build up in my gut, and my efforts to distance myself from it were futile. I had worked months on that presentation, and I believed it was well-received. The woman was impossible. I couldn't speak to her about it right now. I was just too angry. I'd give it some time before—and maybe if—I addressed it. It was like she went out of her way to undermine my confidence.

The problem was our working conditions didn't allow for me to avoid her, so I'd have to suppress how I felt. When I walked out of my office, Dr. Williams sat at the table in the conference room. As an independent contractor, our firm was given office space toward the back of the building, next to another independent contracting group doing a work-study on agent hours and effectiveness. It was early American grey and beige with functional cabinetry, linoleum, and vinyl.

"Good morning," I said. I did my best not to look at her and went to the coffee machine.

I could feel her studying me.

"I left a memo for you with some discussion points about your presentation. I think you did a good job, but I wanted to give you feedback to improve."

"Yes, I read it."

She paused.

"You seem angry. I said I thought you did a good job, and it was clear you put a great deal of time into it."

"Thank you," I nodded and went back to my office. Like an abusive partner, she was great at knocking you down and then playing the role of consoler. It pissed me off.

She came to my door.

"Don't let Michaelson's attitude bother you. He's all about control," she said. I just looked at her.

"His behavior doesn't mean that he didn't listen or doesn't plan to apply what we give him. He just wants to get his pound of flesh from us to make sure we know he doesn't think that much of us."

I thought to myself that there was no shortage of neurotic psychologists, even at the highest level of psychology. I often wondered if neurotic people, fascinated with their own disturbances, were drawn to psychology and then played out their dysfunction. Adjusted people probably didn't spend all day anxious or depressed, obsessed or wondering how to find some god damned comfort in their lives. They just became lawyers or accounts, made money, watched the Yankees, and followed the Kardashians. It haunted me.

Aisha, the admin for our group, came into the conference room.

"Dr. Williams, you wanted me to remind you about your supervision notes, and Trace, you have an agent session in 15," she said.

"Yes, thank you," Dr. Williams said. "I've got to get the CR-32s done by Friday," she said. The amount of paperwork required by contractors was substantial. We may have been Ph.D. psychologists with more degrees than a thermometer, but that didn't mean the government wanted to trust us without documentation. Redundant reports, notes made in special redundant formats, redundant summaries of redundant notes, and redundant plans that drew upon redundant everything else filled the day. You were either doing them or procrastinating doing them. At times, it made me wish I could build something with my hands, fix a machine, or enjoyed hauling large objects around.

My next agent session would be a welcome relief from Eddie Hutchins. Melanie Freitag was an agent on the job for two years, and she had a psychology degree from Vanderbilt. She looked forward to our sessions and utilized them to better herself. It wasn't that she was less well-adjusted or weaker than Eddie. It was that she accepted and believed in the concept of processing things. She didn't hold back her emotions or concerns, she put real shit out there, and the two of us worked on it.

She had periods of insomnia, maybe a couple of times a month. She brought up having trouble letting go of a Sudanese torture video of a husband and wife. Melanie talked about it becoming intrusive into her downtime, and when she tried to repress it, it became stronger.

That's exactly what happens with disturbing thoughts. Your

beer-drinking friends may tell you to think of something else, make yourself busy, or have a few more drinks, but those strategies don't work or at least don't work for long. The technique that "works" is mindfulness.

With mindfulness, you allow thoughts to happen, and instead of suppressing them, you look at them dispassionately like a third-person observer. You acknowledge that they sometimes go away, sometimes lessen, sometimes increase, and sometimes stay the same. You work like hell at accepting that that's the way they work. Actually, you don't work like hell; you work as gently as you can with yourself to not pressure any particular outcome. "Working hard" on thinking brings on the undesired outcome. It goes against western thought but to get more comfortable with thinking and emotions; you need to hold things gently, not demand of yourself to conquer and defeat them. It was this dynamic that uber macho badass agents had the toughest time with. The John Wayne approach was bullshit, and it didn't work.

Whining about things endlessly to a Freudian psychoanalyst didn't work either, and unfortunately, that's what the general public thought psychology was. We were helping agents to see that one agent at a time. Sometimes we struggled with the Eddies, and sometimes we got down to business with the Melanies. It wasn't auto mechanics. There was far more nuance to it.

It was the style we worked on with Williams for years. It was different than behavioral techniques, and it went in a different direction than Cognitive Behavioral Therapy, which encouraged you to dispute irrational thoughts. Accepting versus disputing thoughts is a sometimes subtle but essential difference.

Before Aisha left the room, Dr. Williams checked in with me again, this time looking at her day planner. She still preferred the old school, leather-bound style and encouraged us to use the same time management system, while I kept a calendar on my computer. Williams always had a prioritized to-do list at the ready, handwritten and ready to act on. Part of that to-do list was keeping track of supervisory duties.

"Trace, are your session notes up to date?" It wasn't accusatory but rather matter-of-fact and designed to allow her to check off a task.

"I'm up to date, not including this morning's. I'll have my notes done by the end of the day," I said. I was getting ready to meet with Melanie, but before I could say any more, Aisha interrupted.

"Trace, you had a call on your cell," she said.

I went to my desk to check the phone. I didn't recognize the number, but I did know the area code. It was from Boston, and it made my heart race and my breath quicken. I was hoping it was from Danny O.

Danny O was a leader of an Antifa-type organization outside of Boston. I had reached out to him and traded emails with him for two months. As would be expected, he was highly circumspect about divulging information and, until now, refused to talk on the phone, giving cryptic answers to most of my research-based questions. I pleaded with him in each exchange to get in touch with me, that it would be kept in confidence and \ used for research and understanding, not for investigation, arrest, or prosecution. It was a hard sell.

He didn't trust it.

In our last email exchange two weeks ago, I took a risk and gave him my home address and personal cell number. It was meant to be an extension of putting myself into his trust. It may have worked. I had weighed my vulnerability against his history, and because he had no history of violence on people, he had only destroyed property. I thought my risk was well measured.

"This is Curran," I said, realizing how CIAish it sounded.

There was a pause, and it was a little longer than would be expected.

"You checked out. Your condo looks pretty basic. Functional, nice, but not upscale. Your fiancé is attractive. Your cell phone bill was due last Friday, you know," he said.

I chuckled just a little. It was enough so he could hear.

"Well, you're thorough. I might also add resourceful. Half the time, I can't figure out when my cell phone bill is due," I said.

"You didn't think I'd check you out? You must think Black Bloc is a bunch of disaffected rich college kids with no jobs and lots of time on our hands between Starbucks grandes," he said. It was very close to this morning's presentation. It made me curious.

"As long as it is free-trade grandes," I said to lighten things up.

"Funny." He paused. "You know talking to the CIA would not be something my rank and file would approve of. My neck is out there, so I urge you to keep your word about confidence and my identity."

"You have my word," I said.

"Forgive me if I find assurances from the CIA a bit hollow," he said.

"I'm not CIA. I'm a contractor," I said.

"Yeah...Danny muttered.

"It's the truth," I said. I felt a little too defensively.

"Um, you want to tell me how that works? I mean, it sounds like a bullshit splitting of hairs," he said.

"What would you like to know?" he said, getting to the point.

I felt a spark go off in my chest. This was a breakthrough and had the potential to be a game-changer for our research. I opened the file on my Mac that held my questions.

I wanted my inquiry to sound conversational and not clinical or interrogational.

"Okay, as you might expect, I have a million questions. This will remain anonymous, and if you don't want to answer any specific question, we can move on," I said.

"Yeah, yeah. Trust me. I'm not answering anything I'm not comfortable with."

"All right then," I said. "Let's start."

He laughed a little.

"Yeah, let's before I change my mind," he said.

I gathered myself. My strategy was to go from the least

threatening questions to the more threatening questions. That was an interviewing technique developed by Alfred Kinsey, the sex researcher. He found that when the questions were presented in that order, quickly and without an emotional response from the questioner, interviewees were more likely to disclose. I was anxious to see if it worked.

"How long have you been a member of the group?" I said.

"Five and half years," he said.

"Where is the group located?"

"The greater Boston area."

"Can you tell me what drew you to the organization?"

"I grew really fuckin' tired of watching the minority with all the money rule the majority who were struggling every day. I hated the double talk and the limp-wristed liberals who made a lot of noise but were always standing back instead of taking action. I'm more of a Malcolm X guy," he said.

"Could you tell me what that means, exactly?" I said.

"Malcolm wasn't Martin. Peace is not the answer to everything. Malcolm encouraged his followers to seek a peaceful resolution to issues, but if that didn't work and violence was laid on his people, he believed it was right to come back with violence," he said.

"Is that what your organization believes and practices?" I asked.

"Honestly, I wish we practiced it more?"

"Tell me more about that?"

He paused for a beat to gather his words.

"When the president did thinly veiled racist tweets, we marched. When he opposed pro-choice in his comments, we marched. Nothing happened. No one noticed. No one cared. When the cops killed the guy in Minnesota and we vandalized police precincts, we made the national news. People condemned us, the president condemned us, but our point got across. We had to be dealt with," he said.

"The 'By any means necessary is an ends-justifying-the-means philosophy."

"Yes, of course."

I waited for a second to frame my next question.

"How do you measure; how do you calculate the ends justifying the means?" I asked.

"I don't understand?" he said.

"I mean, is it ever out of proportion?" I asked. I wanted it to be philosophical and not an accusation.

He didn't take it that way or at least chose not to.

"If the German Jews threw rocks at the Nazi propagandists before the invasions and the camps, would it have been justified? Can they be at peace knowing they didn't "overreact" as you suggest? Or should they have tried to kill as many of those motherfuckers as possible as early as possible?"

"I see your point," I said to give him some affirmation. "What lengths are you and your peers willing to go to?" I asked. The questions were getting deeper.

He didn't answer right away.

"That depends," he said and paused. I gave him as much time as he needed. Silence was an excellent tool to get subjects to talk. Just about everyone gets uncomfortable and chooses to fill the gap.

"We react to oppression. We react to all forms of unfair domination. We react to fascism. We are committed." He didn't continue.

I waited.

I decided to break the silence this time. I felt he needed a nudge.

"Committed to?" I said, hoping to lead him into finishing the statement.

"Committed to stopping it by any means necessary. And that is what it says, 'Any means necessary."

"What would stop short of?" I asked. I was a bit uncomfortable leading him to this directly, but he was the one heading down the path.

"Nothing," he said.

I let that hang for a long moment to see if he adds to it.

"Destruction of property?" I asked.

"Yes," he answered.

"Interruption of business activity?"

"Of course," he stifled a laugh.

"Blackmail, cyberstalking?" I asked.

"Ha, our specialty."

"Threat of personal injury?" I had kept the same pace to see if I could lead him into answering.

He waited.

I waited.

"By any means necessary means 'any." He said with deliberation.

"Would you kill?"

"I believe that's been answered," he said.

He hung up.

CHAPTER SIX

I hurried to write down as much of the detail of the conversation as I could remember. I felt rushed because I realized I was late for my agent meeting, and I didn't want any more feedback on my tardiness. I finished up what I could remember and tucked the yellow pad under my arm, and headed out of my office through the conference room.

Dr. Williams and Aisha were around the table with the office planning calendar. They weren't looking at it. They were focused on the flat screen on the wall at the head of the table.

"I got him! He called!" I said, wanting to share the big moment we've been waiting 18 months for. They didn't turn around. It was a CNN special report.

"...reports are two are dead, and another seven are wounded, two critically..." the reporter said.

"What the hell..." I said.

The television featured a helicopter view of a large industrial park. The trailer said, "A group dressed in black opened fire on Consolidated Tactical Industries before the building exploded..."

The camera showed the shell of a recently constructed factory or production building. It was three stories, but now the entire right side was girders, steel, and crumbled concrete. Employees gathered in a pavilion next to a softball field on the building's north side.

The news was unfolding as we watched, so the reporter onsite kept repeating the same information while on a split-screen with an anchor. They were scrambling and didn't seem to know much other than the visuals from the CNN helicopter.

"CTI manufactures police and armed forces anti-riot gear like tear gas and other irritants designed to disperse crowds," the anchor said, clearly reading from some recently found website or file information. "It is unclear the exact motivation for the attack, and one can only speculate as we often see that this will be some sort of disgruntled employee or someone who feels slighted by the company. Yet, one cannot help but speculate, given the industry, that Antifa or Antifa-related forces were behind this."

He was, of course, correct. Most of these workplace acts of violence involve people with a personal motive. However, those circumstances almost always involve a shooting or perhaps a stabbing, not a high-level explosion like this.

Dr. Williams and Aisha remained fixed on the television. No one spoke. Domestic terrorism was part of our study, and this sort of event was going to change our lives. We didn't know how yet, but we know that it would.

CNN now had their homeland security expert on a split-screen.

"It is clear from the extent of the damage that this act has been performed by someone with considerable resources and, I would conjecture, expertise. From the reports we have, this was completed by a half dozen or so assailants who were in and out of a building with a high degree of speed and efficiency. They knew what they were doing. They knew explosives, and they did their homework. That is, if they intended to render CTI unproductive, it was effective because the end of the building destroyed was indeed the manufacturing end," he said.

He was, of course, correct. The damage made this clear that it wasn't a pipe bomb made in someone's basement. But what was it and who had access to it?

The anchor broke in.

"We've been informed that the word "ANTIFA" and a fist have been spray-painted in black at the exit of the building where it is believed the assailants fled." He paused and addressed his security expert. "What does this mean? What is this about?"

"Well, clearly, an Antifa-based organization wanted credit for this work. What the implications are, I don't know. This hasn't been what Antifa has been associated with until recently. Honestly, I don't know what this all means," he said.

As the three of us watched, no one said a word. Finally, Dr. Williams spoke.

"This changes everything," She said. Her cell phone rang. She looked at it like she wanted to see who it was from so she could decline the call. Instead, she quickly picked up.

"Yes, Dr. Michaelson. Yes sir. Oh my God, sir," she paused for a moment. "Yes, I'll be right over."

She left the room.

Aisha and I just looked at each other.

CHAPTER SEVEN

Dr. Williams was back in twenty minutes and came into my office. Her face was cold, and she avoided direct eye contact.

"Can I see you in my office right away?" She said.

"I have a session in five minutes, can we—" She didn't let me finish.

"Cancel it." She turned and walked out.

I grabbed a notepad and went to her office. When I got there, she sat behind her desk, reading a memo. I sat across the way.

"Did I do something wrong?" I said.

"Edwin Hutchins is dead. He shot his wife and two children and then hung himself."

I just looked at her.

"He was found by a postal worker trying to deliver a package shortly after 5 pm. They were all dead. It is being labeled a murder/suicide. It will hit the media this morning. Hutchins's cover is as an auditor with Agriculture."

"I...I...I don't know what to say. He showed no indication of—"

"Trace, do you realize how this makes our work look?"

"Huh?"

"Our highest priority is the mental health of the agents. One just killed his family and himself." She glared at me.

"Eddie didn't buy into the debriefings. He said he knew his

job, knew what he was supposed to do, and accepted that bad things happened to good innocent people. He didn't—"

"Clearly, you missed it."

"But Dr. Williams, I—"

"We will need to go over all the notes, all the assessments and do a full psychological autopsy. Be prepared to report on his feelings of hopelessness, sadness and depression, and his indifference to the future." Her face was almost in a grimace.

"Eddie didn't have any of those things. The last time we spoke, he was talking about his frustration with his golf swing and USC football," I said. I shook my head in disbelief.

"That sounds like the problem. Those sessions aren't to talk about bro stuff like football and golf. Jesus Christ, Trace." She raised her voice.

"That's not fair and you know it!" I had never talked back to her, but she was out of line. My shock and sadness had turned into anger.

She folded her arms.

"The man is dead, and we were responsible for his mental health. You know how this makes us look?"

"Sounds like you're more worried about your reputation and the success of your business than you are about this tragedy." The more I thought about it, the angrier I got. "How dare you! God damn it! How fucking dare you!" I stood up from my chair.

Aisha entered the room.

"Trace, Trace—maybe you should go to your office..."

The room got very quiet. I could feel my heartbeat.

"Yes, it would be best if you went to your office. We will address this later," Dr. Williams said. She slammed her desk drawer and picked up the phone.

Aisha walked me back to my office.

I slammed the door.

"That fuckin bitch! I can't believe—" Aisha shushed me.

"Trace, calm down. She's upset. You've got to calm." She closed my office door and made a pushing down gesture with her hands to encourage me to chill out. She leaned on the closed office door.

I sat at my desk, and all at once, I was consumed with tears. Grief and anger mixed, and I felt sick. I turned and vomited into the wastebasket.

Aisha stayed. She didn't say anything, but she remained while I continued to get sick. I tried to distance myself from my thoughts. I tried to check in with my emotions, but they came way too fast and rolled over me. I threw up again.

"You should go home," she said lightly. "Go on home. You want me to drive you."

I shook my head. My arms were on my knees, and I was hyperventilating. I didn't have anything left inside me to puke. For a moment, the tears subsided.

"What's Williams doing the rest of the day?" I asked.

"She's already back in with Michaelson and will be for the rest of the day. Go on home."

Aisha was right. I was a mess, and heading out would make the most sense. I'd be no good here. There was no way I'd have the presence of mind to get any work done.

I headed home.

I drove home in a trance. Why the hell did Eddie do it? It made no sense. Last week it was about busting my balls, getting through the day, and bettering his golf swing. Yesterday, he shoots his wife and kills his kids? Their photos were in frames on his desk. I pushed down the urge to vomit.

And Dr. Williams's reaction? What the fuck was that?

I know her business is her life, but she was all about looking good and worrying about her ego. There was no concern for Eddie and the Hutchins family. I'd never quite seen that side of her to that extent before. She was driven. She was ambitious. But she was also a trained clinical psychologist whose career is supposed to be based around empathy.

I tried calling Marie again on the way home. I needed someone who loved me to talk to. I needed someone who could somehow make this ok. Or, at least I needed someone to make me feel okay. Again, it immediately went to voice mail. It was the middle of the day. She was probably in a panel discussion. Still, I don't understand why she hadn't checked in. It was a day and a half, and I know we're grownups and all that, but it pissed me off that she didn't want to share her day with me. I had to let that go.

I didn't know who else to talk to. Ray was a friend, a close friend, but the touchy-feely stuff wasn't his strong suit. He'd tell me "fuck that nonsense" and not to take responsibility for another person's actions. He'd especially tell me to "fuck that nonsense" when it came to taking shit from Dr. Williams. Ray was bright, but he still was a bit of an old school guy, and taking shit from women was something he just didn't accept.

My family wasn't an option in this case. They loved me but talking about feelings wasn't exactly their strong suit. No, I was going to have to process this by myself. Maybe some bourbon. Maybe some mindfulness and perhaps some prayer would get me through this.

It was going to have to.

I went to unlock the condo's door, but it was open. Weird, but it wouldn't be the first time I ran out and left the front door unlocked. I stepped inside, and something came over me that I couldn't immediately identify. I stopped, took a breath, and observed my thoughts and emotions. It was the faint smell of Marie's perfume.

"Marie?" I called out.

Nothing.

In the living room, my socks were where I left them, and last night's beer cans were on the coffee table.

"Marie?"

Nothing.

I ran up the stairs to our bedroom. Someone had been here. The closet door was open. There were a few odd socks and a t-shirt on the floor. My side of the closet was all pushed to one side.

Marie's side was empty.

Her shoes were gone.

I whipped around, and her perfume, moisturizer, lipstick, and all that shit was gone from her dresser. I threw open her dresser drawers.

They were empty.

On the bed, there was an envelope in Marie's stationery.

I ripped it open.

Trace,

Please forgive me. This is totally unfair.

I haven't felt right for a long time and just couldn't bring myself to talk about it. I have to leave. I can't get married and can't ever expect you to understand or forgive me.

Maybe in time we can talk and you'll forgive me. Now, I can't expect that to be possible. I'm taking a leave from work. Dr. Williams knows.

I'm sorry for being so secretive. I'm sorry for doing this. I don't know what to say.

M.

I held the letter in my hand and looked at it. It went out of focus. It was hard to swallow. I kept it in my hand. I looked up at the closet, and her luggage and trunk were gone.

I reread the letter. It was her handwriting. Still, it was so distant and without any depth that it didn't seem like her. It made no sense.

Five years and she's gone with barely a paragraph.

I sat on the couch and wanted to cry. I didn't.

I just sat there. I tried to breathe. I tried to notice my emotions. I tried to make space for them.

Nothing.

I don't know how long after that my iPhone rang.

"Trace, it's Jack." My older brother. He never called me. "Dad's dead. He had a heart attack."

That was the last thing I remembered.

CHAPTER EIGHT

"Mr. Curran, the doctor would like to visit with you now." It was my nurse, and it didn't seem to matter to her that my eyes were closed. The clock next to my bed read 10:13, and I had a good idea that it meant AM.

"That will be fine," I said.

A short, pudgy, middle-aged Indian man came into my room with a clipboard and wearing a white hospital coat fulfilling just about every cliché there was when it came to psychiatric hospital admission.

"Good morning, Mr. Curran. I am Dr. Fadhi." He said it without making eye contact.

"Good morning, doctor," I said. I sat up in bed just a bit.

He gave me a half-smile.

"Do you know where you are?" He asked without warmth.

"St. Elizabeth's Hospital on the mental health unit," I said.

"Do you know what day it is?" Dr. Fadhi was not going to win the APA's empathy award this year. At least I wasn't going to nominate him.

"Wednesday the 23rd."

"And what is your name?"

"Trace Curran."

"Very good," he tapped his clipboard with his silver Cross pen. "Who am I?"

"You're the hospital psychiatrist."

He smiled. "Very good."

"Dr. Fadhi, I'm a psychologist," I said. I tried to leave the attitude out. It wasn't easy.

"Yes, I know that. You know the reasons for my questions, then."

I exhaled.

"Yes. I am oriented to time, place and person."

He smiled but didn't respond. He was making a note.

"Mr. Curran, I have diagnosed you with Acute Stress Disorder with Dissociative Amnesia. That means—"

"I know what it means. Did you hear me say I was a psychologist?"

"It means you experienced a traumatic event, and your mind and body have responded in the fashion to protect themselves. It is why your memory is impaired. It is why you feel tired and sleep many hours, and it is why you have experienced parasomnia."

It's a good thing I was a psychologist because I knew Parasomnia meant nightmares.

"Do you remember being admitted?" he asked.

That pissed me off. I looked at him.

"No."

"You were in the parking lot of where you work. You were pacing, and you kept repeating the same words to yourself."

"I hope it was something smart," I said.

He frowned.

"You kept saying 'No, No, No…"

I looked away.

"You have been here for four days. I am concerned about the time you spend sleeping."

"Weren't you the one who gave me the Ativan?" It came out harsh. I meant it to.

He didn't care.

"Yes, I am continuing on this with discharge. I have also recommended that you not return to work."

"Yeah, well, that's not up to you, doctor. There is something about HIPPA regulations." I had gotten harsher.

He smiled without and glee.

"That is between you and your employer. It was Doctor Williams who found you and called the hospital."

That gave me a wave of nausea. I almost threw up.

I didn't want to listen to any more.

"I am referring you to follow-up care, and the nurse will be giving you names and numbers of consulting psychiatrists we work with. Here's your prescription. Please follow up today so we can discharge you." He smiled and left the room.

I crumbled up the prescription and got dressed.

It was time to go home.

PART TWO

CHAPTER NINE

George came in the front door at 11:05, like he did every day.

"Top of the morning to you, Trace," he said, like he did every day.

"And the rest of the day to you, my good man," I said, trying to put some cheer into my voice. I was at the beginning of a 10-hour shift in my dad's bar.

This wasn't where I thought my career was going to take me.

I was stocking the coolers with Bud, Bud Light, and Coors Light. Despite the craft beer renaissance, Curran's still sold tons of domestic shit. The craft stuff was on tap, and all the micro-breweries competed to see who could have the cutest or stupidest tap handle. There were geese, car stick shifts, and fish, all whimsically annoying to me.

SportsCenter was on, and there was a heated debate about the college football playoff and whether Notre Dame deserved to be in the final four teams. They didn't play in a conference, and this year their schedule was a bit soft. With SportsCenter on most of the day, running in an endless loop behind me as Curran's default soundtrack, it never ceased to amaze me how talking heads with skinny ties, perfectly honed facial stubble, and nothing to say could spend all day saying it.

It was identical to what you'd hear if you let CNN run all day. Just substitute different clichés, and you'd have the same back and forth for the mere sake of going back and forth. The hair would be slightly less edgy, and the fashion sense for the female news professionals would mute the overt sexuality that the ESPN anchors favored.

"These guys hate the Irish. Always have," George said. He was a huge ND fan, and he wore his Lou Holtz-era hat on Saturdays when the games were on. It wasn't just football, and it wasn't just football-as-religion for him. It was football intertwined with religion. The "God Made Notre Dame Number One" wasn't tongue-in-cheek for George. It was about right and wrong and good and evil.

"You going back for a game this year, Trace?" George asked.

George was just making conversation. He covered the same conversation points every day, which got tedious. It seemed comforting to him, like by saying the same things, he didn't have to come up with anything new. George was in his mid-70's, never married, and he took care of his mom until she died early last year. He came here to pass the day and was a nice man. Boring as hell, but a nice man. In a sense, his purpose, his role, and his vocation were gone now that his mom had passed. He was here to get through the hours until his day would come. One time, I tried to explain to him how Notre Dame was a school founded by French priests who were not Irish at all, but his eyes glossed over. I never brought it up again.

"Probably not, George," I said. "Flights are expensive out of Albany, and it is tough to get a room during football season. Plus, I know fewer and fewer people out there as time passes." It was the same explanation I gave him a week ago when he asked. I hadn't been back to the campus in the two and half years since I started post-doctorate work.

"Oh, Sweet Jesus, here he comes," George shifted his focus. I heard the familiar scritch-scratch, scritch-scratch, scritch-scratch on the old faded, pitted and stained hardwood, followed by the expansive yawn then the tornado-like twisting and flapping of the jowls. Rocky, my family's 150 lb., black and tan, bloodhound, had risen like the messiah himself, from his storeroom bed to say hello to George. He was big enough to rest his head on George's thigh as George sat on his barstool. Soon, Rock would leave foamy slobber on George's pant leg, but George would just rub it into the fabric of his husky dad jeans.

"Hey, Rock, why the long face? Ha!" George offered his daily greeting, reached into his pocket, and produced a Milk-Bone. He padded Rocky's head a few times and then brought his attention back to the TV. Rock stayed as long as George continued to pet his head. Every fifth or so pet George would scratch Rock's neck. Rocky loved that part. Occasionally, George would get just the right spot, and Rocky's hind leg would go into near orgiastic spasm. George didn't care that Rock smelled like old Fritos or that his 15- inch ears were crusted from dragging them across the bar floor after being dunked in his water dish. Their friendship made me smile to myself every day.

"Man, your dad loved this guy," George said while he got the spot below Rocky's ear. "And his daddy."

"He sure did," I said and exhaled hard. There was something about Rocky without Dad that hurt deep down inside when I thought of it. He was the son of Dad's other dog, Sully. Rocky came to dad's wake and funeral and laid down in the procession line with the rest of the family. He kept Mom company, and she spoke to him when she was alone in the house. Just thinking about it made me almost cry.

Dad was the heartbeat of the place. Structurally, the bar had changed little since 1968 when he opened it. It was now hip again in its styling, merely by not changing. Through the '70s, '80s and most of the 90's it was seen as out of date and passé, but now it fit right in with the retro look of the other bars in Albany's warehouse district. Curran's didn't try to be retro. It was retro. Dad was a character that people came to see, and though he called everyone "Pally," everyone seemed to think it was their own special unique nickname.

"Trace, I think there's a note for you over the register," George said. He didn't mind his own business when it came to anything having to do with the bar or, for that matter, anything to do with my life. George's heart was in the right place 100% of the time, so I gave him a pass on his deficient social skills 100% of the time.

The note was a near-daily occurrence. It came from Jessica, the new, or I guess, new to me, manager, that my brother hired to get the place up to hipster speed. Jack, my older brother, was a lawyer in the Albany District Attorney's office, but he looked after the bar for mom since Dad died. In that six months, Jack didn't ever take a shift behind the bar, drop a dozen wings into the fry-a-lay-tor or mop up college puke on a Saturday night. He did hire Jessica away from managing, The Gasthaus, the German-themed, soccer-crazy, uber-Euro-cool joint across the street. It used to be a plumbing supply warehouse, and now it had the perfect blend of old brick, exposed beams, and intolerable patrons with narrow frames, ironic tattoos, and black skinny jeans. They showed Premier League soccer early Saturday and Sunday mornings and packed the place.

I tried to like Jessica; I really did. She moved Curran's in the right direction, doubled the business, and made the place a stop for people younger than 70. She did it through Trivia Night, Monday Night Football specials, Country Music Night, and, just like The Gasthaus, Premier League Soccer promotions. Myself, I'm not much of a kickball fan, and the posters from the beer distributor of some one-named Argentinian wearing a Tottenham jersey and featuring the EPL TV schedule made me throw up a little in my mouth.

The note read:

Trace,

No biggie, but could you remember to stock the coolers with plenty of Spaten for Saturday morning? Last week it wasn't in the cooler and we couldn't get it cold fast enough for the first EPL game. The German guys who follow Arsenal really like it.

Don't mean to be a bug-thanks!

Jen

There was a hand-drawn smiley emoji next to her name. I did forget the Spaten last week, and it was a mistake because the German guys did drink a lot of it. Somehow, and it bothered me that I knew this, but their countryman, Bernd Leno, played for Tottenham. The fact that kickball awareness was involuntarily seeping into my consciousness disturbed me. I feared that I'd be having the inseam of my denims taken in and that I'd be making a trip to the optician for new eyewear before I knew it.

I tried not to resent Jessica's reminder, but my mental gymnastics only partially worked. Jess was never mean and went to great lengths to protect my feelings since I came back. I'm sure Jack briefed her on my "issues" and was told to handle me with care. She had shoulder-length blond hair and an athletic build that she honed with dedication at a place called Orangetheory fitness. Some of the young patrons were OT enthusiasts, and their allegiance to it as a lifestyle bordered on cultish. Far as I could tell, Jessica was either there, here, or sleeping. She was delightful, very positive, and she worked her ass off.

I guess part of why I resented her was that I use to feel that way about my work, but not in a while. Certainly, not in a long while. She also shared a perfume with my ex, and that didn't help my feelings for her. It was a little too intimate reminder of shit I didn't feel like thinking about.

"Hey Trace, you look kinda down. You still lettin' that girl bother you?" George said. It made me cringe. My broken engagement was never too far from my thoughts, so it wasn't like George was reminding me of something that I didn't think of. Still, I preferred not to verbalize about it if I could help it.

"Ah, I don't know George. I guess sometimes I can't help it," I said, trying again to be civil but not open the door to conversation.

"Lotta fish in the sea, my man," George said.

"Yeah, you're right on that one. Like ridin' a horse. You just gotta get back on," I said, parodying dude speak. I knew George wouldn't pick up any irony. Whether it was fish or horses, the dude mentality did little to help how I felt.

"Atta boy!" George said, and I'm sure he felt like he turned my world around for me. That was okay. George was a good man.

As for getting back on horses and riding them, it was something I knew I had to do, too well, get on with things, but, shit, it felt foreign as hell. Yeah, there were women who interested me but pulling the trigger on anything other than small talk seemed akin to breaking the four-minute mile. I tried, I kept my mind open, but it seemed to be as stale as some of George's analogies.

The door opened, and the harsh mid-day light broke through the bar's darkness. The cool fall air washed through the bar, making me aware of how much the stale spilled beer, old smoke, and deep fryer smell hung in the place. My flannel shirts never seemed to exorcise the funk, and I often feared that it got into my skin. Macy's didn't carry a men's scent with notes of "crispy chicken skin and fermented ale backsplash." I wondered again, like I did about six times an hour, how I got here.

A glance at the Blue Moon clock over the register told me it was 11:45, and that meant a group of regulars and semi-regulars were due. There was often a shift of cops coming off a late overnight, a group of nurses who worked in the emergency room from nearby Memorial, and a couple of construction foreman types who I could count on for an early lunch. Not all of them came every day, but some combination of them usually stopped in. George stayed through it all, two stools away from the TV with Rocky. Rocky would lift his head off of George's thigh to check out the new two-legged scents that came in, but most of the time he put his head back on George's thigh.

I squinted while my eyes adjusted to the light and noticed three detectives I knew and one construction guy, whose name I think was Randy, come in. Agusto, our day cook, wasn't in yet, which made him an hour and ten minutes late. That meant Agusto's special needs kid was having a tough time in school, Agusto's 1988 Corolla wouldn't turn over, or Agusto was still drunk from last night. Agusto worked all the time, at a million different small jobs, and never said no to a paying gig, except when it interfered with cooking here. We paid Agusto's health benefits, and he was loyal to Curran's, if not for emotional reasons, then for financial ones. With his life, I didn't hold it against him for getting wasted once in a while.

If Agusto didn't show, it meant I was tending bar and cooking. That meant bad food and poor bar service, neither of which would be my fault, but I still had a pretty high need for approval and didn't like the muttering and rolling of eyes. I didn't like doing poorly at anything, even if I hated whatever it was I was doing.

"C'mon Gus..." I heard myself say.

"Hey Trace, LaGunitas," Tony Crespo said. Tony worked narcotics and had a rep for being a hell of a cop. He had strong Italian features with a nose that looked like it had been broken as often as a school girl's heart and a hairline that started about half an inch above his eyebrows. Sometimes, a little quick with his hands, which got him into some trouble, and he liked to drink, but there was no denying his work. Last year, he brought down a Harlem to Albany to Syracuse heroin supply chain, and for a long time, Tony's sins were going to be forgiven. Jack rolled his eyes whenever I mentioned him because Tony's extracurriculars made Jack's cases troublesome more than a couple of times. Tony was in with two guys I saw less often. Kevin Morgan and Al Nace, who both were detectives. They didn't talk as much as Tony did, and they had that cop way of keeping to themselves.

"Fightin' anymore?" Tony said when I placed the draft in

front of him.

"I did some sparring a week ago. I haven't been doing it consistently enough to compete," I said. "I was getting steady sparring in Washington with a buddy from work, and I miss it."

It made me think of Ray. It reminded me of all the changes and, most of all, it made me sad.

"Once a week will barely keep you sharp. You gotta get more work if you're going to compete?" Tony boxed 20 years ago and kept an interest in the local goings-on. He even came to the gym once in a while.

"I know, I know. I've been working with Jesus and trying to stay focused," I said. "Not sure about competing again." Jesus ran the city gym. He was one of boxing's characters and a surrogate father to many teenage boxers.

I turned, got the construction guy his Diet Coke, and I took a deep sigh of relief when I saw Agusto come through the front door. He had an Indian complexion with super smooth skin that never would support facial hair. He was built like a laborer with no extra fat, calloused hands, and fingers that curled a little bit with the muscle and the dexterity that comes from working and relying on them day after day. He wore a laundered white t-shirt and faded Carhart pants.

He was a stand-up guy, and I knew the first thing he'd do.

"Yo, Trace, I'm sorry man," he said. His voice had just the slightest hint of an accent. He grimaced. "Carlos was having a bad morning and—"

I cut him off.

"No sweat, Gus. Don't worry about it," I said. It was almost impossible to find cooks that would last more than a week, not steal you blind, and who wouldn't shoot heroin while they were prepping a salad. Agusto was a good man, didn't do any of that shit, and he worked his ass off. He immediately put on his apron and went through the swinging doors to get to work. The day just got a whole lot better.

I was checking in with the construction guy on the other side of the bar to see if he was ready to order. I wasn't sure enough that his name was Randy, so I didn't use it when I approached him. His ambivalence was getting the better of him, and he asked me to give him a minute. My iPhone rang, and I realized I made the mistake of leaving it on the bar when I brought Tony his beer. It was on its fifth electronic ring when I got to it. I saw who it was from and got that sick feeling in my stomach, and I hit "Decline."

I felt my chest tighten, and I got that feeling behind my eyes that I've never been able to put an emotional word to. There was no point in dwelling on it, and I went back to ask the construction guy if he made up his mind on what he wanted to eat. He wanted a cheeseburger, medium, and the sweet potato waffle fries, extra crispy. I passed the order through the kitchen window to Gus.

I scanned the rest of the bar. George was good, and Tony and his boys were a few sips away from a refill. I drifted back over to them.

"I should mind my own business," Tony said, glancing at my phone that I now held. "But, do you often decline calls from the CIA?"

CHAPTER TEN

I should never have labeled the number "CIA" in my phone. I remember kind of laughing to myself when I got the job and entered it into my contacts. I thought it was funny, and even though I was a contractor and not a CIA employee, I left it that way on purpose. Now, I wish I hadn't tried to be ironic. Then again, people aren't supposed to snoop around your phone.

I looked at Tony without saying anything, just a little too long. I didn't want to let this spiral into an argument or an interrogation, so I tried to be nonchalant. I could sense I wasn't pulling it off. Tony dedicated his life to figuring out when someone was full of shit, and I wasn't a pro at lying. Still, I pressed on with the routine.

"As a matter of fact, I regularly decline calls from 'The Company.'" I put a self-mocking emphasis in "The Company," the code name for the CIA that even the most novice of conspiracy theorists knew. I tried to say it like Sean Connery, but I think the best I did was sound like the guy on Saturday Night Live that satirized Sean Connery. I smiled at Tony, who smirked in response.

"I still don't believe they hired a Notre Dame-educated shrink and didn't use him to profile nutjobs and serial killers," Tony said. "I know you're not supposed to say anything, but don't waste your time bullshitting a bullshitter."

We've sparred like this before, and humor was the best tool I had to deflect things. Tony knew I was doing it, and I knew I was doing it, but this is how this game was played, and I wasn't going to bend.

"You see, Tony, Ted Kascinski, Mr. Unabomber, dropped a dime on me, said Rocky over there was talking to him and told him that I was going to go on a spree, maybe shoot up the nuns at Bishop Maginn because Sr. Fredricka spanked me in first grade. That's why 'The Company' let me go," I said.

I Groucho Marx-ed my eyebrows and grabbed the construction guy's lunch Gus at the kitchen window. I brought it to the bored customer who mindlessly watched SportsCenter, and I asked him if he needed anything else. He wanted some ketchup and some Tabasco.

"That story is more believable than the shit you've tried to sell me," Tony said. I was never going to convince him, and I got the impression that he thought if he persisted like I was one of his street perps, he would get it out of me.

"Tony, do I really strike you as a secret agent man type? Do I give off the badass vibe of a federal dude?" I said, smiling.

Tony pursed his lips. "Yeah, you go study brainiac psych stuff for about ten years, get your Ph.D., and they hire you to hold hands with stressed-out staff? Yeah, that's how the government works. That makes a lot of friggin's sense," Tony said and punctuated it with a sneer and a pull on his beer.

"Think about it, Tony," I said calmly. "Over 20,000 people work for the CIA. It's like working for General Motors or the Army or something. Sure, there's all that clandestine black ops or whatever they call it stuff, but there's also a whole lot of boring support jobs. I worked for a company contracted by the CIA. We did support work. That's what I did. I've told you that."

It was mostly true.

Mostly.

Tony took a long sip from his second Lagunitas, gave me his "You're full of shit" look again, and turned his attention to

Kevin and Al, who were muttering stuff about the Lieutenant, skels, and the Arbor Hill neighborhood.

I ducked it, at least for today, and I felt myself ease just a bit. Then, the purpose of the call and who it was from came back to me. I felt my chest tighten up. The feeling was never that far away to begin with, but now it was back front-and-center and eating away at my gut. I did the mindfulness thing and tried to detach from it, telling myself that it was only a feeling and nothing more.

Yeah, "nothing more." What bullshit.

Rocky slunk away from George to the detectives and gingerly sniffed their half-circle. He didn't get any pets there, so he moved on to the foreman and stared at him as he ate his burger. Rocky's eyes followed the burger from the bar to the foreman's mouth and back again. He didn't blink. He had a neurosurgeon's concentration skills, and I know the customer could feel the big brown eyes burning a hole in him, or at least in his burger.

"Hey, Rock," the guy said. "Ron says, 'Have a fry!" There we go, it was "Ron" and not "Randy." I felt like I used some sort of Malcolm Gladwell instinctual cognitive process to not guess on his name, and it paid off.

He tossed the waffle fry in the air with the intention that Rock would do something athletic or at least dramatically snap it out of midair like a YouTube Golden Retriever. Rock wasn't athletic, and the waffle hit him just above his left eye. He wasn't sure where it went for a second, and he looked, first left, then right, in desperation. Then he saw it between his legs. Rocky couldn't catch, but he could vacuum, and the fry disappeared in an instant. He moved back to his bed in the pantry with a profound sense of satisfaction. He was a Zen master.

Before long, Tony and his boys left to go home and go to bed. Ron, formerly known as "The Construction Guy," left crumbs on his plate and went back to his site. Now, it was just George, Agusto, Rocky and me. Agusto stayed in the back, chopping onions, preparing tonight's soup, and making chili. The smells from the kitchen now rose over and above the Buffalo wing and old beer aroma to something new and savory. It was wonderful aromatherapy.

This was the most difficult part of the day. My bar prep work, stocking the coolers, cutting fruit, and wiping things down, was over. Almost no customers, and even George was getting ready to pack it in. The quiet gave me too much time to think, which was the worst.

"Trace," George knocked the bar with his knuckles and shot me with his index finger. It was his trademark farewell, and, honestly, it was a pretty good one.

"See ya, buddy," I said as George headed to the exit. Rock came out of his lair and slowly walked over to George as he made his way out.

"I'll see you tomorrow, my friend," George said, and he gave Rocky his last Milk-Bone of the day. Rocky sat at the door for a long moment after George went through the front door, then he turned and went back to his bed. Like the tide going in and out, such was the rhythm of the day at Curran's.

SportsCenter re-entered my awareness, and three very tall Black guys and a very tiny blond white woman at a desk were arguing whether LeBron or Michael was the GOAT. GOAT, or "greatest of all time," now was its own thing, and I hated it. That, and the fact that Wilt Chamberlain, who averaged 50 a game without a three-point circle, was never in this stupid argument. I pointed the remote at the TV and muted it.

I plugged my iPhone into the sound system, put it on the playlist I put together, and hit shuffle. Waylon Jennings sang "If You See Me Getting Smaller," Springsteen did, "Drive All Night," and Elvis did, "You'll Think of Me." Probably not the selections they chose to pump things up at Orangetheory, more like the songs you'd pick when you broke the seal on a bottle of Slane Irish Whiskey.

I had made the playlist after the breakup. It was utterly self-indulgent, and I cherished the heartache it allowed me to wallow in. There were days I stayed away from it and days I immersed myself in it. I didn't know which was healthier, and when I was tired and the day wore on, I didn't care. She wasn't coming back. It was over, and there was nothing to show for it and no one to complain to. Time to get on with life.

Life being keeping track of important issues like Spaten in the cooler, keeping up with George's conversation, and admiring Rocky's approach to life.

Right now, the Slane appealed to me. Most days, it appealed to me.

Rock got up, went to the end of the bar, and looked at me. His eyes, hidden in the brown and black folds of his skin, focused on me. He whined twice, a high-pitched combination of concern and exhalation.

"I'm alright, Rock," I said.

He stood and looked at me without blinking. He knew when I was full of shit. He hesitantly went back to his bed.

Around three, Tinker showed up. It was his first time in since I came back. Tink was a holdover from the early days of Curran's.

"Good afternoon Tracy," Tinker said. He, my mother, and my sister were the only people who called me by my given name.

I opened a can of Schaefer and poured him a shot of Jim Beam. He didn't have to ask. He and his buddy, Stagger, were the only customers that drank Schaefer. It wasn't easy to get, but it was made in Albany up until '72, and Dad would've wanted us to keep it. Jessica and Jack didn't want it, but I didn't care. Even when they didn't order it, I'd get a case at Westmere Beverage and put it in the cooler without asking permission. Jack and Jessica didn't want to kick up my issues, so they left it alone.

Tinker wasn't a huge talker. He wore his VFW hat and usually an NRA shirt or something that, let's just say, suggested "conservative values."

"You know, Tracy, the old man, used to stand just like

you're standing," Tinker said.

I wasn't aware I was standing in any particular way.

"Huh?" I said.

"He had this way of leaning back on his left leg and shifting his weight back and forth while he had a hand on his hip. Just like you're doin'."

I must've made a face while turning it over in my mind.

"I'm serious,' Tinker said.

"Oh, I don't doubt it. It just isn't something I was ever aware I did," I said.

"Lotta things like that in life," he paused. "I miss your old man."

I nodded. I wish it didn't come up every shift.

"When me and Stagger came back, your old man didn't charge us anything for the first month. We drank for free. He never charged us full price, even after 22 years," he said. "He never made a big deal about being brothers in arms or any of that shit, but he showed it.

Dad went into the service in '64 or '65. It might even have been later. He never talked about it. Born in Ireland, he had dual citizenship and proudly served.

I thought about the free drinks without an explanation. That sounded like dad.

"You've heard the story, right?"

I didn't know what he was referencing. Dad and stories were kind of redundant. His life was filled with stories.

"About when we came back? He never told you?" Tinker finally sipped the bourbon.

I shrugged.

"The three of us were here, drinking during the day. It was probably our third day in a row. There were five college boys who just got done with their final exams. You know, long-haired ones from SUNY. Two of them had fathers in the mayor's office. It was why they drank here. They knew your old man was connected.

They started making comments about our haircuts, and then it turned, and they started saying shit about killing babies." Tinker took a longer sip of bourbon.

"The old man had gone downstairs to get more Schaefer. He was stocking it, and they were keeping it up when he heard them." Tinker drank some beer. "He put the case down and walked around the bar. I'll never forget the look on his face. He walked toward them, didn't run, didn't say a word," Tinker rubbed his eyes a little, and his voice got just a little forced.

"He grabbed the two he knew by their t-shirt collars, spun around, and threw them into the door. They fell over each other. They got up, and the old man just stared at them. Didn't say a fuckin' word. They got up and left. The old man turned and just looked at the other three. They followed behind." Tinker nodded and finished his Schaefer. "He then set us up with another round and poured us shots and one for himself. He never said a word."

I had never heard the story. My dad was the guy who called everyone "Pally." He wasn't a badass.

Maybe he was.

"Those were connected guys who he threw out. I don't know if it ever cost him anything. He never brought it up," Tinker said.

I didn't know what to say.

"Your old man was all right," Tinker said. He finished his beer and threw down his shot. Then he left.

I felt myself well up a bit.

CHAPTER ELEVEN

The bar action picked up again around 5:15 when the state workers' day ended, and by 5:30, I had a nearly full bar. The TV went over to the Spectrum News channel. We all got to hear about a fire in Montgomery County, the polluted Hudson in Hoosick Falls, and the Shenendowa High's varsity football team's undefeated season. Jessica came in at 6:30, checked the register, and looked in the coolers. She had on stretch jeans tucked into low-cut black suede boots and a navy-blue crew neck sweater over a white turtleneck. Her blond hair was pulled back in a simple ponytail, and she wore the slightest hint of makeup. When she walked close to me, I picked up a hint of the citrus-based perfume. The feeling in my gut gave me a quick shiver, but I did my best to let it go.

She was good with people and knew how to manage them.

"Thanks for stocking the Spaten," she said. I knew she was recognizing my responsibility and praising me as an employee. It was okay. "I appreciate not having to hear those knuckleheads on Saturday morning."

"Trust me, I get it," I said to be conversational and to let her know I didn't resent the patronizing; "Thanks for doing what you were told."

"Hey, Trace, was Agusto late today?" She asked matter-of-factly, without hesitating her count of the day's cash from the register.

"Nope, he was fifteen minutes early. You know how he is with that Chili of his," I said.

She gave me a quick smile before she went back to checking the liquor stock. Without looking up, she said, "I can cover the bar until Maureen comes in. It is only half an hour."

I pondered that for a second and wondered if this was a reflection on me somehow. Was my sullenness affecting business? Was she hoping to turn on her charm and make some tips? Was she covering for her friend Maureen who was chronically late and just as often in a state of drama over something?

I didn't think about it real long because I didn't really care, especially if it meant getting off duty early.

"Are you sure?" I said, concentrating on putting some enthusiasm in my tone.

"Yeah, no biggie," she said. "Biggie" was a word she used often.

"Great," I said. I double-checked my day's receipts and logged out of the register. I headed back to the kitchen through the pantry.

"C'mon Rock," I said. He wasn't quite snoring, but he was exhaling in a steady rhythm that was a kind of pre-snore. I bumped fists with Agusto as I passed him and turned the corner around the counter to the backdoor that lead to the stairwell. I was about to climb the eleven steps up to my apartment when I heard Agusto.

"Trace!" I heard him call, not a yell, but not in a regular speaking voice either.

I turned and looked at him.

"Thanks, man," Agusto said and touched his chest with his fist.

I smiled and returned the salute. Rocky passed by him and took his time on the stairs behind me. His long gangly legs made climbing awkward for him, so he took it slow and deliberately. His long day in the bar was over, and it was time for him to unwind. Mom liked when I took him for a few days, so she didn't have to do the revolving in and out back door game.

My phone vibrated in my pocket, and I took it out.

It was a reminder about my earlier call.

Living above a bar is depressing enough. Living above your family's bar sweetens the deal just a bit more. When you look at your pallet coffee table crowded with junk mail and magazines, and you noticed that your framed doctorate diploma is at the bottom of that pile, it provides all you need for a night of hopeless despair. I just couldn't bring myself to hang it on the wall. It somehow would stand there as a constant reminder about the dissonance in my life.

Rocky had things to do. He sniffed the perimeter of the kitchen. He stuck his nose into the threshold from the kitchen to the living room and concluded that there wasn't anything new to explore. Instead, he headed to his bed under the kitchen table, did two full turns, and collapsed. He let out a half sigh, half grumble.

"I know what you mean," I said aloud.

I was going to have to return the phone call. It didn't matter if I didn't want to or if I felt I would be prodded or manipulated into something. I still had to do it. I thought about cracking a beer and watching the national news, and I thought about throwing some gear on and going to the gym. Inertia was getting ready to kick my ass when I heard something at the door.

"Shithead! You in?" It was my little sister Molly.

"The shithead is indeed in," I said, and I felt myself smirk. Rocky recognized the voice and bound up so quickly he bumped his head on the kitchen table, which caused him to tornado his jowls.

Molly came up the stairs and immediately ruffled up Rocky's ears while kissing him on his nose. His tail wagged so much his whole body shook. Molly did it again, and Rocky responded in kind.

I stood and watched, not dreaming of interrupting the ritual.

"I only come to see the Rockstar. You can get me a beer,"

she deadpanned.

I opened the fridge and threw her a Boomsauce Double IPA.

She raised her eyebrows and looked the can up and down.

"You don't fool around. This is 8%," she said.

"7.8," I said.

She pursed her lips at my correction and rolled her eyes.

"So, what's up? Killin' it downstairs, are ya?' She said.

"Oh yeah, checking off all my life goals," I said.

She looked at me for a long moment.

"Self-pity or self-loathing?" she asked with only a hint of her usual sarcasm.

"Combination of both, with maybe a little broken heart shit mixed in," I said.

Molly frowned at me and scrunched her eyebrows.

"Bro, get over her. She showed her colors, and I know it hurts but better learn now, then later," she said.

"Man, those are such refined empathy skills you got there," I said. "Your ability to console is exceeded only by your snappy rejoinders."

"Rejoinders? Did you say that sort of thing a lot when you were engaged? Geez, no wonder she left you..." she said.

I chucked the sofa cushion at her, spilling some of her beer, and we both fell into laughter. She was the only person in the world who could bust my balls like this and make me laugh. I loved it.

"I'm sorry, Tracy," she said after we got done laughing. "It sucks."

I nodded and frowned.

"Yeah, it does," I said as casually as I could.

There was an awkward pause. She drank from her beer.

"I miss dad," she said, looking at the can's label. "A lot." I could see her eyes well.

She was the proverbial "Daddy's Little Girl." He cherished her, and it wasn't lost on anyone that Molly probably wasn't part of the Curran family planning. Mom and Dad were well into their forties when she came along. Molly could do no wrong with the old man, and she was blessed with the gift of being able to make him laugh no matter how dark his moods got. They got plenty dark, and Molly's role was crucial to all of us.

"Yeah, me too," I said. "I worry about Mom."

"She misses him. She doesn't talk about it, but sometimes she gets this far off look," she said. "Then, she says something Irish to Rocky and goes over and pets him. I think she likes it when you take him, so she doesn't constantly feel the pain of missing dad,"

"Jesus, Mo, I can get sad all by myself. Thanks for coming over," I said. I watched her drink the beer.

"Sorry, I think about it a lot," she said.

"Tough Irish Catholic, mom is," I said. "How's the fourth grade?"

"I got some great kids. I really do." She smiled to herself. She was in the right line of work.

"Is it ever weird being back at St. Teresa's. I mean, do you ever get lost thinking about the old times?"

"You mean do I ever go down to the tunnels and smoke cigarettes and neck with Jimmy Maio?"

"Yeah, something like that," I said.

The coolest thing about our school was the tunnel that ran from the school to the convent with a hatch in the middle of the softball field. Any eighth-grader worth his salt knew how to pick the lock and head into the underworld. It was where I found my first dirty magazine, smoke my first cigarette, and had my first underage beer.

"The tunnels are there, but I think today's kids spend more time on video games and AAU tournaments. I don't think they see the adventure in going underground to look at discarded dirty magazines," she said.

"Not with Pornhub on their phone."I switched the subject. "What do you make of Jack lately?"

She winced and scrunched her face.

"Jack's Jack. He seems to be in a state of perpetual annoyance, like the rest of the world is failing to live up to his expectations," she said.

"Funny, I thought it was just me. Like, being a lawyer was so much more real, so much more badass than being a psychologist," I said.

"Well, to him, yes, psychology, anything, actually involving human feelings is a waste of time," she said.

"Or anything that doesn't make money," I added. I thought about it for just a second longer. "Is there some sort of added life pressure being the oldest?"

"I don't know. He's 38 and not married and not seeing anyone. Maybe he just needs to get laid. He's probably all backed up and just needs someone to help clean out his pipes."

I shook my head in mock disapproval of her language. She spoke this way just for the negative attention it would bring, except I thought it was a riot coming from her.

"You ever use the expression 'clean out his pipes' when you're talking to mom?" I asked.

She looked at me with exaggerated eyes of mock fear.

"I would have to go immediately to see the monsignor for confession!" she said.

"How exactly would you confess to the monsignor that you used the expression 'cleaned out his pipes?' I mean, how would you tell him you said those exact words?" I asked, setting up her next line.

"Uh, maybe I'd say, 'I referenced an explosive ejaculate to my mother.'" She deadpanned.

"You're going to hell," I said.

"For referencing an explosive ejaculate?" she asked while feigning confusion. She giggled a little. It was an all-star giggle, and its mischievousness would excuse her from anything.

"Nice. What about you? How's Julien? That going any better?" I asked, knowing I was on shaky ground.

"Hmm, Julien, how do I describe..." she said. It was a sore subject, and I wished I hadn't brought it up at all.

"Never mind, you don't have to," I said.

She took a sip, a big sip from the beer, and finished it.

"Last week, he called me a cunt," she said, trying to be nonchalant.

I felt my jaw clench and my stomach tighten.

She looked at me.

"Don't, don't—I called him a loser. I started it." She looked at me like she wished she hadn't said anything. "Don't go all protective big brother on me."

I just looked at her, not knowing what to say. I wanted to scream and shake her. I wanted to find Julien and punch him out. Instead, I just glared at her. I got really quiet and didn't look at her. I walked out of the room and sat on my couch in front of the television. The room got even quieter, if that was possible.

I turned on the TV. It was the local news. I just didn't look at her. I hated to hear about her being mistreated.

"Are you going to say anything? Please say something," she said. There was some desperation in her infection.

"Why do you put up with that shit?" I finally broke. I shook my head, knowing I just delivered the type of platitude that would push her away.

She started to cry, got up, walked past Rocky, and went down the stairs and out the door. Rocky stood up and looked at me without blinking. He looked down the staircase and then back at me. He just stared at me.

He did that when he thought I was an asshole.

I thought about going after Molly, but that was never a good idea. When she didn't want to deal, she didn't deal. Maybe I'd hear about it later, or maybe she'd never mention it again. The undeniable point was that she wanted me to hear how much she hurt, even if she was going to make light of it. It was probably why she came over. Molly was rarely direct.

Rocky was still standing at the top of the stairs, only now he was facing the direction Molly went. He eventually turned and looked at me.

He wasn't pleased.

CHAPTER TWELVE

I was sorry Molly's visit ended on a down note. Like no one else, my kid sister could bring me out of a funk, and she did for a moment or two before I steered her into her own funk. It was a Curran thing, an Irish thing, and Dad had it and Mom had it. Jack was too angry all the time to have it.

That funk was my biggest weakness. Sure, I was a supposed expert in such things, but I fell short when it came to solving my internal battles. I was embarrassed by it, and though it was not uncommon for psychologists to be fucked up, insecure messes, I still felt like there was something sadly deficient inside me for failing to live life without so much baggage.

Of course, the pending phone call just raised all my insecurities. It was from Dr. Williams. She had granted me a mutually agreed upon leave after my, uh, I've never found the correct term for it, thing, I guess. Sometimes I liked to refer to it as the time I went bad.

Williams tried to make it clear that she wanted me back, but I wasn't sure whether she meant it or even if I wanted to go back. In addition to being a brilliant researcher and clinician, she had this way of making you want to follow her, get her respect professionally, and not let her down. She was difficult to negotiate with, and she was very convincing. I also didn't like the fact that I knew I hadn't lived up to her expectations.

There was nothing left to do but call the number.

"LW Psychometrics," Aisha said.

"Hey Eesh, it's Trace. What's up?" I said, doing my best to be upbeat.

"Trace! What's going on. We miss you!" Aisha was one of the happiest and most centered people I ever met.

"I'm okay. You know, getting by," I said, trying not to sound self-absorbed.

"You stay at it and get yourself back here. I miss arguing with you about, well, everything," she said.

"I miss telling you your wrong about everything," I said.

"Oh, now you're going to go there, huh?" She laughed.

"You know I will," I paused. "Hey, Dr. Williams wanted to talk to me. She in?"

"Sure, Trace, we're all working late tonight. Hang on, let me put you through," she said.

I waited and noticed the tension in my gut and that I was gripping my iPhone like I was trying to crush it.

"Trace, thanks for getting back to me," she said when she picked up. Her voice was feminine but also strong and confident.

"Of course, Dr. Williams. I'm happy to. I just not sure I'm ready to come back," I said. It was premature. I winced to myself for not letting the conversation develop.

"Trace, it isn't unusual for someone to have the feelings you are having after what you've been through. You understand that."

The hard part about my field is when work conversations bleed into psychotherapy discussions. It was part of what made me hesitant about making this call.

"I know, Dr. Williams, I do. It is just...oh shit, I don't know," I didn't know exactly what to say. I know what I felt, but I didn't want to share it with her.

She stayed silent in that therapist's way of allowing and encouraging you to speak more. I knew it as a technique, and I have used it. The thing was, this wasn't therapy, and she was my boss, not my shrink. Sure, there was all that transference and counter-transference stuff that psychology supervisors were supposed to go over with their staff, but in real life, it rarely happened. Supervision usually turned out to be about getting paperwork done.

After the uncomfortable pause, she continued.

"I know you know this but, the very first thing you're supposed to do after a trauma is process it. That's critical incident debriefing 101. Trace, you've never processed it. You've avoided it by going on leave," she said. Her tone wasn't condemning, nor was it apologetic. If I had to put a descriptor to it, it would be "scientific."

"That leave was mutually agreed. At least I thought it was. And, all due respect, Dr. Williams, you don't know if I processed it. You know I haven't processed it with you," I said. It came off more belligerent than I intended.

Again, she paused. I knew her well enough that she took time to formulate a response when she was caught off guard.

"Trace, I've known you for years. I am your direct supervisor in a behavioral science field. It is not a controlling request to ask you to go over the incident with me. I also think it is unfair to somehow suggest that," she said.

"I didn't mean to suggest that. I'm just saying that the agency is not my entire existence, nor do I want it to be. In fact, I might not want it to be at all," I said.

"That is something we need to talk about. I need you to come back to headquarters to go over some things," she said.

This time I paused. I checked in with what I was experiencing. Not just what I was thinking but also what I was feeling. Being mindful of it helped me make decisions.

"Trace?" she seemed a little impatient for her nature.

"Yes, Dr. Williams. I was just thinking that over," I said.

"It is an important part of your duties. Your position comes with responsibility, and I need to go over some things with you," she said.

"Some things?" I asked.

She took a moment and then answered.

"Yes. Hutchins was an agent, and we need to know some things about the event," she said.

I gave that some thought.

"I think we know what we're going to know about the "event," I said with just a bit of sarcasm mixed in.

"Yes, and please don't make light of the situation," she said with the tone of an angry parent.

"Trust me. I don't make light of the situation. You've got a lot of nerve—" she didn't let me finish.

"That wasn't fair, Trace. I'm sorry," she said.

I didn't say anything. I let the silence get awkward.

"Please come to headquarters. I'll have Aisha schedule it," she said. "She will call you with arrangements."

"Fine," I said, and we ended the conversation.

The conversation left me uneasy. I don't know if there was anything I would have responded to differently or anything I should have stated or declared. Dr. Williams was powerful, not just because she was my supervisor and not just because she used to be my doctoral mentor. She had a strength to her that was difficult to deny. I had wanted to please her while I was still in graduate school, and that desire to please her had continued since I took the job with her company. It wasn't just the usual need for approval that I burdened myself with. She had something else that hooked me somehow. I followed her directives, and it bothered me that I didn't often question them.

My time away had led to me questioning things a bit more. I wasn't comfortable with it because I had worked so many years to get where I was. Now, I stocked Spaten for soccer fans, and, all joking aside, it wreaked havoc on my soul. I knew I wasn't put here to pour drafts and keep George company. I just wasn't. At the same time, I couldn't envision just going back to work, not after what happened to Eddie and his family and not after I failed to stop it.

I went to the Bible my father left me. It belonged to his

grandfather, and it was purchased in his hometown of Derry, Ireland. The thought of Dad went through me, and I felt it behind my eyes. He wasn't gone all that long, and his sudden death rocked the entire family. He was the center of our family system, the foundation, and the bedrock. I knew I hurt, but I just couldn't let myself really feel it. It was too much, and with everything else that had happened, I didn't think I could work through it.

It was something else I could add to the list of things I had not dealt with. That list seemed to be growing every day.

The Bible was bookmarked with a folded newspaper article at Luke 12:22. It was my favorite passage and one I found myself rereading regularly. Handling worry seemed to be one of the chief goals in my day-to-day existence. It read:

Then he said to his disciples, 'That is why I am telling you not to worry about your life and what you are to eat, nor about your body and how you are to clothe it.

For life is more than food, and the body more than clothing.

Think of the ravens. They do not sow or reap; they have no storehouses and no barns; yet God feeds them. And how much more you are worth than the birds!

Can any of you, however much you worry, add a single cubit to your span of life?

If a very small thing is beyond your powers, why worry about the rest?

I tried to let it sink in, and it connected with me, but at the same time, prayer always left me a bit self-conscious. I wasn't sure if it was real, if I was doing it right, or just trying to be a good boy. I did my best to observe those thoughts and move on to concentrate on what the passage held.

The passage also held another purpose. It was the holding place for the neatly folded newspaper article. I kept it, preserving it here for some reason. It was ridiculous to think I ever could've forgotten the account of the incident that the article chronicled.

LANDOVER, MD.—Maryland police believe a senior analyst

with the Department of Agriculture killed his wife and three kids before taking his own life at the family's home in Landover, Md. this week.

The five bodies were discovered Wednesday morning at 53 Fair Road, following a fire. Maureen Hutchins, 44, was found dead on the first floor. Her husband, Edward Hutchins, 45, and two children, 7-year-old Carlton and 3-year-old Maryann, were found dead upstairs, Prince George District Attorney County District Attorney Adam Gold told reporters Thursday.

During a short news conference at 6 p.m. in Landover, Gold said evidence indicates that Mr. Hutchins was the assailant in what authorities have classified a murder-suicide. Gold said officials from several Maryland agencies are still combing through the family home, located in the northeastern corner of the state about a half-hour from Washington, looking for clues.

The causes of the deaths are part of the ongoing investigation. The bodies were taken to the chief medical examiner's office in Baltimore for autopsies, she said. Gold could not provide much more information about when the family died, whether weapons were involved or how the fire started.

The department of agriculture released a written statement Thursday, saying Hutchins "built a reputation both domestically and internationally as an agricultural expert."

"Ed was smart, knowledgeable, dedicated, and hardworking," the statement said. "He was a devoted father to his two wonderful children and a true friend to everyone in our agency."

"We are each devastated by loss and extraordinary sadness, but are comforted and grateful for having shared Bill's infectious spirit and energy.

"We pray for his family and those who loved him."

The fire was reported shortly before 8 a.m. It took about 90 minutes to extinguish, according to The Capitol.

The reference to the Department of Agriculture brought a smirk to my face. It was deliberately meant to cast him as a faceless federal employee and discourage anyone in the press or the public from jumping to any conspiracy theory-type conclusion.

Of course, the truth of the matter was that Eddie spent all day watching—studying—the most disturbing things imaginable.

I thought about how bored and annoyed with the sessions Eddie was and how he just went through the motions. I swear he gave off no signals about any problems at home. I didn't sense this was below the surface. I didn't know about any issues with his wife. I let him go through the motions. I let him keep it on the surface. I let him live in denial.

Now, because of it, he and his family were dead.

CHAPTER THIRTEEN

I just couldn't keep thinking. It exhausted me. I had prayed a little bit, which helped, but I was spent emotionally and physically. Despite that, I needed to move and push my body to clear things. Working out, specifically boxing, was something I learned long ago that I needed to do, not for fitness or vanity but for the release it brought. It was hygiene, and my body craved it like it craved breathing when I was underwater. As a teenager, it delivered me from the depths of hopeless insignificance, and since then, I had gone to it when I needed to exorcise something or, maybe closer to the truth, fight back against something.

Rocky snored while I threw on my tattered ND hoodie that had hung on the rusty roofing nail behind the door to my bedroom. I had cut two inches down the front of the sweatshirt to make it fit just a bit looser, and it was so old that there was little pill left to the fabric. My grey sweatpants were still on the floor by the unmade bed, well, mattress, from yesterday. My five-year-old Adidas boxing shoes, which I couldn't bear to part with because I was afraid the newer models wouldn't fit right, were harder to find because Rocky liked them. I spotted one on the other side of the dog bed, but the other was nowhere to be found in the bedroom. I walked out to the kitchen and listened to Rock under the kitchen table. Just the top of the shoe's toe was sticking out from under his belly. He only chewed them, really just held them in his mouth, for a moment or two, and then he liked to cuddle with them. I was flattered that my sweaty foot odor brought this creature comfort. I pulled it out from under him quickly and as smoothly as possible so that I wouldn't disturb him. He exchanged one snore for a sort of snort but didn't come to, and I got my second shoe on without lacing it.

I took a moment to look at Rock and take him all in. One hundred and fifty pounds, slightly overweight and black and tan, his pronounced sense of smell made him perpetually curious. He looked at people as possible sources of affection and food, and his first assumption was that they were all good. Yet, he could sense something he didn't like in a creature, and that would cause him to keep his distance. He moved away from ambivalence. Today, in the bar, when he sniffed around the cops and then moved on, it was because he sensed that their interest was elsewhere and they were indifferent to him. He didn't spend time with creatures like that, I guessed because he assessed there was no joy to be gained from them.

He kept those who showed him love consistently close. He loved George, and though he may not have been broken-hearted every time George left, he maximized his time with him without being clingy or needy. He let George know he appreciated him.

Rock also could sleep like a champ. He lied down and went totally limp like he had no bones. His mind was clear. He appeared satisfied or at least at peace with the way the cards were dealt, and when he slept, he gave his all to the process.

Rock had it figured out. I patted his head and went across the street to the gym.

I loved boxing gyms. The smells of leather, sweat, and BO melded together along with the hint of chlorine and disinfectant, though usually not enough of the latter, to let you know you were someplace different without anything needed to be said. The Cleveland Street gym had it, and the Albany gym had it. They were authentic.

The cacophony of sounds brought me a training symphony;

the backbeat of the speed bag, the bass drum of fighters going through their paces on the heavy bag, and the blues call of the coaches calling out one-word gospel verses at the sparring fighters; "Jab!" "Move!" "Touch" and the most common refrain, "Work!" The cacophony was improvised blues at its roots.

The bell sounds at the end of three minutes for a one-minute intermission before the next instrumental begins. There are ten seconds of quiet in that space, then the awareness of the rap music blaring from the cheap 80s boom box and 30 seconds of abbreviated conversations before the bell sounds to start over. I liked the workout, but I loved the meditative rhythm and the place's cadence. The structure eliminated the need for thought, and it brought me peace.

The entirety of the gym brought my thoughts back to Ray. Maybe the pending trip to DC could lead to a meet-up with him or perhaps even a workout. I missed him, and I missed the camaraderie we shared. It was the one thing I was certain of when it came to the old job, really, my old life.

I unfurled my yellow hand wraps and began the ritual of readying my hands. Every time the same way, loop the thumb, three times around the wrist, up and over the knuckles, in between each finger, three more times over the knuckles, and back down for four more times around the wrist. A Tibetan monk's altar had nothing on the Albany Parks Department Boxing Gym.

I began at the heavy bag. It was an excellent place to start because it allowed for long smooth movement, slowly bringing in to focus the body's balance, alerting the physical system of what muscle groups remained tight and inefficient. The bag gave the body feedback about where to focus attention. It let me know where tension existed, where soreness needed to be worked out, and directed what kind of workout I should have and the pace.

The speed bag was next. I was proficient in its use, but I avoided the gadgety and showy theatrics that some guys loved. I preferred the same four movements done in the same manner and pace over three minutes. It was meditation, but it also worked my traps and trained them to be able to hold my guard up while in the ring. After three minutes, I could feel the burn below my neck and in between my shoulder blades.

I shadowboxed in the auxiliary ring after the speed bag. I did my best to concentrate on movement and the pantomime of real sparring but struggled to keep my mind from becoming lazy. I worked jabs and crosses, first moving straight forward and then moving straight back. I circled, adding a bob to each side, followed by a jab, cross, hook combination before changing direction and repeating the combination in the other direction. I tried to blend a planned pattern and the improvisation of a real sparring duel. It was why karate guys did kata.

When the bell sounded, Jesus called my name.

"Trace! You want some work?" He yelled. He looked at me and nodded.

I nodded back, and instantly I felt it. It came every time I knew I was going to get in the ring with another man—some fear, some excitement, some concern, but definitely a lot of energy. Sparring cleared the mind while you focused on your opponent, hitting him, not getting hit hard by him while continuing to move, and keep a gauge on your reserves. You had to empty your mind, or your opponent would remind you by punching you in the face.

I fixed my headgear, and Jesus helped me get the 16-ounce gloves on, closing the Velcro and rolling down the cover. He had it down to a system, and his fighters knew to get geared up within the minute rest period and not miss the start of the next round. Jesus was a Marine for ten years, winning their bantamweight boxing championship twice, and he was all about structure and routine.

I was working with Nick, one of the few other white boxers in the gym. Some people will tell you that boxing gyms are devoid of racism, but I don't think that's entirely true. In the world of boxing, the white man has to prove he can fight because it's presumed he's softer than his Black counterparts. Black guys have to prove themselves, but they aren't necessarily assumed to be less tough. That was just the way it was.

I had Nick in experience, and he had me in youth, overall strength, and punching power. That might seem like he had the advantage, but boxing's beauty was that movement and experience could neutralize a good portion of power. It was like a Rubik's Cube because each move brought subsequent challenges. You could also get hurt by a lucky or unorthodox punch from even the most rank novice. Not every strong guy could hit hard, and there are plenty of skinny guys with no muscular definition who could really bang. I'll never completely understand why, but I think it had something to do with the complex chain reaction of body weight shifting. It is sort of like the power of a whip and how it is loose and limp until the exact moment of its cracking when all of the power comes to get at precisely the right time to get the snap. Great punchers knew how to be like a whip.

The bell sounded, and Nick touched my outstretched glove. It was part readiness check, part sportsmanship, and part acknowledgment of each other's courage even to be doing this.

We circled. I threw a double jab, mostly into Nick's gloves as a sort of way-finder. It measures distance, gives your opponent a distraction, and moves them off their mark. Mostly, it was a mental thing, like annoying flies that kept you from paying attention to the hamburger you were grilling. I threw a few more, made the mistake of being far too predictable, and Nick was ready, poised, and parried my jab with his left hand and countered me with a straight right. It landed flush on the bridge of my nose, letting me know my timing was off and my guard was down—Instant and reliable feedback.

It was the kind of punch that hurt the head and strained the neck, and I knew I'd have a dull headache for the next few days.

"You left the jab out," Jesus said. He was succinct, and he knew he was stating the obvious. It was like he was highlighting a sentence in a textbook so you would pay special attention to it and remember it. Boxing offers its own feedback system and, like Jefferson once said, "That which hurts, instructs." Still, Jesus's yellow highlighter made sure I'd remember what Nick just typed on my face.

I clinched for a moment, maybe a moment longer than I needed to, but I wanted the flash of minor nauseous to pass. It did, and we resumed circling.

Nick's a good guy, but the shot he landed put blood in the water, it revved his aggression engine, and he tried the move again, this time leading with it instead of timing and countering. He got greedy, and that was a mistake.

It was my turn, and I hit Nick with a jab as he came in, and because he was moving in, it magnified the force. It put him on his heels which eliminates a fighter's chance of getting anything off. My balance was square, with my momentum going slightly forward. I hit him with my straight left. It was a good shot, and Nick took a turn at clinching. Shortly after, the buzzer ended the round, and I think we were both a bit relieved.

The next round brought more circling and jabs. Jesus called for us to jab constantly, and he was right because just about every effective combination started with the jab. It distracted the opponent, got his hands moving, and ultimately led to openings. If both fighters are doing it, it can lead to a silent contract of sorts with both combatants not willing to move in. That's what the second round was like. It would go in the bank as a deposit on ring generalship, and it would pay off over time. All of the sparring was good in that it gave you time on task and presented you with more puzzle pieces to assemble.

Two rounds were plenty. It was just six minutes of exertion, but I'd feel it for a few days all over my body, and, thanks to Nick's shot, I'd have a bit of a dull headache. Just how difficult it was, was hard to understand and even harder to explain. It cleared my mind like nothing else, and I was soaked in sweat, and my breathing was labored. I decided it was enough for the day, and I began to undo my hand wraps.

"Looked good in there, champ," the voice came from behind me. It was Kayla. She was one of the women who trained at the gym and one of the very few who got in the ring.

"Yeah, I don't know about that," I said, and I blew the drop of sweat off the end of my nose. "Just happy Nick didn't take my head off."

Part of the boxing gym code was to be self-effacing, especially about how you worked in sparring.

"Yeah, yeah. You know you were moving good. You just won't ever admit it," Kayla said. In the past, we had a bit of a repartee that I liked, but this was as forward as I ever remember her being. It stirred something. She was tall with angular features, deep brown eyes, soft white skin, and a muscular physique. She was 5'8" or so and looked me nearly in the eye.

"You getting in tonight?" I asked.

"Nah. no one to work with," she said with more than a bit of disappointment.

"I'll work with you," I said. It wasn't unheard of for a male fighter and a female fighter to pair up, but it didn't happen often. There were the issues of size and experience, and men were almost always stronger, which meant they hit harder. The main reason it didn't happen, though, was ego and the discomfort of being in with a woman. Guys would spar with beginners who had no skill, acumen, or coordination, but they wouldn't go in even with an experienced woman.

If I was honest, I wasn't 100% comfortable with it either. It didn't hurt that it was Kayla who was looking for a partner. I liked to think I was evolved, but you don't leave your upbringing behind, nor did the gym culture not seep into you, no matter how mindful or aware you were. I was probably the only Ph.D. and licensed clinical psychologist at the Albany Parks Department Athletic Club, a background I never mentioned to anyone there. The new guys knew me as the white guy who bartended across the street. There weren't many old-timers around who remembered me as a teen.

The other reason I didn't mind getting in with Kayla was, honestly, she had an amazing body, all sinew, sharp angles, and taut muscles and tendons. She wore her hair pulled back and under a worn Yankees ball cap, and I never saw her with makeup on. The sparse look accentuated her looks, and I thought she was beautiful. She had straight white teeth, probably the product of some good adolescent orthodontics, though her front tooth was chipped ever so slightly. Her dark brown eyes and aquiline nose were elegant and way too delicate for the boxing ring where I thought they were in danger. I've paid attention to her from a distance, and I felt a kind of nervousness and wondered if something else was happening.

When she smiled, a series of dimples and laugh lines formed around her eyes and her mouth that seemed to give her a dimension of character. When she laughed, her forehead scrunched just a little bit, which made me smile. Her presence was welcome, even if in some twisted way it brought back the thoughts and feelings around my last relationship. Any positive emotion around a woman seemed to trigger a conflict within me. It was something I didn't quite understand and something I wanted to escape.

I had talked to Kayla enough to know she was a first-year graduate student in the University of Albany Social Work program. I thought it was cool that she was here, boxing, not at Orangetheory with yoga pants on, checking her heart rate.

She took off the ball cap, put on her headgear, and Jesus helped her with her gloves. Her hand wraps were tattered and worn, which told me she has been at this for a while. There was no polish on her nails, and they were short but still feminine. To his credit, Jesus made no jokes about us sparring, nor did he treat it differently than any other round.

"I want you guys to go easy, feel each other out. Mostly jabs, use your twos to the body. Lay off the power shots upstairs," Jesus said. It was what he said to everyone before they sparred together for the first time unless both fighters were known quantities and had plenty of ring experience. Having guys with lots of ring time blast beginners was bad for business because only the most masochistic novices would come back for more punishment. Getting beat up was also a poor way to learn. You had to learn how to take a punch, learn what it felt like, and go through the discomfort of it little by little in increments. It was a deliberate process if done right and Jesus did it right. Fighters just didn't come back if they were humiliated the first time they went through the ropes.

We went to work at the bell. Kayla circled me in the same way that Nick did. Her stance was tight the way it should be, and the way she moved it told me she wasn't carrying much nervousness.

She jabbed at me to be doing something. It fell short, and I didn't have to reach to parry it. I was relaxed and probably felt some internal compassion for her being in with a man who was 40% bigger than her. Just then, she adjusted her bodyweight, shuffled in, and followed a jab that fell short with a second one. After that landed, she dropped a straight right hand down the middle that landed perfectly into my solar plexus. It took some of my wind.

The jab hurt, and in about five seconds, I began to taste blood.

"Time!" Jesus called out. It was the universal command to stop. "C'mere," he said, and I looked over.

"I'm good," I said. "No big deal."

Jesus frowned. It meant to shut up and do what he said. Kayla stood off to the side in what would be a neutral corner had this been an official bout. She paced back and forth in short turns.

"Sorry, Trace," I heard her say.

"C'mon, it's a bloody nose," I said, trying not to sound defensive.

Jesus toweled the blood and put his index finger together with his thumb on the bridge of my nose.

"Ah!" I winced.

"You probably broke it, but it stayed in the middle and won't need to be set," he said with the confidence you'd expect from an emergency room doc. "Get out, no more tonight."

"C'mon, Jesus, "I said, "I'm good."

He frowned again, and I stepped out. The blood continued to run down my upper lip. I needed some cotton. Jesus already had the mitts on and preserved the rest of the round, working Kayla on the mitts.

I struggled with the elastic closure of my right glove but got it flipped down, put my glove between my legs, and pulled it off. I undid the left glove and went over to Jesus's desk, and got the cotton out of the top left drawer. I stuffed a couple of cotton balls up my left nostril. It was uncomfortable, but it was better than tasting blood and making a mess down the front of my hoodie.

The gym knew what happened. No one said anything, but there was a distinct change in energy. Would I take shit for being made to stop by a "girl?" I was still a bit of an unknown quantity at the gym, having been there steady for just a couple of months, and I had built some cred by getting in the ring. They didn't remember me from years ago. They knew that I held my own and didn't talk shit. There probably wouldn't be a lot of BS because they knew me but not well enough to kid me about sparring.

"You all right?' Kayla asked. She had finished her mitt round. "I mean, I hope it isn't broken." She was a bit embarrassed, and she let her polite nature override the gym code of asking about a ring mate's welfare.

"I'm going right to intensive care so they can put me on a ventilator," I said. I adjusted the cotton in my nostril.

"Can I at least buy you a drink tonight?" Kayla was hesitant at being forward, but it made something in me sharpen my attention.

I had that tell-tale hint of a spark go off somewhere in my gut. It was small, and I didn't recognize it at first, but I observed it and felt it spread a little. It scared me just a touch.

"Pity? A chance to gloat? A celebratory toast to woman as conqueror?" I said, doing my best to be cool.

She smiled at me, looked down, and then back up. She tilted her head.

"All of that, and later we can document your nose for Instagram," She said.

I smiled.

"Glad to do my part," I said. "Where we going? Is it okay if we don't go to Curran's? I'm not a big fan of The Gasthaus either."

"Let's go to The Orchard," she said.

CHAPTER FOURTEEN

The Orchard was a 100-year-old place, famous for its football-shaped personal pizzas and intensely loyal customer base. It wasn't a big customer base, but it was a loyal one. I got up there once in a while, but they didn't know me well.

I toweled off the dripping sweat and grabbed my clean Albany Patroons Championship hoodie from my bag. I kept the short white towel around my neck Elvis style to dab at my face's remaining sweat. My grey drawstring sweats and boxing shoes completed my old school ensemble. With my cotton-filled nose and BO, I was ready for my date.

Kayla drove and took us up Clinton through Arbor Hill and turned right on Henry Johnson Boulevard at the mural of the African American World War I hero for which the street was named. The Orchard was on Arbor Hill's fringe, behind Bleeker Stadium, still in the ghetto, but close to the industrial park. It was an anomaly in the city because it survived 100 years despite being in a rough neighborhood in a building that barely passed inspection. White people felt comfortable bringing their kids there because they went to The Orchard, and their parents before them went to the place too.

"Hey Kayla," The bartender said when we came through the door. There were three other people at the bar. Without asking, he drew her a Guinness.

"Mike, this is Trace. Trace, Mike owns the place."

Mike was a forty-something guy with a round face, a balding head, not much of a chin, and only a hint of a smile.

"You tend bar at Curran's, right?" he said. "What can I get you?"

"Boomsauce, please," I said. I made sure I was polite to people who worked in the bar business. Boomsauce right after a workout with an empty stomach and a slightly dehydrated system would hit me as hard and fast as Kayla did.

One of the four TVs was on a classic Jeopardy. The other three had SportsCenter, Spectrum News, and a college football game from Northern Illinois. No one seemed focused on anything, but Jeopardy and the patrons shouted out mostly wrong answers to every question Alex Trebek posed. Uh, I mean every *answer* he posed.

The volume was up for Jeopardy, and it seemed a bit out of place for a bar, but I think it was one of the idiosyncrasies that made The Orchard singular.

"The study of head landscape, it was believed to diagnose mental illness," Trebek said.

"What is Phrenology," I said reflexively.

Kayla lifted her eyebrows and let her jaw go slack in mock astonishment.

"He introduced the Person-Centered approach; his style later carried his name." The next question—the next *answer* in Jeopardy terms—came.

"Who is Carl Rogers." I spit out.

Again, mock surprise from Kayla.

"This style, often used with addicts and juvenile delinquents, emphasizes the individual's strengths and goals." Alex continued.

"Motivational Interviewing," I said. I celebrated with a fist pump.

"Wrong," Kayla said.

"What do you mean wrong?" I said, acting incensed.

"You didn't put it in the form of a question," she said with a sinister grin.

"Psychology for $2,000, Alex, the champ, Stephen said. He was wearing a brown shirt and matching brown tie, the monochromatic look screaming for a pocket protector.

"The Daily Double!" Alex exclaimed, masterfully maintaining his enthusiasm. "This therapy pioneer broke from Freudian analysis to focus on Epictetus and the world of rational thinking."

"WHO is Albert Ellis," I said, making sure I over-pronounced the 'who.'

The brown guy said "Wayne Dyer," which was ridiculously insulting if you respected Albert Ellis.

"No, no, no...I'm sorry," Alex consoled. "It was Albert Ellis, Ellis."

Kayla looked at me for a long beat after that.

"If you can do it, it ain't bragging, Ali used to say," I said and winked.

"I'm guessing you're the only guy in the gym who could have finished the category like that, notwithstanding your error of not putting it in the form of a question," Kayla said. She made intense eye contact and didn't break it for an extra beat. She wanted an explanation.

"Maybe, but I'm also the only guy who got his nose broken tonight by a bitch," I said.

Kayla punched me hard in the shoulder.

"Bitch?" she said, pretending to be angry.

"I'm sorry. I shoulda said 'girl,'" I said.

She punched me again. The shots were starting to hurt.

"You know, this is getting close to physical abuse. I could have my own 'MeToo' thing going soon," I said.

"You wish," Kayla laughed and made a fist again. This time she threw a slow-motion punch and let it linger on my shoulder for just a second.

The "Special Report" slide interrupted Jeopardy and our interlude. The bar got quiet, and an uneasiness enveloped the bar like only the silence of an ominous "Special Report" could.

"There's been another terrorist act with mass causalities and massive property damage," Lester Holt said. He was even more intense and sincere than usual. "This time at Maximus Corporation in La Grange, Illinois. Maximus produces pharmaceuticals, perhaps best known for their HIV drugs that have been quite successful in limiting the advancement of the disease."

Holt threw it to his correspondent.

"Our Miguel Almaguer is at Maximus. Miguel," he said.

"Lester, this is what we know so far. Late this afternoon, six assailants dressed in black with their faces covered entered the Maximus plant armed with semi-automatic weapons. They proceeded to shoot three members of the private security force at Maximus. They then proceeded to the laboratory, where they armed it with explosives. They shot and killed four employees who tried to stop them along the way. They then detonated the explosives as they drove away," Almaguer said. "And Lester, once again, ANTIFA was painted near where they entered the building."

Lester Holt continued to reiterate the same facts as the news switched to an overhead view of the factory, the collection of law enforcement vehicles, and the media staging area, which had grown to around fifty people, with satellite trucks, bright camera lights, and microphone stands. A scroll along the bottom of the screen read: "Seven people believed dead in the Maximus Industry shooting in La Grange, Illinois.

Everything that went through my mind was a cliché.

I thought these acts had become so routine that they hardly shocked people any more. I thought about how a group so disturbed could go unnoticed by the people around them. Don't people somehow, somewhere, know this shit is being planned? Will a neighbor be interviewed tomorrow and say about one of the members, "He was quiet and kept to himself?" I wondered how they got the weapons and why citizens can get a firearm that can kill so many so easily.

All clichés.

Then there was the Antifa thing. I had spent years studying them, and the most salient point about the organization was that it was no organization, or at least there didn't used to be. Antifa was a movement, not a group of people. It was more a philosophy. There were no Antifa headquarters. These latest things might mean some group had co-opted the name.

What was about to follow in our culture turned my stomach. People will offer prayers for the victims, and others will angrily insult those who pray. Some will point out that they used licensed guns, and therefore gun regulations are not effective. Others will say they used unlicensed firearms, and we shouldn't punish law-abiding citizens who happen to own guns.

It will go on for a while, and you won't be able to escape it. We will learn the shooters had a cache of weapons and posted or left behind a manifesto.

Then, the conversations will stop until the next time, and it will be over.

Over, except for the people who will have to investigate the whole mess and people who will have to endlessly watch the footage of it and cull through every piece of evidence until it burns a scar into their psyche. It will affect those people more than anyone knows.

And it will affect the people who counsel them. And it will burn a hole in them.

The whole story, and the thoughts that came with it, didn't do much for my mood. I knew I couldn't escape my past, and I definitely knew I couldn't control my thoughts, but I struggled when it was thrown right in my face. I could feel my thoughts race. I could feel a wave come over me that made me feel out of touch. It was like I was there, but I wasn't.

I caught Kayla looking at me with the corner of my eye. I got the sense she was uncomfortable with how quiet I had gotten.

"You all right?' she asked.

"Sure," I said, not moving my glance away from the television.

The news stayed the same. Helicopter view of the factory,

occasional cuts to employees evacuating from a back exit, and a middle-aged woman from the plant in a hairnet crying. Then back to the overhead shot of the factory, the scroll repeating.

Seven people believed dead in shooting at Maximus Pharmaceutical in La Grange, Illinois...Shooters yet to be identified...Antifa logo painted at entrance...Maximus manufactures HIV drugs...

"Hey, earth to Trace, earth to Trace," Kayla said. Her voice interrupted my trance.

"Oh, uh, sorry," I said. I felt awkward, like I had a poorly kept secret.

"This stuff gets to you, doesn't it?" She said. "I mean, it gets to me, shit, I'm sure it gets to everyone, but it seems like something else is going on. I don't know..."

"We've gotten used to it," I finished her sentence.

"Yeah, that doesn't seem right," Kayla said the obvious. It was like she felt guilty.

Mike came over.

"Another round?" he asked.

My stomach churned, and my nose and forehead were beginning to throb from sparring.

"Sure," I said. "You okay with having another?" I asked Kayla.

"I got no place to go," she said.

"Can I have a Slane, too?" I asked. It was a night for a bit of whiskey. The Slane would calm the anxiety for a bit. It would make the morning's worse, but I didn't mind renting some peace.

"Trace, you're not just a bartender, are you?" Kayla's tone was serious.

I raised my eyebrows at the question. I preferred to be just a bartender at the gym without a complicated past. I smirked, didn't say anything, and sipped the whiskey. It burned the back of my throat and then mellowed into warmth as it spread down my throat to my gut.

"I mean, what's with acing the entire Psycho Facts column on Jeopardy? Not many could hang with you there," she said.

"You don't think Jesus is versed in the use of Jungian Mandalas?" I said, conscious of the fact that I still danced around the questions.

"So, you're a shrink of some sort?" Kayla said.

"That's kind of like calling a mechanic a grease monkey," I said 'We don't care for derisive, dehumanizing labels," I said and moved my eyebrows up and down.

"So, you *are* a shrink." This time she stated it.

I sipped my Slane and chased it with the Boomsauce. I put the pint glass down and looked Kayla in the eyes.

"I'm a licensed clinical psychologist," I declared.

She held my glance for a couple of beats, then smiled and looked down like she knew an inside joke.

"That's funny to you?" I said.

She giggled a little. It was the first time tonight that she seemed at all girlish, which, it dawned on me, flew in the face of the fact that she broke my nose.

"I've just sensed for a while that you weren't just a bartender who boxed after work," she said.

"Serving drinks is an honorable profession," I said, adding some pretentious base to my voice. "Are you saying I box like a guy with too much education?

She giggled again. It was a sweet giggle, and I liked it.

"You might as well say I fight like a bitch," I continued with the self-effacing humor.

She giggled again, but there was something in her eyes that didn't join in.

Lester Holt's broadcast interrupted us. He was interviewing a former FBI profiler. They discussed whether this was an act to get attention, disrupt business, or simply to inflict pain and outrage.

"This company was recently embroiled in a firestorm of

controversy surrounding what AIDS advocates described as *usury-level price gouging* for their AIDS treatment cocktail. It has gotten the attention of anti-fascist groups who have called for doctors and hospitals to utilize the less expensive competitor, Phaseron, manufactured by Capstan Pharmaceuticals in Germany," the profiler said.

Kayla listened, and I could feel her looking at me when she spoke. I kept my eyes on the television.

"That's weird, isn't it?" There was a little frustration in her voice. "I mean, aren't they always disgruntled workers who just got fired or didn't get a promotion or something?" She said.

"Almost always," I said without taking my attention from the screen.

"Otherwise, it is just totally random, right? That makes no sense. I mean, even the mentally ill have to have some justification in their minds, regardless of how twisted it is."

"Deranged is exactly what it sounds like, 'deranged.'" I said, still focused on the broadcast. "Don't forget, Son of Sam, David Berkowitz, killed eight people because his neighbor's Labrador told him to."

Kayla didn't say anything but appeared to be thinking it over, turning it around in her head like she could make sense of it. No one could make any sense of it. At least I never met anyone who could make any real sense of it.

Now another NBC reporter was interviewing someone in the plant. She was a frantic middle-aged woman with dirty blond hair pulled off her face into a messy pigtail and a gap between her front teeth. She wore a Chicago Bears hoodie.

"I can't believe it. Why?...Why?" She buried her face into her hands, her right hand, still holding a cigarette.

"Do they have to stick a microphone in traumatized people's faces?" Kayla said. "It's cruel."

"The American way. Our culture loves this stuff. We're the same people who devour the Serial podcast and make a cult figure out of Robert Durst," I said. I realized too late that I had just pontificated a mini-lecture.

Kayla went silent.

I drank the rest of the Slane and had half a pint of beer left. Between the drinks, the workout dehydration, and the surreal television broadcast, my mind buzzed. Things seemed less real but now in a slightly more comfortable way.

"This shit is different for you," Kayla said. It wasn't a question.

I looked at her, and our eyes met for a second or two. I looked away. I wasn't sure what to say.

"Why?" she said.

"Why what?" I asked.

She didn't repeat the obvious. She just continued to look at me. I marveled at her ability to turn on the intensity when she felt it, despite being the early twenty-something who was giggling just a moment ago.

I waited. It wasn't going to go away. Kayla had a forceful presence. I waited a little longer.

"I worked for the CIA. I counseled agents who watched terrorists and such on video all day long," I said. "I did ongoing research on Antifa."

I tried to read her reaction. She didn't tip her hand much about what she was feeling.

"What happened?" She asked.

I exhaled hard, and I felt the wall go up inside of me. It was the wall that shut things off. It was the wall that brought me back to Albany. The wall was bartending. The wall was living above the bar.

"Trace?" Kayla persisted.

"Uh, it isn't something I talk about," I said.

She just continued to look at me. There was a warmth to her that I couldn't exactly describe.

"I'd like to listen if you'd like to talk," she said.

"An agent on my caseload, Eddie Hutchins, never was much into processing things with me. He thought therapy was bullshit,"

I paused. It felt like someone else's voice. "I didn't press him."

I took a sip of Slane.

Kayla didn't say anything, but I felt her hand lightly on my thigh, and her eyes never veered.

"Eddie went home one night and shot his wife and two children," I said. The last words were a struggle.

She put a hand on my upper arm and looked at me hard.

"Let's get out of here," she said.

CHAPTER FIFTEEN

We didn't speak on the way out or during the drive. She drove to her apartment without any explanation. We pulled into a parking place on Chestnut Street and went in the side, street-level door of a four-story 19th-century brownstone. Kayla rattled her keys and opened her apartment. It was pitch black until she switched on a floor lamp a step from the entrance. It lit a rectangular room with mismatched furniture consisting of a worn brown leather sofa, a colonial-style rocking chair, and a tan, old-school leather club chair. There was an Asian rug on the floor, and her walls had a series of abstract paintings in dark reds, browns, and blacks. They were in oil paint, and I guessed Kayla dabbled in art.

"We need to shower," she said matter-of-factly.

She reached for me with both hands, grabbed my hoodie by my ribs, and helped me lift it off. I moved my hands down and awkwardly took both of her hands in mine, leaned over, and kissed her lightly on the lips. She pulled back gently, bit her bottom lip and looked into my eyes.

I leaned forward to kiss her again and closed my eyes. I felt her hand reach up and hold the back of my head as she kissed me deeply. I responded by holding her as close as I could.

"C'mon," she said, putting her hand inside the drawstring of my sweats and tugging. She had a sense of urgency to her. She undid the knot and guided my sweats down my legs. I awkwardly fumbled with my boxing shoes, and while I did, Kayla let her sweats fall to the floor. She was far more graceful than me getting her shoes off, and we stood naked in front of each other.

She grabbed my hand and pulled me down a narrow hall past the bathroom to her bedroom.

"Never mind about the shower," she said softly as we passed her small bathroom.

She pulled me down on her bed on top of her. I noted the coolness of the comforter but only for a second as she shimmied into position underneath me. I couldn't remember ever feeling like this. The combination of desire, arousal, and deep longing ran all the way through me. I so much wanted everything in this moment, the physical, emotional, and sexual.

Our bodies were wet from sweat. I felt her nails dig into the muscles of my shoulders, then my lower back, and finally, she grabbed my cheeks, pulling as deep inside of her as possible. She let out a deep moan that cascaded into a breathless shriek, and I felt her spasm underneath me. Her nails dug deep into me as she pulled harder and harder. I let go, and it shook me like a current of electricity. It intensified Kayla's experience, and we both lost control. I had never experienced anything like that.

We stayed in that position as our breathing slowed. Sweat ran down my face, and I placed my cheek next to hers with my face buried in the pillow.

"Don't move," she whispered. "Please don't move." Her hands now lightly stroked my back in a way that was almost cooling. We stayed like that for a long time. When it got a little hard to breathe, I finally rolled off her.

We were lying on our backs, shoulder to shoulder. Kayla rolled onto her side, putting her head on my chest and absent-mindedly stroked my chest hair. It was a long time before either of us said anything.

"You know, that was pretty awesome for a guy who hits like a bitch," she said. Kayla looked up at me and smiled. She made a fist and hit me on the chin with a slow-motion right hand. We fell asleep like that, and I slept like I haven't in months. There was the usual stuff floating around my head, but it was easily quieted.

A harsh electronic alarm shook me awake. The red LED lights read 5:30.

"Shit, I got a meeting before my early class," Kayla sat up fast. She seemed comfortable in her nakedness and paused, running a hand through her hair. "I got to get in the shower."

I lied on my side, looking at her. She eyed me from head to toe, pretending to be suspicious of me, like she was wondering how I got there.

"Hmm...you always wake up like that?" she said. She widened her eyes in mock fashion and looked down my body.

"I think it has a lot to do with what I was dreaming about," I said.

"I've got to get ready," She bit her lower lip. "Wow, someone is at full attention," she said, reaching for me.

"Shit, I'm gonna be late," she said as she got on top of me. She smirked and looked at me with humor in her eyes. "We're going to have to go fast," she said.

I didn't say a word. She slid down on top of me.

"Whew..." she said.

Her looked regained its seriousness, and she started to move. We both let out a slow hard breath. I managed to exhale and roll my eyes, acknowledging what she was doing to me. She stopped being playful. She braced her hands on my chest, and despite her claim to be in a hurry, she began to move slowly and deliberately.

I concentrated, using my mindfulness, and did my best to stay in control.

She let out a bit of a whimper, and her breathing escalated. Her pace quickened, and her breathing became fast and deep. The whimper became more of a groan and then changed into more of a high-pitched cry.

I pulled her down from her riding position and forcefully rolled her over. I supported myself with my hands on either side of her as I drove as hard as I could. It didn't last long like that, and we both ended it with a series of groans and shrieks until I had to pull myself away from the hypersensitivity. Our sweat melded together, and my hair was soaked. We were a mess.

Without warning, Kayla rolled, actually almost flipped me over so she was back on top of me.

"What the...!" I shouted.

"Jui Jitzo," she said, climbing off me and scurrying toward her shower. "Let yourself out—I'm late!" she yelled, closing the bathroom door and turning the water on.

CHAPTER SIXTEEN

I got dressed shortly after Kayla left. When she was gone and the daylight streamed in from her windows, I felt out of place, like I was somewhere I didn't belong. It happened whenever I left the structure of the day-to-day life I was accustomed to. I headed to my apartment to get ready for work.

I haven't had many nights like the one I just experienced. The evening's intensity from the excitement of heading out, the weirdness of the latest Antifa act, the disclosing about Eddie, and the winding up in bed, it all left me, I don't know, maybe a bit disoriented. I functioned in a world of predictable structure. The predictable suited me and last night wasn't anything I could predict. Maybe the predictable suited me, and perhaps I saw its comfort, but there was an awful lot to be said for last night.

Still, getting dressed and heading to the bar on this particular morning felt different.

I had been drawn to Kayla at the gym. I had noticed her, traded a few pleasantries, and she made me curious. Like I said, I felt drawn to her, but I hadn't spent a lot of time thinking of her. Now, after last night "drawn" wasn't strong enough. I had to see her again.

My mind was spinning, and it all confused me. I dreamed of being able to just be in the moment, just have the ability to enjoy things without turning on the super analytic mechanism, but that just wasn't to be. I was going to turn this over in my head a million times. That analysis put a bit of a damper on my life. Still, in this case, even with that analysis, it would be a long time before I didn't remember this as a peak experience emotionally, psychologically, and sexually.

I don't know why my analytic nature wouldn't let me just chalk it up to the birds and the bees. I wish I had a mind that allowed me to not compulsively analyze everything down to its roots. It was exhausting, and it sapped the joy out of so many of life's subtleties. I couldn't just experience things. I had to know all the whys and wherefores and had to understand the intentions and the cause and effect of each variable. Like I said, it was exhausting. I hated myself for it, and it was why drinking appealed to me. It quieted the voices and stilled the arguments.

I knew one thing for sure, though. I sure wanted to see Kayla again, and soon.

I was scared that wouldn't happen and scared it would.

As I put on a clean pair of jeans and my t-shirt and fresh hoodie, the conversation I had with Dr. Williams came back to me and provided cloud cover from Kayla's sunshine. I just didn't want to deal with what happened to Eddie. My stomach flipped when I thought of it. Of course, I knew about trauma and the psychological implications of clinical debriefing. I knew I hadn't talked about it, and I knew what it was probably doing to me. I knew about it every day while I poured Coors Light for George and served wings to Randall or Rodney or Robert or whatever the fuck his name was.

God, how I knew it.

Regardless of all this high-level drama, I needed to get to work and serve those Coors Lights and wings. I picked up Rocky and took him around the block, and got to the bar in time to open on schedule and prep my station. Routine, structure—it was what kept me going.

I was cutting up my third lime when Molly came in.

"Why aren't you at school?" I asked her. I noticed she was

wearing what she wore last night. I looked at her long and hard and recognized it. She was drunk. It was a bender drunk.

"I'm in troublllle," she said, trying to laugh it off.

I had had my suspicions about her drinking.

"You're supposed to be at school—have you called in?" I said with more than just a little desperation.

"Trace, so responsible," Molly said in that embarrassing drunk way.

I got my phone out of my pocket.

"What's the number?" I said.

"Trace, relax," Molly said.

"You teach fourth grade, and it is 10 am. Do you want your job?" I said.

Molly's eyes welled.

"Don't be mean about it," she said, choking back tears.

"Mean? I'm being mean?" I said. "You're drunk on a school day at ten in the morning, and somehow I'm a bad guy?"

Now the tears were full-on. She put her head in her hands and just let go. She broke after a moment to breathe and sniff. She tried to speak, and I think what I heard was:

"I miss daddy!"

This was turning pathetic. I had fifteen minutes until customers started coming in, I was trying to process my own strange interlude from last night, and I was awaiting a call back about my future.

I put my hand in the center of Molly's back, and she leaned into me and kept crying.

"I'm sorry, Trace. I'm sorry. I'm such a fuckup!" She sniffed hard again and wiped her eyes. She didn't look at me.

I waited a moment or two.

"You've got to call school," I said as calmly as I could.

She finally looked at me.

"And say what?" she said with drunken desperation.

I thought about it for a moment and knew I needed to come up with a big brother-worthy solution.

"Food poisoning, terrible vomiting, just back from the ER. You couldn't call until they got the Meclizine hydrochloride into you,"

"Meclizine hydrochloride ?" she said.

"Anti-nausea med, controls vomiting," I said. "You want me to call?"

She gave me the look I've seen for 24 years. I never could say 'no' to it.

"Give me the number," I said. She did, and I called.

I asked for the principal and gave him a series of first-class lies. He didn't require a doctor's note and told me to tell Molly to take all the time she needed. Molly heard all of it. She stood up and hugged me. She smelled of sour wine, and she held on too long. She started to cry again. It was just as George was walking in.

"Hey, Momo, no school?" he said, oblivious to what was going on. It was exactly what was needed.

"Yup, special holiday," She slurred. "Just checking in on Trace," she said. Her voice bounced back to normal. George loved her.

"Atta girl, that guy behind the bar needs to be checked up on!" he said with mock concern.

Molly kissed him on the cheek and headed out. Her apartment was walking distance, which was a good thing.

I went back to the bar, set up, and got ready for George.

"Top of the morning to you, sir," he said. Of course, he did. I replied and got him his Coors light.

"That Momo, she's a pistol," he said. He had no idea.

"She sure is," I said without any irony. Inside, my stomach churned. Molly crying over Dad, being drunk after an all-nighter, missing work—she was turning into a dumpster fire. She was beautiful, bright, and could charm anyone, but she also seemed to be dying on the inside. I was powerless to do anything. If I ever found out her pain was related to this piece-of-shit boyfriend, I swear to god I'd give the guy a beating.

I was wiping down George's side of the bar when my phone binged.

"How's the nose, bitch?" It was from Kayla.

A sweet post-coital reach out, I thought to myself. Actually, it was clever enough. She was touching base, busting my balls without getting all lovey-dovey and needy. I felt relieved. I wasn't sure how to approach the morning after.

"I've been violated in so many ways in the last 24 hours #Metoo, #mynose," I texted back, hoping it had the right mix of edgy humor and suggestiveness.

"Maybe sometime I can punch you in the nose and get a chance to violate you again soon," she texted.

That made me smile, and it stirred something.

"Of course, I'm sure now there's a government file on me," she texted.

"Count on it. Come by Curran's when I get off?" I felt just a hint of anxiety sticking my neck out like this.

She didn't return that text as fast as the others.

"Did you know any of the football players at ND," George said. His timing was exquisite. I was staring at my phone, looking for a response.

"What's that, George? Oh, football guys? Yeah, I knew the punter and a couple of backup linebackers. No one who was really famous," I said. C'mon, c'mon, where's the ping, I thought.

"We're they decent guys, or were they conceited?" George was relentless.

C'mon...

C'mon...

"Uh, they were regular—" the phone binged.

"See you 'round 6," she texted. Whew.

I felt myself exhale.

"They were regular guys, George. Good guys," I said.

"Well, Notre Dame is special like that. All regular guys. Wouldn't take anyone else." George added. He was wrong, of course. There were plenty of douchebag jocks, guys who had been entitled since they won the genetic lottery and got put on the five-year-old all-star teams in Pop Warner, T-ball, and AAU basketball. It was all big business, and too much money was involved at the college level to ignore it. George didn't need to hear that, nor would he want to. He just wouldn't believe it.

Agusto came in right on time, we bumped fists, and he tied an apron on and headed off into the kitchen. That was one thing I didn't have to worry about and, for that, I was grateful. It was 11:05, and it was already a busy morning setting up the bar and dealing with the emotions that came with family stuff.

My iPhone buzzed, and I noticed the 202 area code. I swallowed hard and answered.

"Trace, it's Aisha." Her voice was friendly, and there was just a hint of her Atlanta upbringing.

"Hey, Eesh, what's up?" I said. "I didn't think you'd be calling so soon."

"Dr. Williams sees it as urgent. She wants you down here tomorrow." She was nice to me, but she did whatever Dr. Williams asked of her.

"Tomorrow? What the hell? I got things to do around here,"

"She originally wanted me to tell you to be here today. I couldn't make it work with the available flights."

I exhaled. I didn't get the rush on things.

"Dr. Williams would like you to have available any session notes you have on Hutchins, and she wants you to be prepared to discuss the ongoing Antifa situation," she said.

"Eesh, I know this isn't your call or anything but, don't forget, I'm on leave. I don't have to go back to work," I said.

There was a pause. Then Aisha continued.

"Trace, Dr. Williams is adamant about seeing you. I wouldn't play around with this, leave or not," she said.

She gave me the flight information and told me she'd see me tomorrow. I know it's the CIA, but my role was research and staff support. The urgency didn't make sense to me, and Dr. Williams's control trip rubbed me the wrong way. She was within her rights to request session notes, but she wasn't supposed to do so capriciously. There were matters of confidentiality and HIPPA laws. If agents knew that what they said while processing difficult things was subject to constant review, it would fuck up the therapeutic process.

Still, duty called. Whatever that meant.

"Everything ok, Trace?" George asked. I hadn't been conversational in almost 90 seconds, which threw him off.

"Yeah, sure, George. The boss at the old job wants to talk to me, and I don't feel like it."

"Damn spy stuff. They act like they own you for chrissakes," he said, doing his best to be supportive. I didn't want to correct him about the spy stuff.

"Just a pain in the ass, is all, George," I said. I knew full well it was more than that.

It was a particularly slow day behind the bar. I did my best to keep myself busy, but wiping down liquor bottles, mopping the floor, and cutting fruit can only occupy the mind so much. George was on autopilot and we covered football, the damn liberals, and how much he loved playing basketball in high school.

Happy hour picked up. Jessica came in, and I got a text from Molly letting me know that she sobered up and was grateful for my help. She promised to clean things up and get on the straight and narrow. I realized that I was starting to hear classic alcoholic rhetoric from my little sister, which scared me.

At around 6:15, I felt the butterflies. Sure, I was a super cool Ph.D.-psychologist-boxer- CIA-bartender, but I was still scared to death of women, relationships, and everything that went with them. Thank God the first night of sex went well, or I would be obsessively excoriating my performance and my entire masculinity. It wasn't easy being me. Or more precisely, it wasn't easy being in my head.

Just after 6:30, she came through the door. She wore stretchy jeans, leather equestrian-style boots, and a tan V-neck over a white t-shirt. She was fit, and her body was firm but still feminine. Her black hair was pulled off her face into a relaxed ponytail, and her smile seemed to magically light up her eyes. I felt something inside.

"What's a girl got to do to get a beer around here?' she said and raised her eyebrows.

"Not break the bartender's nose would be a start," I said, really pleased with my opening line.

"Ah, the bartender needs not to leave his jab out after he throws it," she said. I poured her a Guinness, hung up my bar rag, and asked Jessica if it was ok if I clocked out. She agreed, and I poured myself a Boomsauce and took the barstool next to Kayla. Jessica, always the professional, only looked at me next to Kayla for a second or two longer than she normally would. I was internally embarrassed at how excited I was.

"Once in a while, a fighter will let a lesser boxer land a punch or two. It is good to train the body to be hit without risking it on someone with real power," I said with mock pretention.

"That so." She smiled and tilted her head. "Hmm…I guess if a greater fighter hit you in the nose, it might've come right off your face, huh?"

"Perhaps…" I said. The problem with cutesy banter is transitioning to actual conversation. It wasn't easy, but if you didn't make the effort, you eventually wound up in an absurd discussion that went nowhere and felt forced. I thought I'd make that move now.

"What's the coursework like this semester?" I said, aware that I was trying to return to a normal tone of voice.

"Group process, Theories of Counseling Two and my internship and my practicum," she said without a lot of enthusiasm. "I've got to get to a study meeting soon."

"Where are you doing the practicum?" I asked.

"St Teresa's grade school. I'm working with the social workers developing a playgroup to explore trauma," she said.

"You're kidding me!" I said.

She looked confused.

"What's so hard to believe about that?" she said.

"My sister teaches fourth grade there. Molly Curran?" I said, smiling.

"No way! Molly is your sister?" she said. "Molly's great!"

"Yeah, she's the best," I decided I didn't need to share this morning's adventure.

Kayla paused for just a moment. She looked like she was mulling something over. She gently chewed her lower lip.

"I've got to go to Vermont tomorrow. Wanna come? I have to pick up something up from my cousin. We could look at the foliage, maybe hit a couple of the craft breweries," she said. I noticed she started to speak just a little faster. I could sense she felt she was taking a risk.

I frowned and remembered my calls from Dr. Williams and Aisha.

"I shouldn't have asked. I—" I didn't let her finish. I grabbed her wrist.

"No, no, no…I got called to DC to meet with my supervisor. Shit, I'd much rather go to Vermont," I said.

She broke into a relieved smile.

"Next time," She smiled and held my gaze a beat longer than expected.

"Yeah, definitely," I said with the requisite amount of enthusiasm.

We finished our drinks. I decided to head back to my apartment and walked Kayla to her car.

"I really do want a rain check on Vermont and, well, a lot of things," I said.

She looked up at me and chewed a little on her lip again before she kissed me gently on the lips. She got in her car and drove away.

It made me dread my trip to DC even more.

CHAPTER SEVENTEEN

United has direct flights from Albany to DC throughout the day. I was on the 8:15 and, like I usually was, I was at the airport ridiculously early.

I admired the people who flew all the time and had all the travel stuff down to a science. When I'd see attendants with luggage the size of a lunch box, I wondered how they did it. No matter what I set out to do, I always found it necessary to bring four or five extra pairs of underwear and socks, you know, just in case I shit my pants once or twice and needed a change. As an adult pushing 30, I wasn't in the habit of shitting my drawers, but there was always that chance, and I didn't want to be left ill-prepared.

Headphones and a notebook were my essential travel gear. If the guy next to me was a loud chewer, a lip smacker, or if he liked to swish his food around in his mouth, it would make my flight experience unbearable. I've gotten so angry at lip smackers and saliva-tors that I had deeply developed fantasies of choking them out MMA style. No jury, I was convinced, would ever convict me.

The notebook was essential for organizing thoughts, identifying the irrational ones, and finding strategies to think more sanely. I had stacks of notebooks filled with my insecurities in several boxes back at my apartment. I rarely went back to review them, but on the occasions that I did, it always struck me that what bothered me in the present was remarkably similar to what bothered me as a teenager. Sure, I had grown in my ability to describe shit along the way. I had developed an advanced psychological vocabulary, learned mind gadgets and techniques to deal with difficult emotions, but the bullshit that bothered me as a 16-year-old high school junior was almost identical to the shit that bothered me as a 29-year-old licensed clinical psychologist. This remained true even as I worked as a bartender.

It always centered around self-worth. Was I good enough for Cindy to go out with me when I was a junior at Bishop Maginn? Did Marie still love me? Has she found someone else? Was I making the right decision? And, maybe my most constant theme: Was I tough enough, or was I a pussy because of all my fears?

Last night with Kayla, interspersed with the events in Illinois and combined with my conversation with Dr. Williams, gave me plenty to sort out. It was the first night of sex I've had since the breakup, and my feelings about it were complex. It was nice to know I could still do it, it was amazingly pleasurable, and I truly liked Kayla.

"Liked" isn't strong enough.

In some ways, there was just too much to process and way too soon in the game for me to get internal clarity. That's what I always sought—clarity. Things needed to make sense in my head, and even when I knew that life was often random, I wanted things to form a logical equation. Life seldom delivered that.

I prayed a little on it. More just spoke to God, asking for clarity to understand what I should do, where I should go, and the courage to go after what I should go after.

The plane was full. A big muscular guy with a broken nose and a little cauliflower growing on his ears took the seat next to me. He had on that woodsy cologne that I smelled all over the place but didn't know what it was. He wore a black turtleneck that went all the way to the jawline and a hard part on his slicked fade haircut.

"How you doin'?" he asked. "Business or pleasure?" I wasn't looking for conversation, but this dude looked like he might be interesting. The nose and growth on the ear suggested a fighting background.

"All business. Not anticipating any fun at all," I said.

"Sounds like you work for the government."

"That obvious? What is it the vague look of torment on my face?"

He snickered.

"Yeah, something like that?" I said.

"I was military. Spent some time stationed at the Pentagon. I hated it."

"What did you do?" I asked. It was more entertaining than writing in my journal and ruminating on my love life history.

"Nothing cool. Logistical shit. It was 15 years ago. How about you?"

"I'm a consulting psychologist. I work for a private contractor."

"Research shit? Probably for FBI, NSA, CIA. I know enough not to ask," He smirked again.

I just nodded. We were quiet for a while after that.

Now that the conversation had ebbed, I found myself resisting getting the pen out and starting to work on the last 24 hours. If I didn't, it would lead to a lazy feeling and the same feeling you get when you forget to brush your teeth or something. Sorting out my thoughts was a type of hygiene, and when I neglected it, which lately I did more and more, I felt unkempt.

My thoughts drifted to Maria. We had slowed the frequency of our lovemaking by our third year together. Grad school demands, familiarity, and fatigue were the excuses I used. I didn't recognize her indifference and ambivalence to our relationship. Now, after the note, I could put together some hind-sighted pieces.

There's a real temptation to give a new relationship…is that the word? That's WAY too soon. Sex partner? That's way to base…great significance when juxtaposed with the past. "Now,

I can move on!", "She was so much better!" "I was ready, and it was the right time, so I'm healed!"

They were all ridiculous arguments but assigning significance to an intense night of sex was hard not to do.

Still, last night was an unexpected thing akin to winning some sort of scratch-off payout. The intensity was so high it was almost uncomfortable, but it had forged a place in my brain's pleasure center that I knew would never be extinguished. It was also a potent elixir for my self-worth, though it bothered me that I still heavily looked outside of myself for validation. I wish I could just experience something and not have to dissect it, diagnose it and apply the scientific method to it.

"Hey, uh, sorry to bother you," the black turtleneck spoke up.

"Yeah?"

"This is gonna sound weird, but I'll never see you again, and you're a shrink…ah…never mind."

"No, go ahead." I didn't mind. This sounded like it could be interesting.

He closed his eyes like he was concentrating.

"Alright, I'm sure you've heard enough weird shit. This won't even compare. Is it normal to still think about a girl, woman, whatever, that has been out of your life for a long time? I mean, the whole, 'One that got away,' bullshit. I mean, even when you're with someone new?"

I let out a small laugh.

"That's funny?" he furrowed his brow.

"Only because I was just doing it. I had an engagement go bad a while ago. Last night, I, well, you know, did it for the first time with someone new who seems cool. Now, all I'm thinking of is the ex."

"I guess it ain't too weird after all," he said with some relief.

"Well, or the two of us are fucked up," I said.

We both laughed at that. He moved his fist for a bro bump. I gave it to him. The fist was oversized.

"Good luck with yours," he offered.

"Likewise, here's to not fucking it up," I said.

We got quiet again shortly after that, and I began to think of my trip's purpose. It forced me back into a world I was trying to deny. It pushed me to bring forward thoughts and feelings I had buried in the coolers with the Spaten. I didn't want to make this trip, but I had to. Was it duty? Honor? I wasn't Jack Nicholson, and I wasn't living in "A Few Good Men," but I felt I had to do what they wanted. It was important, and I felt cowardly resisting it.

Even considering that and having an awareness of my reluctance, I couldn't figure out exactly why she wanted to speak with me. We processed and counseled agents regularly whose assignments involved careful study of traumatic events. Hutchins had spent six weeks reviewing a beheading, slowing the video down to an almost frame-by-frame reading. Sometimes it was to study the background looking for landmarks, specific furniture, wall hangings, artifacts, or even wall paint. Other times it involved listening over and over to speech patterns, accents, and dialects. Still other times, it involved the video itself for anomalies, edits, and camera angles. Meanwhile, blood might be spurting from the torso where a head was just severed, or someone might be raping a prisoner, a woman deemed unfaithful, or a child.

The agents who denied it had any effect, said they were used to it or made crude jokes, were cause for more concern. The only person who could be genuinely flippant about such horrendous acts would be those with personality disorders. That would mean functioning without a conscience, and folks with that personality just couldn't be trusted in other areas. Anti-social personality disorder types were liars, thieves, and narcissists, and for them, a field that required a sense of duty and honor and concern for the good of humankind was not a good fit. For others, the secondary trauma insidiously got into their lives.

In short, their psyches or their bodies failed them because the disturbing things they were exposed to laid beneath the surface and came out sideways in their lives. Trauma counseling didn't make their lives unicorns sliding down rainbows. It affirmed what they witnessed and acknowledged it was disturbing, and gave them an outlet to share that. That was how it worked.

It wasn't that the CIA or any other government agency cared deeply for their employees and wanted them to feel good when they tucked themselves into bed at night. They were a needed investment in time, training, and resources. If they freaked out, it set investigations back, pure and simple. Our jobs were to keep the motor running by keeping agents in front of their video screens.

All of that, the denial, the machismo, the false bravado were characteristics that trained psychologists were expected to deal with. Our mission was to get through that and help the client process their experience. Of course, it was a shared responsibility with the client, and, of course, therapy was a two-way street, but labeling an agent as resistant was ridiculous. Of course, they were resistant. They are supposed to be. For a psychologist to just go through the emotions with agents in denial was negligent and irresponsible.

That's what I couldn't accept in myself. I had worked long hours and had my real struggle with secondary—and I guess tertiary—traumas. Still, I knew the kind of guy Hutchins was, and after a while, I didn't press him or even confront him on his attitude. He lost it somehow and killed his family and himself, and I couldn't live with that. I couldn't live with myself.

The fact of the matter was that Eddie Hutchins demonstrated no mental illness. That means I missed it, failed to uncover it, or identify it. There was no way around that fact and no amount of processing or reframing that would make it so.

It was something that I had to carry and something I just had to live with. That was something that I found impossible. I said a prayer asking God to help me find the insight to come to terms with all of this so I could keep on.

I closed my eyes and did my best to just focus on my breathing.

I repeated Psalm 131.
"Peace, be still."
Thoughts kept interrupting.

CHAPTER EIGHTEEN

The Behavioral Science Division was on the main campus in a two-story, gray building surrounded by neatly trimmed hedges, set off by well-cared-for marigolds. It could've been an insurance company or even a junior college, except that everything seemed a little too tidy and organized.

Like a lot of businesses, the front doors were darkly tinted, and the lettering was neatly stenciled in all capitals. I happened to know from the company orientation that the doors were also bulletproof and could sustain an SUV's crash at 55 mph.

I went inside and got ready to go through security. A fiftyish man with a salt and pepper flat top, a blue blazer, grey pants, and a red and blue patterned tie sat behind a glass partition at his desk. He was trim and fit, with a musculature that looked like he could still max out the Marine PFT.

"Trace Curran for Dr. Williams," I said. Something about the place seemed to encourage an economy of words delivered in short staccato bursts.

"One moment, please," the man said. Polite and efficient and with a complete absence of warmth. This was not a warm business, and the security guard with a name tag but nothing describing his duties or job title was a microcosm for the whole place—just the appearance of efficiency, a polite but "short tip of the cap to social convention and a back to the business at hand" attitude.

"Jack Spearow," the name on the tag read, and he told me to have a seat. Dr. Williams would be right with me.

I've been through this plenty of times before, but I found the officiousness cold and a bit silly. It's like the people who work here act the part to fit Tom Clancy's novels. There was no reason in this division and, for that matter, many others, to act like a Navy Seal.

In a moment, Dr. Williams appeared behind Jack the security guard and waved me in. Her mouth formed a smile, but her eyes didn't cooperate and it made her seem all about business. Her close-cropped hair created an androgynous look, and she was wearing a tan suit with a black silk blouse. Two buttons were undone, perfectly in the boundaries of fashion while devoid of any attempt at sexiness. She was in her mid to late fifties, but she ran obsessively, was put together well, but she didn't give any vibe of sexuality. She wore fashionable two-inch heels, I guessed ankle-high stockings under her suit pants, and little or no makeup. There was a scent to her, but I was positive it came from an over-the-counter deodorant and not a perfume.

I heard the click of the lock on the double doors, and I went on through. Just inside, another guy dressed like Jack manned the metal detector. He was a middle-aged African-American with a well-manicured mustache and large, strong hands. I emptied my pockets, putting my keys, $31 cash, three Halls honey-lemon cough drops, and a gum wrapper in a bowl. He slid it through the machine, and I walked through the detector. He gazed at the monitor, then gave me the once-over with the wand.

"Have a nice day, sir," he said with no eye contact and without anything to suggest that he desired any more in the way of conversation.

"How was the flight?" she said while he shook my hand. Her attempt at social convention was only marginally warmer than the security guards.

"It was fine," I said. "Flights are good times to think," I said to keep an awkward conversation moving along.

"Coffee?" She said as we walked down the long corridor to her office.

"Nah, I'm good," I said.

Her office was still neat, almost sterile, and as I remembered, there were hardly any distinguishing knick-knacks or photos to warm things up.

"I want to say again, I appreciate your making the trip, especially considering what you are going through," he said.

"What I've been going through" was a good phrase. It implied caring, suggested the weight of the issue but didn't uncomfortably identify that I was on leave for what amounted to emotional reasons. It was intended to make me feel less of a pussy. Still, I wasn't sure if this was a meeting to process my adjustment or if Dr. Williams had some ulterior motive.

"First of all, how *are* you?" She said with particular emphasis on the *are*.

"I'm good. I mean, I'm good for now," I felt like I was stumbling. "I mean, for the time being I'm okay. My goal in life isn't to be the day bartender in the family business."

"How's your mental health?" Her approach wasn't the warmest or the most sophisticated I had ever heard.

"I'm okay. Of course, shit still bothers me," I said. This wasn't exactly excessive self-disclosure.

"That makes sense. Take your time. Process things. Don't rush yourself," she said with all the complexity of an Oprah self-help manual. This was getting weirder.

There was an awkward moment when neither of us said anything. Dr. Williams looked briefly out her window and then back at me.

"We were hoping you could help us in some other ways," she said.

"Other ways" had me curious, but I felt it was prudent to be compliant.

"I'm happy to help," I said. "Though I must admit, I'm not

even sure how I can be of help."

"All background. You know how it goes. We won't know what will help until we talk about it." She was overdoing the laid-back thing.

"I'll tell you what I know."

"Okay. Hutchins was reviewing several things at the time of his death. One was the Allied Security shooting. What did he tell you about that?"

I thought for a second. It was about seven months ago, and I had sixteen agents on my caseload. I had gone over what Hutchins had said in my mind many times. It wasn't about remembering what he was talking about as much as it was about my self-flagellation for missing his emotional disturbance.

"Well, we talked a lot about it," I said. "Are you looking for a specific topic or issue?" I asked.

She opened her hands and turned them over, palms up, while raising his eyebrows. I took her non-verbals as saying, "You tell me?"

"He talked about the 'poor sap' security guards. I remember him using the term 'poor saps."' I said. "He commented on the fact that that these employees had no idea of what their fate was about to be on a Monday morning," I said. I paused and tried to remember more. She sat upright with her elbows resting on the desk. She had a yellow legal pad in front of her, inside of a rich burgundy leather portfolio, and it looked like she had made three notes. From my vantage point, I couldn't read what they said.

"He said something about how the Antifa guys killed so efficiently and without hesitation. He said the guys in the hallway were in the wrong place at the wrong time and should've not tried to be heroes. He—" She interrupted.

"What did he mean by that, that they shouldn't have tried to be heroes?"

"I guess he was remarking at the absurdity of how life can be normal in one instant and be gone in another. I believe he thought the guys in the hallway were using bad judgment for fighting back," I said.

She tapped her pen on the desk and looked at me. Her eye contact was intense.

"You sure that's what he was getting at?" he said.

I looked back at her, made eye contact, and then looked down to diffuse it. Her intensity was off-putting.

"Well, I guess I'm not sure exactly what he was getting at," I said, confused at the importance Dr. Williams gave my statement.

She nodded, tacitly acknowledging one human being can never really know what another human being is thinking.

"What else did he tell you?" she said.

"He didn't admit to anything bothering him, which to us isn't a good sign," I said.

She tilted her head.

"Why is that?"

She obviously knew the answer to her question. She was a psychologist for chrissakes.

"Well, you know, it is a denial mechanism. It shows he's not being truthful with himself," I said. She was well aware of those dynamics.

"How so?" she said.

I decided to play along and answer rather than question why she was asking about things she knew.

"Well, if a human being watches a group of other human beings get slaughtered before his eyes, the normal response would be to feel some degree of emotional distress," I said.

"Wouldn't it be good for an agent to be like Hutchins?" he said. This was getting weird. It was like she was testing me.

"Only in the short run. If an agent at the beginning of his stint lies about the work's effects, he can probably tough it out mentally. Over time, the repressed secondary trauma takes its toll, and that's where we start to see dysfunction," I said. She knew all of this. It was part of the job.

"What did he have to say about the operation?" She asked.

"Excuse me?" I didn't get the question. It was a non-sequitur.

"You know, generally, was he a happy agent? Did he grouse about the department?" she said.

"Not that I recall. He bitched a little about the long hours and being away from home," I said.

"What do you think that was all about?" She asked.

I gave it a little thought, mainly to demonstrate to her that I was putting in the effort.

"I think it was just to have something to talk about. Kind of bravado against authority," I said.

"Bravado against authority? Are you saying Hutchins had tendencies toward subversion or insubordination?" She was fishing and making way more out of it than it was. It was obvious.

"Oh God, no. It was more like a guy bitching about his boss because that's what men do. Hutchins was loyal and motivated, in my opinion. Like a lot of agents, he was tired and overworked," I said.

She tapped her fingers on the desk with her right hand as she thought. It dawned on me that the whole thing wasn't making any sense. Why the urgency to get down here? Why the dramatic plea? It just didn't add up.

"Did he talk about other members of the team? Did he talk about his supervision?"

Now she was asking what Hutchins thought about the team, which included her. Was he worried that Hutchins didn't like her? How did that fit in with the CIA badass, get-the-job-done thing?

"No, I never heard him bad mouth anyone or complain about another member of the staff," I said.

"But you said he complained about overworking…"

"I did, but not to any great degree. He said it to be saying something. You know what I mean?" She looked at me for a beat longer than social convention. It was like she thought I wasn't giving it my all or holding back. There really wasn't anything to hold back.

She started to nod. She leaned back in her chair and exhaled.

"What were his feelings about Antifa?" Dr. Williams asked.

I gave it some thought. I remembered him making a comment once.

"Uh, I don't know, he didn't talk about it much. Maybe once or twice," I said.

"And what were his comments?" she asked.

"It wasn't a big deal. I think he said, 'this didn't look like other Antifa operations.' That the Antifa members were usually nerdy limp-wristed college liberals, that these guys were too organized and knew what they were doing," I said.

"What did he mean by that?" she asked with a little too much intensity.

"I don't know if he meant anything by it especially," I said.

"Well, he said it. It must've meant something," she said as if she was angry with me.

I didn't respond. I just looked at her and tried to get why she was so pissed off.

"Can I ask something?" I said. I decided to take a risk. It was a long trip down, and I was beginning to feel annoyed.

She raised her eyebrows, signaling me to go ahead.

"What's this really about?" I said. I looked straight at her.

Her eyebrows went up, and then she furrowed her brow before speaking.

"I told you it is about background," Williams said, a little too casually.

"Background," I said.

She nodded.

CHAPTER NINETEEN

I was so happy to get out of there and get away from her questioning. Something didn't feel right. The questions veered into a weird place, and I not only didn't get it, I also knew there was an ulterior motive. There just had to be. After all, this was the CIA, and maybe the conspiracy theorists were right—maybe nothing was as it appeared. One of my favorite adages was, "Just because you're paranoid doesn't mean that they are *NOT* out to get you."

Meeting up with Ray was a welcome diversion. I missed him and his no-nonsense approach to, well, anything. It was how he boxed and how he approached his job as an agent. I admired how, unlike me, Ray didn't worry about what others thought. He processed situations, evaluated them, moved on, and let go of them. In the ring, if you tagged him, he didn't get mad. He simply adjusted what he was doing after quickly evaluating it. It made him a great sparring partner, and it made him a great agent.

"Holy shit, look what the cat dragged in," Ray said with his slight southern drawl when I came through the door at Slick's. It wasn't so much a southern accent as it was him reverting to his roots of being a Black guy, originally from Detroit. In the office, he spoke with no discernable accent. It came back just a little in the gym, and when he was comfortable with you, he revealed it.

"Uh-huh, don't worry about any cat, worry about you getting

soft with your hands in my absence." As I blabbered on with the requisite macho greeting, Ray smiled, and we bumped fists. I ordered an IPA, put my jacket on the back of the barstool and let out a heavy sigh.

"Man, my extra sensitive spy sensibilities tell me you're a little weary. What you all knotted up about, besides the usual?" Ray said. It was one of those rare friendships where nothing was out of bounds when it came to ball-busting. He knew why I was on leave, and he was giving me some shit while also asking, in his way, why I was back down here.

"Weary, is the right word, my friend. I just spent two hours being interviewed about bullshit. I don't even know the point," I said.

"Ah, yes, the ways of the agency and, uh, in your case, contractors to the agency. What makes you think there's a point?" Ray said.

"Yeah, I guess that's true. They could be doing it with the sole intention of fucking with me," I said.

"Now, you're talking some sense," Ray said. He took a big sip of beer and briefly checked in to SportsCenter. "You know, that boss of yours, she was straight CIA for a while a few years back?"

"What, Williams? No, I didn't know that."

"She was doing behavioral or whatever you call the shit you do, when she was young, just got her Ph.D. She got pissed when she went for Michaelson's job and didn't get it. That's when she went back to academe-ah."

Ray pronounced *academia* in a mock intellectual way.

"Funny, she never mentioned it. That might explain the contempt she shows him, besides the fact that he's a prick," I said. "Do you have any idea why they would call me down here and grill me on bullshit for two hours? They said it was urgent, and she asked me nothing but background."

Ray let out a breath.

"How long you been working around the agency?" He said

and opened his eyes wide like there was something obvious.

"Year and a half, maybe a little more," I said.

"You haven't noticed the amount of bullshit that goes on? You haven't noticed the self-important attitude of the powers that be and their intent on making even the simplest shit seem clandestine and covert?" He said and shook his head.

I sipped my beer and didn't respond. I just let it sink in. He was right. Ray was always right.

"Uh-huh, that's what I thought." Ray drank and looked at the television. "Now, why don't you let it go and tell me about what you've been doing in the ring up in Smallbany. Do I detect just a wee bit of swelling around the bridge of your nose?" He said.

"Man, what are you, some sort of special secret agent? I didn't think it was even noticeable," I said in somewhat mocked astonishment.

"Hmm. Man, you have forgotten who you're dealing with. Twenty-five years in gyms, and you never stop sizing up opponents. Of course, I gave you the once over. Who lit you up?"

Now, I was screwed. I hesitated.

"Who, man, who lit you up?" Ray persisted with some good-natured intensity.

"Fighter named Kayla," I said.

He spit his beer across the bar and laughed so hard he had to support his head with his right hand.

I rolled my eyes and drank while Ray continued to laugh.

"Fuck you," I finally said.

He put his hand on my shoulder.

"Now, I know you've been through some tough times, but damn, man!" he said and continued to laugh that great laugh.

"Hey, I got in with a woman, and she threw a good right hand after a couple of jabs. It caught me just right," I said.

Ray looked me in the eye and laughed at me again.

"Alright, alright," I said. "Does it make it any better if I told you we hooked up afterward?" Even with Ray, I felt a little cheesy talking about this.

"Pity, my friend. The woman took pity on you," he smiled.

"Perhaps. Had I known pity worked, I would've tried it long ago," I said.

"Trust me, Trace, you've always been pitiful," he said. "Glad to hear you made a step toward moving on."

He said without mentioning names or by prying. He just said it, and I knew what he meant.

"You hear anything about her?" As soon as I said it, I wish I hadn't. It was almost a reflex, and I knew I had to not act on that reflex anymore to get on with my life.

Ray got a funny look on his face. He pursed his lip and looked down at his beer. He didn't say anything.

I got the sense that he knew something. I should just leave it alone.

"What?" I said. I couldn't leave it alone.

"C'mon, man," Ray said. "Let it go."

I tried to but I couldn't. I just couldn't."

"She seeing somebody?" I said. Now I felt pitiful.

Ray winced.

"You're asking. I didn't bring this up, but you're asking," I said.

"Yeah, man. I'm just curious," I said. "Really, I'm good."

Ray raised his eyebrows calling bullshit on my "just curiosity."

"Look man. You're looking for gossip? Do I look like a guy who traffics in rumors?" He paused. "I've heard she and Dr. Williams were working late into the night in their office." He had chosen his words carefully.

"Nothing unusual about that. We often worked long hours. Williams demands it." I said.

There was an awkward pause. I tried not to overreact.

"Yeah, I know. I remember you working late a lot." Ray almost said it just to be saying something. After that, it got weirdly silent and the conversation felt forced—or at least I imagined it did. I didn't want to know anymore or find out what Ray implied. I was pissed at myself for going down the Marie rabbit hole and scratching at that scab. I was also pissed that I turned my meetup with Ray weird.

Stupid.

Fuckin' stupid.

CHAPTER TWENTY

Ray and I hung around Slick's for another beer, and the awkwardness waned a bit. I had that social intuition that our time for interacting was up, and I decided to head out. I begged out of there to catch my flight even though I still had three hours to kill. The whole day left me uneasy, first with Williams and her obtuse non-sequitur questions and then with Ray and me getting weird with the Marie questions.

I did best when I just let Marie and her memory go. I'll never know what happened or why and an explanation would most probably be inadequate. The long and short was she didn't love or at least didn't love me enough to marry me. There were no guarantees in a life filled with constant uncertainty.

I didn't do well with uncertainty, and when emotion was mixed in, it made it even more challenging. I took a deep breath and tried to distance myself from it, but it wasn't easy. It never was when deep emotion was around, and Maria was deep emotion. It made me think, what good was all this mindfulness mumbo-jumbo if it didn't work when you had intense feelings. The promise wasn't that it would make you feel better. The promise was that you could defuse from intense discomfort—whatever the hell that bullshit meant.

Sometimes the best I could do was observe my thoughts and feelings and notice them like a third party.

My phone chimed a text notification, and it shocked me out of my reverie.

"Missed you in Vermont. See you soon...I hope." It was Kayla. I found myself smiling and allowing just a little hope that maybe life held something for me.

There was no reason to hang around DC, and getting home now had some reason. I felt out of place, like an actor asked to take on a new role. I wanted to cut some limes, go to the gym, and I wanted to see Kayla.

In moments like this, I inexplicably thought of Dad. He wasn't the father who sat you down for life lessons. He wasn't the dad that passed down some legacy-rich code that all Currans practiced for centuries. No, in fact, a lot of times, he wasn't around. He had things to do, politics and whatever came with that, and he'd be home after whatever was over and he had a few drinks. There were always a few drinks.

Still, when he called me "Pally," it lit me up. It was what he called people he cared about, and, as a kid, I was thrilled enough to be in the company of other Pallys. I wouldn't bring my Marie issue to him, but I know just having him around would somehow make it better. Like I had this force in the world that was on my side. I haven't felt that force since he died.

BWI was full of business commuters looking to get home and salvage some part of their day. I got there two hours early, not so much because I'm a responsible air traveler but because I didn't have any place else to go—that and the fact that airports had bars and right now I could use an adult beverage. One stool was left at "The Runway," a ridiculous aeronautical-themed pub with faux vintage plane stuff all over the place. There was a rusty propeller behind the bar, and the help wore pilot shirts with little wings on their name tags. They had beer and Irish whiskey, so it was fine. There was also an open bar stool, which made it my lucky day.

The bar patrons were quiet. The bartender, a 20-something Latina with severe eyebrows, bright red lipstick, impossible blond hair, and a diamond nose stud, was standing perpendicular to the bar but with her eyes transfixed on the television. The patrons weren't on their phones, and they weren't drinking or talking.

They were watching the television.

Lester Holt, Miguel Almaguer, and Gabe Gutiérrez were in special report mode again, this time from Bradenton, Florida.

Holt was narrating.

Another Antifa terrorist act has left the city of Bradenton in shock. Not all details are in but here is what we know," Holt reported. "Around noon today, a group of six, dressed all in black and armed with assault-style weapons, stormed the offices of Trident Incorporated, a defense contractor, recently in the news for the attack of a Syrian terrorist stronghold that killed 31 innocent civilians. The Trident Incorporated H2 Disperser, an anti-riot explosive designed as a preventative weapon, malfunctioned and led to several casualties before troops were overrun and opened fire on the crowds. The attack has drawn protests worldwide, and some rioting believed to be fueled by Antifa organizations.

"Fucking Antifa—they should fuckin' nuke the shit of them!" The fat guy next to me with the undone tie and deep pit stains said.

I didn't feel the need to go into my research and let him know that "Antifa" was not a single group but a movement that sprang up to combat Mussolini and Hitler. That they weren't even a "they" like the Mafia or the Taliban.

These latest acts of terrorism were being done by a group that had co-opted the name.

Miguel Almaguer reported:

Members of the executive leadership team were executed. They had convened for a quarterly meeting and were in the corporation's board room when they were attacked. Explosives were then affixed to the basement level mainframe computer and detonated as the group drove off, believed to be in a white Econoline van similar to the vehicle used in the Allied terrorist act one week ago. Five more employees were killed in that explosion, bringing the number of dead to twelve.

"Fuckin' Antifa!" The fat guy started in again. "Fuckin' snowflakes! This is fuckin' America!" he said.

Like most of the American masses, the dude had a sound bite's amount of knowledge about what was in front of him. The Antifa movement probably had more in common with the founding of 'Merica than today's political parties—either side—but his wave of terrorism and killings did not fit their history. Our studies focused on the movement over the years and the threat the current organization presented to the general public. That was changing now. It just seemed to be different than what the movement had done historically.

Almaguer continued:

This makes five acts of terror in the last six months for which the group calling itself Antifa has claimed responsibility. The National Security Office has yet to issue a statement on Antifa, and the critics of the office are starting to have a louder voice.

I thought to myself that the reason the NSO hadn't said anything yet was that they didn't have a clue what was going on. This wasn't the Antifa they knew.

CHAPTER TWENTY-ONE

The next morning, I was back behind the bar like nothing had happened. I never thought I'd feel this, but it was a relief to be back at Curran's. Lunch was uneventful, and by mid-afternoon, Tinker paid a visit.

Today, he was wearing his Ted Nugent t-shirt that said: "Re-elect that Motherfucker!" Subtle, no. Clear message, yes.

George raised his glass from across the bar.

"Good afternoon, Sergeant," George said by way of greeting.

"Oooh-ah!" Tinker responded. "Here's the mail. The post guy was dropping it off when I was coming in."

The two cops and the three nurses in as customers didn't even raise their heads. They'd been in before, and like the constant hum of the coolers of the repetitive percussion of SportsCenter, it all blended in like the white noise app on my phone.

I gave Tink his Schaefer and bumped fists with him.

The mail consisted of a restaurant supply catalog, a flier for a school board candidate, the weekly ad paper, and a white envelope with my first name and the bar address.

"What's new, kid?" Tinker said. "Kid" wasn't patronizing when Tinker said. I took it as a sign of affection. Some others who knew my dad not nearly as well and me not at all called me "kid," and I despised it.

I put the junk mail aside and opened the envelope.

"Can you put on the news?" Tinker asked. It was early afternoon, and SportsCenter had repeated itself five times. A glance around the bar told me no one would notice. Of course, with Tinker and George, the "news" meant FOX. I could tolerate FOX as much as I could an NBA talk show, so it didn't really matter. I found it kind of amusing.

The envelope had a newspaper clipping. No note, no sticky, just something from a newspaper.

The pretty FOX blond with a hostile attitude was blaming Obama for current crime, domestic terrorism, and economic problems. No matter he hadn't been in office for close to a decade.

"Thanks, Obama," I heard myself say. Not sure who would pick up on the sarcasm.

"Say what you want about President Obama, but there's no doubt he left us in a place more vulnerable to outside terrorism," Tinker said. It was a road I didn't want to go down.

"Yeah, I guess. They used to say that at work," I said. I didn't want to get into it, and restating a fact neither encouraged an argument nor did I risk getting into a pissing match.

The article was from the Boston Herald. The date was September 2, 1991

Boston University Uprising Leaves One Dead, Several Hurting

A protest near the Boston University campus turned tragic last night. A crowd protesting the US involvement in Afghanistan assembled near the student union. Initially, the protest was peaceful, with students and a group from off-campus holding signs and chanting against the increased US military involvement in the Middle East and the bombing of Iraq.

Lorelei Campbell, a senior at the university, was restrained by police, hit her head on the pavement, and became unconscious. She was dead at the scene from a massive brain injury.

"I can't believe she is gone, I can't believe she is gone," Lin Williams 20, a Boston University sophomore, repeated about the

death of Campbell. Williams said the two were in a relationship.

It was a young Dr. Williams.

I looked at the article again. I put it up to the light to make sure it was real. It looked like any other newspaper clipping. I didn't understand why it was sent to me or from whom.

I remembered I was on bar duty and brought my focus back to the bar. I was hoping my far-off look didn't trigger a lot of questions from the customers.

Fortunately, Stagger Lee came through the door.

"Tracy, what's up? Tinker, how are they hangin'?"

"High and to the left," Tinker responded on cue.

"Georgie! How the fuck are ya!" Stagger yelled across the bar. He saw me wince. "Sorry Kid, sorry…What's the blond bitch talkin' about? Man, Follow the money!" He stopped and looked at me. "Ooh, sorry kid, I forgot."

Stagger liked to yell "Follow the money!" at every news story for reasons only known only to him. He must've been a huge Hal Holbrook fan or something.

"Talking about how the lefties are responsible for the mess we are in today," Tinker responded. I checked on George, who was staring straight ahead and hadn't taken a sip in twenty minutes. It was sort of a nap he took with his eyes open before he got ready to leave. I set the cops up with a couple more and didn't interrupt the nurses who were still talking and not really drinking.

The FOX news shifted and reported on last week's Antifa terrorist act.

"Oh, these fuckin' faggot snowflakes," Stagger said. He was looking at the screen. He didn't look down for a count of three. When he did, he saw my eyebrows were raised. "Oh, sorry, Trace."

I listened to the commentary. They pointed out that Antifa needed to be treated as a terrorist group, not a group of protesters. They had lost that designation years ago and didn't deserve to be given any special consideration.

"Fuckin A right! Follow the money!" Stagger said. "Open fire on 'em," he said, quickly followed by a "Sorry, kid."

For a moment or two, Stagger rested his commentary. The news team continued.

"The Antifa guys of today share a lot with the hippies who were against Vietnam. They both followed the idea of 'by any means necessary.' Am I right, Tracy? Isn't this your thing?" Tinker asked.

I sipped my Diet Coke and thought about whether to join in, whether it was worth it. I thought, why not?

"Pretty much. In fact, both groups—almost all groups—start with an honorable cause. With the Antifa groups, it was stopping fascism before it starts with whatever it takes. If you grew up under Mussolini or Hitler, you'd be hard-pressed to argue. For people who didn't want to go to Vietnam and who questioned what we were doing there, stopping it in any way they could made sense to them," I said. I was on somewhat delicate ground.

"Yeah, except there was a bunch of us young men who were over there with no choice. Kinda fucked things up for us," Stagger said. He offered no apology for cursing this time.

"You're right, Lee, but so is Tracy. It was unfair to us, but they were protesting the bullshit we were involved in," Tinker said.

"No doubt. It was fuckin' bullshit," Stagger added.

I appreciated Tinker's input and was glad he agreed.

"This shit today with Antifa has gone too far. There's a world of difference between fascism and just being a Reagan conservative. I mean, I don't think much of those assholes either, but I don't think it is right to just sucker punch Republicans walking down the street,' he said.

"Of course, but that's what happens with movements. There is almost always a lunatic fringe," I said, "This stuff with the blowing up businesses and industries is way out of line. So much so it doesn't even seem like stuff Antifa gets involved in."

"Because they've lost their way..." Tinker said.

"Yeah...I don't know..." I let it trail off.

"What do you mean "You don't know?" Tinker said.

"It isn't what they've ever done. It isn't even what their fringe elements have done. I don't understand it," I said.

That kept the guys quiet for a moment. FOX had gone to the weather. It was a good few beats later that Stagger broke the silence.

"Follow the money!" he said.

"Huh?" Tinker said.

"That's what fuckin' that Watergate dude, Deep Throat, told Bernstein, isn't it?" Stagger said.

"Yeah…but what has that got to do here?" Tinker said.

"C'mon, Tink, someone's always makin' money. Whose making money off of that shit?" Stagger said.

Everyone got quiet. FOX was running the long-form "My Pillow" commercial.

Who's making money? What money was there to be made?

Stagger had me curious.

"Trace!" I heard Gus yell my name. "Trace!" Gus was not one for drama or for losing composure. I hurried into the kitchen.

"What's up?" I asked with just a little urgency. Gus was near the exit to the kitchen. He had a green garbage bag in his hand.

"C'mere," he motioned with his hand for me to follow. We went out the kitchen's back door, where the bar's trash cans were lined up. Next to them was the door to my apartment. Gus nodded for me to look at the apartment door.

It had been pried open, and it was pulled away from its frame. Someone had broken in.

"I just saw it when I brought out the trash," he said.

I went up the stairs two at a time with a feeling of dread running through me. The apartment had been tossed and everything, which wasn't much, was thrown on the floor. My pallet table was on its side with the magazines and books open and on the hardwood floor. The glass in my diploma frame was shattered. In the kitchen, my refrigerator was open, and the contents on the linoleum. Ketchup had spilled, and an old container of chicken lo mien was splattered across the floor.

In my bedroom, my mattress was flipped over, and all of the drawers in my dresser were pulled out and emptied. The clothes I had hanging in the closet were strewn across the floor, and the four shoeboxes full of papers, pens, tie clips, sticky notes, and whatnot were scattered across the room.

My bible, with the newspaper clipping, was splayed open like someone had rifled through it. The article was a foot or so away from it, and it looked like it held no special meaning. I went back into the living room, and I could feel my heart racing. I tried to still my mind and distance myself from the emotions. It was hard. The emotions were muddled, and they came at me hard and fast.

"You okay?" I heard a voice say. I looked up, and it was Tinker.

"Yeah, yeah, I'm fine," I said. I let out an exhale.

"What'd they take?" Tinker asked. Stagger came up the stairs behind him. He had a pistol in his hand.

"For fuck sake, put that away!" Tinker said. Stagger looked at him and paused. He reached down and pulled up his jeans, and put it in an ankle holster. Great, I thought to myself. Stagger is always packing.

"I can't see that anything's missing. I didn't really have anything of value up here."

Tinker scrunched his face and panned the room.

"Fuck, this bullshit," Stagger said apropos to nothing.

"Tracy, did you have any drugs up here? Fentanyl or even a substantial amount of weed worth stealin'?" Tinker asked.

"No, nothing like that. I don't do that stuff," I said.

"You sellin' it?" Stagger asked.

"Of course not."

Tinker took a step forward, nosed a textbook on perception with his boot, and took another long look around. He let out a sigh.

"Kid, why'd you leave the job?" Tinker said. He looked straight at me.

I felt my mouth go dry. Tinker was a lot of things but being full of shit wasn't one of them. He was somebody you didn't bullshit.

I looked away from his stare.

"Someone wants something you have or, at least, what they think you have," he said. "They at least want to know something about the way your life is going."

I just shrugged.

"I mean, no offense, but this is a dump. If you're not known in the drug business, no one would target this place for theft. I could see them going for the cash box downstairs, but there'd be no reason to do this.

"I have no idea…" I let my voice trail off.

"And it happened in the middle of the day when someone would know you're working," Stagger said.

"And they had to have the balls, or for that matter, the skills, to do it while Gus was right down the stairs," Tinker said.

I had a sickening feeling come over me.

"Kid, why'd you leave the job?" Tinker said again. He looked straight at me.

I heard him, but I didn't react. I didn't look up, and I didn't say anything. His words froze me.

"You don't have to tell me. You don't owe me nuthin'," Tinker said.

"My own shit, Tink. It is my own shit. It had nothing to do with anything. It certainly had nothing to do with any spy shit," I said.

Tinker nodded, but he didn't say anything. He kept nodding.

"You know, kid, what division me and 'Ol Stag were in when we served?"

I had no idea where he was going with this. I let the question just hang.

"Special forces. We did shit that people didn't know about. We worked with your outfit a lot," he said.

"My outfit?"

"The Agency," Stagger said. "C-I-A," Stagger said.

I was lost. I had no idea what they were getting at.

"Your place has been tossed because they were searching for something. We did this sort of thing," Tinker said.

I just shook my head.

"I counseled people. I did research..."

"It could be a brother from Arbor Hill ransacked your place. You always have bartender cash with you. That's always a possibility," Tinker said with a rational tone. "But then, again nuthin' is missing."

I could see he was using the Socratic method, Tinker style, to push through my denial.

"Dad ever keep anything up here?" Stagger asked. Tinker shot him a look.

"Huh? It was an apartment he always rented," I said.

"Yeah, but did he keep anything up here," Stagger persisted.

"That's enough!" Tinker scolded.

Things were getting weirder. I had no idea what they were getting out.

"What's this have to do with dad?"

They both got quiet. Neither would look at me. Stagger put his hands in his pockets.

"What's this have to do with my father!" I almost shouted.

"He never told you," Tinker said. It wasn't a question but a declaration.

"Told me what?" I demanded.

Tinker pursed his lips.

He took a deep breath.

"Never mind, kid. Never mind," Tinker said.

CHAPTER TWENTY-TWO

I had to get back to the bar.

It was one thing to deal with Tinker and Stagger's craziness serving them drinks. It was altogether another one when they were thrusting themselves into my personal life.

What was the shit with dad?

I knew dad served in Vietnam. I knew he saw action. I never heard anything more than grunt stuff. Of course, if he was doing something covert, I might not know. He couldn't or wouldn't tell me. Would mom know? Would I even risk asking my mom about something that would upset or confuse her?

Man, my head was racing. I did my best to distance myself from my thoughts and try to watch them go by like leaves on a stream and breath through it. I asked God to help me with it as I went through the kitchen. Gus took over for me behind the bar, something he didn't like and, honestly, something at which he wasn't particularly competent.

"Everything okay, Trace?" George said. Rocky was by his side with his ears up, indicating he wasn't relaxed and he wasn't looking for treats. He was wondering where I went.

"Yeah, someone broke into my apart, is all," I said, doing my best to be nonchalant.

"Damn, neighborhood keeps getting worse!" George said with legitimate anger, "Thank God my mother is gone and doesn't have to deal with this crap."

George rarely mentioned his mom. It was like it was still too painful, and he did his best just to pretend it was a period of his life that was over and that he no longer had to deal with. A common strategy that we all use, and as good an explanation as any for George's daily dosage of Coors Light. We all do what we can to deal with the pain.

He seemed to relax a bit, even if Rocky didn't. Rock came to the side of the bar and looked at me. He didn't whine. He didn't scratch. He just looked at me with his ears up.

"It's alright, Rock, relax," I said.

He stood there with his ears up.

George had an extra Coors, probably because of his concern for me and because the incident evoked memories of his mom. He got an even more far-off look in his eye than usual.

"Trace, things cool?" It was Gus looking through the kitchen window.

"Yeah, man, someone broke into my place. You didn't hear anything did you?" I said.

"No, I had the dishwasher and the sink going. I'm sorry man. I shoulda heard them. When I took out the trash, I saw your door." Gus shook his head like he had failed me.

"No, no, no…no way you could've. Not your fault, Gus."

He shook his head, clearly mad at himself, and went back to his kitchen duties.

It was almost four, and the place started to fill up with new customers. The light broke through the dark bar, and the sounds of women giggling echoed off the walls forming a strong contrast with what was in the room.

"Tracyyyyyyyy, look what I found…your secret is out…you're in troubllllle." It was Molly, and she was even more filled with mischief than usual. As my eyes adjusted, I noticed her companion.

It was Kayla.

You've got to be kidding me, I thought to myself. My crazy

little sister and my, uh, what?...were pals. Kayla had a grin on her face like she had one up on me. What that might be, I don't know.

"Oh geez, talk about an unholy alliance." It was the best I could come up with, and what happened to come out of my mouth.

Kayla smirked in mock offense.

"Momo! Where's my kisses!" George shouted, coming out of his reverie.

"Georgie!!!" Molly ran over. "How could I ever forget you, you handsome man!" She smothered him in a big hug, and he kissed her loud on the cheek.

"That's better," George said. "Who's your friend?" he nodded toward Kayla.

"Hmm...maybe you should ask Tracy." She made her eyes wide and looked at me. George turned in my direction. He looked at me with anticipation. I knew he would require an explanation.

"Trace?" George said.

"George, this is Kayla. Kayla, this is my good friend and friend of Curran's, George," I said as formally as I could. "Kayla and I are new friends," I said and awkwardly cleared my throat.

"Atta boy, T! Way to get back on that horse!" he said, having no idea the can of worms he just opened. "Nice to meet you, Kayla."

Kayla smiled and offered her hand. George took it and gave it a kiss. Kayla blushed.

"George, don't forget, you're my man!" Molly said. Rocky had made his way over to Molly, wagging his tail and finally relaxing his ears. She got the spot behind the ear, and Rocky mooed a little.

"Oh my God, what a gorgeous dog!" Kayla said. Rocky sniffed his way over to her. She got on one knee and roughed up his ears and kissed him on the snout. Rocky's tail thwapped the floor.

George looked over at me and gave me what he thought was

a subtle thumbs up. Then he did his bar top knock and headed toward the door. Rocky broke free from Kayla and escorted his best buddy to the door. He got his last Milk-Bone and watched George head out.

"So, you weren't going to tell your little sister about the social work intern in her building?" Molly said. "You know, you can't keep secrets from me."

I looked at Kayla.

"Tell me you don't have to work with her?" I said.

"Sorry, Trac-y," she was mocking the "y" that she now learned people used with my name. "I am providing all the family counseling and student interventions for your sister's classroom." She smiled like she had something on me.

I just nodded.

"What can I get you two to drink. I might as well do my job as long as you're my only customers."

"I'm going to go girly. Use your mad skills and make me a Cosmopolitan," She feigned an awful aristocratic accent.

I looked at Kayla.

"That sounds awesome," she said. She was still smiling.

"How was the day manning the Curran's stick," Molly said. "Oooh, I didn't realize how homoerotic that sounded!"

Kayla spit out her first Cosmo sip.

"Well, it was going swimmingly until I found out someone ransacked my apartment,' I said, knowing I dropped a bomb.

Molly and Kayla went quiet.

"Serious?" Molly said.

I nodded.

"That sucks," Kayla said.

"Tell me about it…" I said.

I realized I had changed the mood, and I regretted it. I felt shitty all of a sudden.

"What they take?" Kayla said.

"That's the weird part. Far as I can tell, nothing," I said. "They tossed my place from front to back."

"That doesn't make any sense," Molly said.

"Yeah, I know."

"It not like you had anything of value up there. Rocky's bones aren't worth anything," Molly said with a smirk.

"Yeah, Tinker and Stagger think it was CIA-related."

The two of them just looked at me for a long time.

"Is it?" Molly said. She glared at me like I was supposed to divulge something.

"Geez, Molly. You too?" I shook my head. "I was a counselor and a researcher. I had no Matt Damon-type duties."

"That you'll admit to..." she said with annoyed sarcasm.

"I'm not going to dignify that with a response," I said. "Hey, by the way. Tinker alluded to Dad's military duties. He ever tell you about what he did in the army?"

"Oh great, talk to Tinker. That guy's looney tunes. Dad told me he shot bad guys and tried his best not to get killed."

"That all?" I said, trying not to call attention to my curiosity.

"Yeah, why? What else would he have done?"

I shrugged and just decided to leave it alone.

"I think he told Jack more about army stuff, ask him," Molly said. "You need any help with your apartment?"

"Nah, I'll straighten up and fix the door jamb."

"Well, then, my work here is done." She said. "I've delivered Ms. Kayla, and I hope I made you sufficiently uncomfortable. That is, after all, my mission."

"Mission accomplished," I said.

CHAPTER TWENTY-THREE

When my shift ended, Kayla insisted on coming back to my apartment. She said it was to help out, but I think it was as much curiosity as anything else. Rocky came along.

We climbed the eleven stairs, and I opened the door.

"Shit..." Kayla said. Rocky paced around the room, sniffing. He could tell other people were in here recently, and he didn't like it. Some way, he could tell they weren't the treat sharing, behind-the-ear-scratching type.

"Honestly, it doesn't look that great even when it hasn't been tossed," I said. "I flipped the mattress back over and made the bed as much as you could make a bed that was on a makeshift pallet platform. Kayla started stacking magazines, and I moved into the kitchen, where I screwed tops back on containers, wiped spillage, and tried to find the best way to clean up week-old lo mien. Diploma.

"So, you don't have any idea who did this or who would want to do this?" Kayla asked, trying to make it sound like she wasn't prying.

"Nope, not a clue," I said. It was the truth.

She was quiet for a long time.

"And, excuse me for being naïve, but it has nothing to do with your job?" She said.

"Like I poured someone a sour beer or something, and they

wanted to get back at me?" It was a smartass response, and I knew it.

Kayla tilted her head and gave me an annoyed frown. She didn't ask a follow-up. I gave it a second before I responded.

"Like I've said and like I tell everyone, my job at the CIA was as a contractor who counseled agents and as a researcher. I didn't interact with Carrie and Saul on Homeland. It was like being the employee assistance counselor at a company that made lightbulbs, hooded sweatshirts, or toilet brushes. There are 20,000 employees, it is a federal job, and they need counselors."

She looked right at me.

"Except it is for the CIA," she said. "I tried to look up what you do and your position on the internet, and I couldn't find anything."

"It is under human resources," I said. "I think it says something about employee assistance services and research."

"Yeah, I saw that. Not a lot of detail," Kayla didn't look up as she swept up some of Rocky's kibble that got strewn around. Rocky sniffed and tried to get some extra snacks as she did.

"It is hard to prove a negative, so I guess you just have to believe me," I said. We were quiet for a little after that. Rocky nuzzled Kayla's thigh, imploring her to stop the meaningless cleaning and to scratch his head. She did.

"What's Rocky's deal?" she asked with a much lighter tone.

"What do you mean?" I said.

"He's your mom's?" The topic brought a sadness I could feel in my stomach and behind my eyes.

"Dad always had bloodhounds. He had Rocky's father, Sully, and before that, there was Paddy, and before that, there was Duffy. All big, all related, all with sweet dispositions," I said. "They loved him, and they did whatever he wanted. I never saw him spend a second on training. It was like his aura or something let them know he loved them and he should do what he wants."

"He's your dog, or is he your mom's dog?"

"He's a Curran. He's ours. Mom loves him, but I get a sense

Rocky makes her sad because he was such a part of Dad. That and his 150 lbs of love can be hard for a 70-year-old woman to handle."

She thought about that for a long time.

"Your family's tight," she said.

"Yeah, I guess so," I said. "I love them, but it was good to be away."

"Why?"

I exhaled and gave it some thought.

"Well, it would be too simple to say I needed to find myself, but I think that's part of it. Family is such a priority it can be easy to get lost in it like you aren't an individual, but merely part of a unit," I said. "I think that comes out in all of us. Jack does nothing but work and seethe at life. Molly loves fun but maybe a little too much, and she has her own pain."

"And what about this stuff about your dad's CIA involvement?"

"Uh, I don't know about all that. It could be the delusions of a guy who drinks too much and has had a fair amount of head trauma," I said.

"Or..." she left it open-ended.

"Or, I guess he could've been J. Edgar Hoover's boyfriend or something else."

She smiled, but it turned sad so she looked away. She put her head down and picked up the broom, and started to sweep an already swept floor.

"What's the matter?" I said.

She kept sweeping and didn't say anything.

"Hey, what's going on?" I said. She kept her head down, and I heard her sniffle.

I went over and took the broom from her hand. I gently lifted her chin and looked her in the eye. She bit her lower lip.

When she went to speak, her lips trembled.

"George said something about you getting back on a horse..." she let it trail off. She looked straight at me.

I took a breath. My mind raced, and I did my best to hold the feelings at a distance.

"I was engaged. She left without warning, and I don't know where she went," I said. It felt like I got punched.

"Is that why you're so angry, so sarcastic? I mean, you're sweet and wonderful and sensitive, but there's an edge that seems constant.".

No one has ever been so right or put it so succinctly. I didn't know what to say or how to think.

"Um, uh..." came out of my mouth.

"Makes me wonder if there will ever be room for an 'Us,'" she said.

I took a deep breath. I didn't know what to say. I didn't want to say anything that wasn't true. I didn't want to not respond.

"You don't have to say anything," she said and kissed me very gently.

She took my hand and led me to bed.

CHAPTER TWENTY-FOUR

The next morning, I took Kayla to her apartment, and Rocky came with us because it was time for him to go back to Mom's. It was a wonderful night and, thankfully, one that didn't require a lot of conversation. Bringing Rocky along for the ride was good because he tended to dominate the conversation.

Dad's Cadillac was on permanent loan to me. It was a big champagne-colored, '98 DeVille with 48,000 miles. Dad just drove it around town and never went on long trips. Rocky was in the back seat, or at least some of him was in the backseat. He came up to the elbow rest to nose me in the neck and lick Kayla.

"Oooh, Rocky, you're such a good boy!" she said. I had made coffee and poured it into a travel mug. She guarded it carefully while petting Rock's nose as we drove.

"Do you get sad bringing him back?" She asked while scratching behind his ear. Rocky had lifted a paw and rested it on her shoulder in approval.

"Maybe a little. It is never for long, and I guess I'll get him to Mom or Molly will drop him off at the bar for George to see him. The beast gets more love and attention than I ever did," I said.

"Well, maybe not last night," Kayla said and smiled at me.

I smiled at the thought of it. There was a feeling of unfinished business and the hanging notion that a necessary conversation was to come, but if she wasn't demanding it, I thought I'd let it take its course. It wasn't a long trip to her apartment, and it didn't seem like it was going to be hard to put the conversation off.

Rocky whined when we got out of the car, and he jumped into the front seat to take Kayla's place as we walked to her door. He had his whole upper body out the window when we stopped at the door.

"Thank you for last night. I'm sorry about your apartment," she said while fishing for her keys. Rocky barked at us.

"I think I should be the one thanking you."

She smiled and gently kissed me on the lips. Rocky howled.

"Better take care of the boy," she said.

"Yeah," I said. I started to head back to the car. I only got a few steps.

"Trace," she called, and I turned around. "You owe me a conversation some time."

I stop and nodded.

She didn't come cheap, and I respected that. Rocky barked plaintively while we pulled away, and Kayla called to him and said she'd see him soon.

I hoped so.

It was another ten minutes to Mom's, and when I pulled in the driveway, Rocky's tail went turbo. He bounded out of the car, ran up the steps of the porch, and began scratching on the front door. I lagged behind, taking a second to wipe the drool off the leather seats.

I was on the steps when Mom opened the door. She braced herself, and Rocky jumped up and put his paws on her shoulders by way of greeting.

"Go ahead, boy, welcome home," she said. He jumped down, ran around her, and through the house looking for his friend Otis, Mom's orange cat. "Tracy, that dog's gonna kill me!"

"Me too," I said.

"C'mon in for coffee. I just put on a pot." She had on her mom jeans and a green cardigan over a yellow t-shirt. I recognized the scent of her Dove moisturizing bar that she swore by. Rocky found a bone and, secure in the belief that his loved ones were present, did a few spins on his kitchen bed before collapsing. Mom poured a coffee into one of the many Notre Dame mugs she had in the kitchen.

"How's things at the tavern?" She always called it "the tavern" and never "the bar."

"Well, of course, it isn't the same, but everyone knows that," I said. "Business is good. Jennifer knows what she's doing."

"And your friend, George?"

"Never misses a day. Never misses a Milk-Bone," I said.

Mom sipped her coffee and waited a beat. I could tell she wanted to ask me something.

"Honey, are you going back to Washington?" She seemed a bit strained asking. It was like she knew she had to but didn't want me to feel bad.

"I haven't decided. I worked so hard to get there but then with everything that happened all at once, I don't know. I just don't know..." I let it trail off.

"You take your time. You don't have to do anything," Mom said, trying her best to be reassuring. "You can do whatever you want."

I smiled. It was great to have someone in your corner, even if you knew she was feeling sorry for me.

"How'd it go when you went down there?" she asked.

"It was okay. I can tell they value me. It is a weird place, you know. It is probably related to what they do. I guess it has to be."

I was bracing for her to bring up Marie. So far, she hadn't.

"Well, all that spy stuff..." she said and took the tiniest of sips.

"Yeah, mom, I wanted to ask you something." She looked at me with just a touch of apprehension.

"The other day, crazy Tinker was talking..." She interrupted.

"Crazy is right..."

"He mentioned Dad's military service, like he did something, I don't know, maybe clandestine? Did you ever hear anything about that?"

She sipped her coffee again. I got the impression she was trying hard to be relaxed.

"Your father, a spy?" She let out a laugh.

I waited. She didn't say anything else.

"Was he?" I said. I noticed my tone had changed just a little bit.

"You know your father never talked about the war. Not to me, not to you kids, not to anyone. It wasn't his nature," she said.

She didn't make eye contact. She wouldn't, and I knew when the door was shut and not going to open. I let it go. She drank her coffee and looked briefly at her nails.

"What do you hear from Molly?" She changed the subject. "She been to visit?"

"Of course, she comes around to check on me and bust my chops," I said.

She smiled. "That's my girl." She took a second and did her best to suppress a smile. "She tells me you have a new friend?"

Great, thanks, Momo.

"Some nice girl who is a social worker with her at school..."

I smiled. "Yes, Mom, but it is no big deal yet."

"Yet, but that doesn't mean it won't be..." She smiled. "You deserve to be happy."

"Thanks, Mom. I'm happy when I'm with you." I saw her bite her lower lip and shift her eyes toward the kitchen window and our backyard. That was her tell. I knew she was about to say something that wasn't easy for her. I've seen her do it my whole life.

"Honey, does that man's death still bother you? I mean, of course, it does, but you weren't at fault. He was troubled beyond anything you could do," she said.

Even when I just thought about it, the topic made me sick to my stomach. People have avoided it. No one has asked me this directly before, not Dr. Williams, not Michaelson, not Aisha…no one. I did my best to detach from the feelings and just observe them, but it wasn't easy.

"Oh, I shouldn't have. I'm sorry, Tracy," she said. It made it worse. I hated doing anything that made my mom feel bad.

"It's okay, Mom. It is just that I've never really talked about it. I know on some level that I'm not responsible, that this is the line of work I'm in, but then I think I missed something. That's my training; that's what I'm supposed to be good at it. I wasn't, and now, a whole family is dead," I said.

She shook her head.

"You're a psychologist, not a mind reader. How could you have known?"

"Mom, Mr. Hutchins didn't like to talk about stress or the job, and he didn't. After a while, I didn't pressure him, and I let him go through the motions." I felt myself tear up. I didn't want to acknowledge it, and I foolishly tried to pretend it wasn't happening. "I can't help but think if I confronted him more or harder that…

I started to cry without control. I put my face in my hands, and I felt my mom's hands rub my back. It felt wonderful and awful at the same time. I was too old to be consoled by my mom. At this stage in her life, I should be comforting her.

"Oh, Tracy. You've always been so hard on yourself. That's mine and your father's fault. We should've gone easier on you."

"Stop, Mom. It is not your fault. I am a grown man. It is not your fault," I said as the tears subsided.

"I want you to have peace with this. This and the whole thing with Maria. I just don't think any of this is fair. And your father, it just isn't fair. I pray for it all the time."

Now, mom was the one crying. It broke my heart. She looked out the window again, and the tears rolled down her face.

Rocky awoke and whined, sensing the people he loved were not doing so good. It brought a distraction.

"Oh, Rocky. We're okay. We're okay, boy," Mom petted

him as he approached. “It’s just an Irish thing.” She scratched behind his ears, and it made his leg spasm, not as much as usual, but it still shook.

Mom did it better than anyone.

CHAPTER TWENTY-FIVE

Leave it to a mom to get at the heart of your shit. I mean, I've spent, I don't know, ten years studying human cognition and behavior, and it took a kitchen table discussion with my 70+-year-old mom to get at the core of my issues. I didn't know what the resolution was, but I knew I needed to process this whole thing more.

It ate at me at the bar the next day, and I couldn't concentrate. I screwed up Ron, the construction guy's order, and I was a little short with George. Rocky glared at me to let me know I was being a prick. After lunch, the bar patrons filed out, and after George left, I was alone. I didn't know what to do, and against my better judgment, I concluded that I had to do something. Rarely a sound decision process, but I was committed.

I looked up Eddie's obit and found that it mentioned a cousin, Carlton Brooks, who lived outside Newark, Delaware. A Google search paid off, and I found his number. I called before I would let myself think it through. He picked up on the second ring.

"This is Carlton," he had a bit of rasp in his voice like maybe he was a smoker.

"Carlton, my name is Trace Curran." I felt the need to clear my throat. I noticed my anxiety kick up. I did my best to distance from it. "I worked with your cousin, Eddie."

He didn't say anything for a long moment.

"What can I do for you, Mr…what was it?"

"Curran."

"Yes, Mr. Curran." His tone changed immediately. It was like he stiffened. I guess as I thought about it, why wouldn't he?

"Um, I was a psychologist at the CIA, actually contracted by the agency, to work with agents like your cousin. What happened, to be honest, has been very difficult for me, and I wanted to reach out and…"

Carlton interrupted.

"It was very difficult for me, Mr. Curran," he said.

"I can't even imagine. I was wondering if we could meet, you know, face to face…if it wasn't too much of an imposition," I said with zero confidence.

There was a long pause.

"Meet? Why would you want to do that?"

"Uh, Carlton, I'll be honest with you. I was Eddie's counselor. He wasn't much into talking to me. I liked him very much, but he didn't really want any part of the therapy thing. He seemed to me to be very much in control. What uh, happened has made me…well, I've left my job and…"

"Are you looking for forgiveness? Absolution? A way out? Mr. Curran, maybe you should be calling a priest or a minister or something," he said.

"I don't know what I am looking for, Mr. Brooks. I want to understand more. I want to know what I missed," I said. I was pleading at this point.

He exhaled.

"If you want to make the drive to Delaware, I'll spend some time with you. I'm not sure what we'll accomplish. And Mr. Curran, as you might think, this isn't my favorite topic. Drudging it up isn't my favorite thing to do."

"Of course, I understand. It isn't for me, but somehow I feel like if I don't…" I didn't finish. I couldn't.

"Okay, Mr. Curran. C'mon down."

I let him know I'd leave right away and I'd be there in the

early evening and hung up. I already felt exhausted. It was a five-hour drive, and it would be tight calling Jessica to get a sub, but I didn't care. This was something I had to do. I called and left a voice message that I had an emergency and that Gus would cover for me. Not the best solution, but I wasn't concerned with quarterly bartending performance appraisal.

I filled the time on the way down with a mix of music. The sad playlist again, an audiobook on Acceptance & Commitment Therapy, and some Christian meditative stuff. Sometimes you can find just the right mix to make a long drive put you in a zone, and sometimes your choices just make you more fidgety and restless. This was one of those restless trips.

My GPS was on the mark, and I pulled into the parking lot of Carlton Brooks condominium complex at 6:17. Two minutes faster than Google Maps said I would. I felt awkward as hell but kept focused on my goal and made my way to the door.

Carlton came after a rang his bell almost immediately.

"Mr. Curran, you're right on time. C'mon in." His place was a classic 90's condo layout. Kitchen to the left, dining area to the right backed up with a living room area with sliding doors opening up to a patio area. It had the requisite patio furniture and a silver gas grill that looked like it didn't get used.

Everything in the place was new, leather and real wood, and looked like it came off the showroom floor. The wall hangings were nondescript and the kind of the thing a well-meaning woman would pick up at Home Goods because it matched the color palate. The floors were some sort of laminate, and they were immaculate. On an end table there were two 5 x 7 framed photos. One was of Carlton in a wedding picture, and the other was him with Eddie wearing Redskin jerseys.

"Coffee? Drink?" he said. "For me, it is the cocktail hour, so I'm going to pour myself a Manhattan. Be happy to fix you one," he said. He was much more cordial in person.

"It was a long ride. I'd love a bourbon with a couple of ice cubes," I said.

"Good man," he said with approval, almost to himself.

He looked like a slightly older, thinner version of Eddie. He had less hair, and he seemed like a man who spent a career in an office, not a life working with his hands. Not soft, but also not hard and calloused. He had reading glasses on his nose.

"To Eddie," he said and motioned to clink glasses. He took a seat in the leather Barco-lounger, and I sat on the couch.

"Mr. Curran—"

"Please, call me Trace," I interrupted.

He nodded. "Trace, I don't think I was too friendly on the phone. Your call took me by surprise and, as I said, this isn't my favorite topic. If I was rude, I apologize."

I nodded and raised my glass slightly in a tacit thank you.

"What can I tell you about my cousin?" He said and sort of settled into his chair, taking a sip of his Manhattan.

"Eddie and I met every week or so. It was part of a program the CIA started for the mental health of agents like Eddie, who spend so much time studying disturbing acts. That's what Eddie did much of the day," I said.

"He talked about it with me a bit. Nothing he wasn't supposed to, but in general. Beheadings, rapes, tortures…" He shook his head in that way that people do when they're trying to get something out of their minds.

"He didn't take our sessions seriously. He'd tell me that the stuff didn't happen to him and why should it bother him. He'd bust my balls about Notre Dame football and be kind of sarcastic. It wasn't rude toward me. It was more like he just wanted to let me know that he thought it was all bullshit."

He laughed to himself. "That sounds like Eddie."

"Did it bother him?" I asked.

"I saw what you saw. That was Eddie. He wanted to golf, watch football, and fish. He knew he had a few years left, and he had already calculated his pension, Medicare, and Social Security stuff. He was biding his time." Carlton took another sip.

"Was his relationship with his wife in trouble?" I wasn't sure if I was getting too intrusive at this point.

"Nah, he and Mare were married 25 years. They got on each other's nerves like every couple I ever met, but they didn't fight or argue. Biggest thing was she'd get on him about how much golf he played," he said.

"The kids?"

"Teenagers. Good kids. Usual pain in the ass stuff. Getting ready for college, proms, football practice that bullshit," He had some more Manhattan.

"Two kids getting ready for college and retirement. Things must've been tight." I asked.

"Not really. Eddie said he had their tuitions already covered. After my wife died and we were upside down with credit cards, he set me up here. He was a good man. We were more like brothers than cousins."

"He helped you out with a down payment?" I asked.

He shook his head.

"Paid in full. Said his investments went off the charts. His hobby was the market, and he went through some sort of tech bubble or spike or whatever they called it and hit it big. He could've retired already, but he kept at it just the same. That's why the whole thing doesn't make any sense."

I paused to think. Eddie was a lot of things, but he didn't strike me as a market shark or a man of means.

"Yeah, I know what you're thinking. Eddie? Yeah, it surprised me too. That is until he set me up here." He looked around the room for emphasis.

"Yeah, that's for sure," I said to be saying something.

"You know right after it happened when the woman from the CIA came to talk to me, I told her the same thing and—"

"A woman from the CIA came to talk to you?" I asked. I wasn't sure I knew what he was talking about.

"Yeah, she said routine follow-up. They asked me background questions. They knew he had bought the condo. They just did some routine follow-up," he said.

"Sure, do you remember her name?"

"No, not really. I was in a fog."

"What did she look like?" I asked.

"That, I remember." He sort of smirked.

"Why's that?"

"Well, at first, I thought she was a light-skinned Black woman, but I also noticed her eyes were a bit almond-shaped like she had some Asian blood or something," he said.

CHAPTER TWENTY-SIX

He had just described Dr. Williams.

But what the hell would she be doing there? And how does an agent who makes about 100k a year buy a condo for a cousin and have tuition for his teenagers' college years already? Something wasn't right.

I didn't have much more to talk about, so I let Carlton know I'd get out of his hair. He apologized again for what he thought was rudeness. He said he could tell that I had cared about his brother. That meant a lot.

While getting on the road, I called Ray to find some shit out.

"Hey, what's happenin' brother?' Ray gave me his usual greeting. "You get KO'd by any chicks lately?"

"Oh, fuck you," I said as we continued our bro speak. "I gotta ask you something."

"Yeah? Like what? No, I never really was trying back when we used to spar, and no, I'm not surprised now that you get your ass kicked by women."

"Again, fuck you. Look, what kind of money do agents make? Specifically, a guy like Eddie Hutchins. You know, the guy on my caseload that took out his family and then himself."

"Clearly, not enough. I don't know, a guy with ten years in...hard to say exactly. An entry-level agent starts at about fifty now. Special agents, guys with super high clearance, might top out over a 150," Ray said.

"So, Eddie was inside studying video, occasionally called in for strategy stuff but not a guy out in the field. What could he have been pulling down?"

"How many years in?"

"I would guess close to 20," I said.

"Ballpark? 100k, somewhere in there," Ray said. "Hey, why the hell do you care?"

I thought for a second and then realized it was Ray. If I asked him shit, I sort of had to tip my hand.

"I was just visiting a cousin of his. Guy said Eddie bought him a condo and paid cash. Said he already had two college tuitions paid for his kids' future. That sound like something an agent could do?"

Ray hesitated.

"I'm still stuck on you saying 'I was visiting Eddie's cousin.' What the hell are you doing?" Ray never held back on speaking his mind.

"Uh, I wanted to find some shit out," I said. I know it was weak.

"Yeah, great idea, genius." I could tell he was pissed. "That's fuckin' great—meddling in a CIA agent's death."

"I'm not meddling."

"No, so this in the scope of your position?"

"C'mon, Ray. I got some shit tied up in this. You know that," I said.

He didn't say anything for a long while.

"I didn't know Hutchins, but if you're asking me, would he have the disposable income to pay eight years of college and a good condo in cash? No, that would not be typical of any agents' income that I know." Ray was annoyed, but he gave me the information I wanted. "Unless he inherited it or something weird."

"Yeah, that's what I thought. Where does a guy get that kind of money?

"I don't know, but there's one thing I do know," he said.

"What's that?"

"It's none of your goddamn business, and you're opening yourself up to a world of trouble making it your business," he said.

"Technically, I am an independent contractor. I don't even work for the Agency."

"Great, let them know that at the grand jury you get called in to."

"Yeah, yeah, yeah…I'm just a sensitive psychologist trying to get closure. That's all," I said.

"You're a goddamn fool, is what you are."

I took a breath and collected my thoughts.

"And why would Dr. Williams be there?" I asked. That one gave me a weird feeling.

Ray didn't respond right away.

"Dr. Williams visited Eddie's cousin? The guy said that? You got me on that one. You sure? It would be inappropriate as hell and as fucked up as you going there."

"He described a woman sounded just like her who said she was a psychologist," I said.

"Brother, that's not exactly the same thing as *knowing* it was Dr. Williams."

"Look, Ray, you know—" I got another call on the line. I could see it was Kayla. "Hey, Ray, I got another call, and I got to take it," I said.

"Sure, you got your information, and now you're done with me. See 'ya, asshole." I think he was half kidding.

I picked up Kayla's call.

"What's up?" I said.

"Where are you?" she said. There was panic in her voice.

"I'm in Delaware. It is a long story, but—" I didn't get to finish.

"Somebody's following me. I'm scared. Two guys in a light blue Malibu have followed me to school, the gym, and back home. They're outside my apartment right now." I could feel her anxiety.

"You sure?"

"Oh my God, of course, I'm sure." I could hear her cry. "Trace, I'm scared as hell."

"Okay. Okay, relax. I'm calling a friend who will come get you and take you out. Someplace public. It is the safest thing to do," I said.

"What? Who!"

"Don't worry about it. You'll be safe. Expect him in 20 minutes or so. I gotta go. Try to relax. It is going to be okay."

I didn't know what the hell was going on, but I knew what to do.

I called Tinker.

I tried to keep the car at 85. Keeping my thoughts from speeding out of control wasn't as easy. Kayla didn't deserve this. She isn't CIA, damn, we just met. What the hell was going on?

I turned on the radio to have some background noise. Five hours in the car, especially when you're in a hurry, can be brutal on the psyche.

No music. I didn't have the space to enjoy it.

Sports talk was just too inane.

Investment call-in show, hell no.

The radio version of CNN would have to do. There was talk about the hurricane getting ready to hit New Orleans. There was a trade imbalance with Mexico threatening the economy, and there was a shooting in Chicago. I was not quite twenty minutes out of Newark when the phone rang.

"Trace, she's secure." It was Tinker. "We're having a drink at Curran's. Our friends are parked outside. I'm teaching Kayla how to drink bourbon. You can thank me later."

"Oh, thank God, Tink. I appreciate it." I sighed some relief.

"Not sure who they are—plain grey car but not typical government. Look too stodgy to be private. Too clean cut to be terror-based bad guys. I'll have to think about it. Regular plates," Tinker said.

"I can get Jack to run them," I think Jack would do that. He might get pissy.

"I already took the liberty. Hope you don't mind." Tinker said with some pride in his voice.

"Did he give you are a hard time?"

"Not like he would you. I know what it's like to be a little brother. I'm the crazy friend of his old mam's. I know how to work a system," Tinker said.

"I owe you big for this," I said.

"Umm, not really. The debit shit goes back a generation here, kid. Your old man didn't keep track, but I know for sure he did me more than I ever did for him."

"Tinker, can you stay with Kayla until I get back?" I asked.

"No problem. She can stay with me, or I'll stay at her place if she wants."

"Make sure she does one or the other," I said.

"Roger that." I could hear him slurp his drink. Undoubtedly a Schaefer. "Oh, and Trace? My buddy Colt joined us for the night out."

"I'm sure Colt knows his place, and even if he's there he doesn't have to interject himself."

Tinker laughed. "Understood. You want to say 'Hi?'"

"Sure, put her on," I said.

"Trace?" Kayla sounded a bit more relaxed but not entirely herself.

"Kayla, you can relax now. You're in good hands," I said.

"I guess. Can we stay together tonight?"

"Of course. Tinker won't leave till I get there," I said.

"Ok, good. Hurry," she said.

CHAPTER TWENTY-SEVEN

I felt my shoulders unclench just a bit. Tinker was nuts, but he was also as good a security man as there was. He was also the kind of family friend you could just ask anything of. He liked doing favors, or at least seemed to.

Now I felt I could keep the car under 85 and turn on the radio. My mind raced as I thought about Kayla, how scared she must be, and even more so about what this was all about. First my apartment and now stepping into the life of a person I had met.

CNN radio was repeating essentially the same stories they aired from earlier in the ride.

Then they broke in.

This is a special report...

The ominous words that always sent fear into every American heart, probably since Kennedy was shot.

We are interrupting your programming because there have been two explosions just moments ago at a rally featuring conservative talk show hosts Sean Hannity, Bill O'Reilly, and Pat Buchanan in Tampa, Florida at the Amalie Arena. The explosions came as the crowds were filing out at the north exit to the arena.

The reporter spoke in the way they do when they go live without all the information.

A man we spoke to, Brendan Noonan, from nearby Venice, Florida, said the explosions came as the rally ended and spectators were heading to the exits. He said the noise was deafening and that people began to panic. He said many near him were down, and many more were bloodied.

You could still hear ambulances and crowd noise in the background.

The conservative rallies have been met with counter-protests in each city. The one leading up to tonight's rally quite large, drawing thousands but was mostly peaceful. The speakers at the rally entered the arena with armed guards, smiling and waving at their supporters.

He paused and stuttered a bit before saying.

We have Homeland Security spokesperson Charles Ignatius on the line. Charles, do we have any information on who is responsible for this act?

"Right now, the FBI, Justice Center, and Homeland Security are sending resources here to investigate the situation to get additional information to see just what have might have transpired. Right now, the effort is in getting all the resources on the ground at the arena and get as much information as we can."

We can hear the crowd and the confusion in the background. We've heard from people at the scene that there were many people injured. Do we have a sense of causalities yet?

"No sir, not yet. This is all in progress."

He hadn't answered the question.

Is there any indication that this is foreign terrorism?

"We are still gathering information. We do not have any clear information, nor did we hear any credible chatter leading up to this event."

Is there any indication that this could be an act associated with Antifa?

"Again, not at this time," the Homeland Security representative said.

The reporter paused again.

We are now getting reports that twelve are dead, and at least 22 have been wounded. That is not confirmed at this time. We have a report from Lara Brillstein from WFLA in Tampa, who is on the scene. Lara...

"George, it is chaos here. There are more injured people than there are EMTs to attend to them. One is reminded of the Boston marathon incident or the Manchester bombing at the Ariana Grande concert. It seems—"

Sorry, Lara, we have a report in and, just a minute, it is confirmed that the ANTIFA logo was painted as it has been at other events near the entrance of the arena.

I waited for it, and it came. My head was spinning.

The radio kept repeating the same information without anything new. Eventually, they went back to their regular programming with half-hour updates to the story. I drove in a near trance.

I was to Poughkeepsie, about an hour outside of Albany, when the phone rang. The identifier made my pulse skip.

"Hey, Curran." It was Danny O. "Watching the news?"

"Listening, Danny. What the hell is going on?"

"Well, well, well..." His flair for the dramatic rivaled a Chandler novel. "More bullshit from the right."

I wanted to keep him on as long as possible. The longer the conversation, the more potential information. It meant humoring him. I hit the Tap-A-Call button on the iPhone.

"Well, well, well, *what,* Danny?" I said.

"C'mon Doctor Curran." He gave "doctor" a long sarcastic pronunciation. "You've used that overeducated mind of yours to study the big bad Antifa for years now, haven't you?"

"Yeah, so?"

"So, when have you seen any of anti-fascist groups do anything that resembles this? You've probably have memorized the Congressional Research project report, or help me here, didn't you help write it?"

"My mentor was part of it," I said, thinking of Dr. Williams.

"Ah, yes, Dr. Williams. How well do you know her, Curran?"

I had no idea where this was going.

"Dr. Williams? She was my doctoral advisor for two years. Before that, I had her as a professor, and for the last 18 months, she's been my employer. Why?"

"She never mentioned her time with us?"

I thought of the newspaper article.

"No, what are you talking about?" He was starting to piss me off a little.

"In her youth, she was in the movement. That is until her lover was accidentally killed. Tragic. At a Boston protest. Word was she left after that. Now she 'studies' us from afar, like lab rats. I know she's not a big fan."

"I had no idea, but what does this have to do with anything?" I could feel the tension in my voice.

"Probably nothing, but it is food for thought. I'm sorry for the digression. Please let's get back on track—tell me, Dr. Trace, the findings of what ANTIFA recommends its members do to take action. Feel free to paraphrase."

The arrogance made me crazy, but I wanted him to stay on.

I started.

"One, develop a social media presence; two, monitor the activities of fascist groups; three, recruit new members; four, hold counter-demonstrations; five, pressure organizations to cancel fascist events; six, remove or deface fascist posters; seven, publicize info about enemies and eight, develop legal self-defense skills."

I, of course, was well familiar with what he was talking about.

"Very, very, very good, Doc." He paused for effect. "Now, what don't you see?"

"I don't see a lot of things."

"Don't get cute, Curran." He flashed some anger.

"I don't see blowing up an arena to kill innocent people," I said.

"Fuckin-A right you don't!"

"So, what the hell is going on?" I matched his intensity.

"Someone is setting up a false flag project to frame the ANTIFA effort. That's what the fuck is going on!"

I didn't know what to say. I kept quiet, hoping he would rant.

"Curran, you there?"

"Yeah, I'm here."

He changed his tone.

"What is going on? Who is behind this? And Why? Is it just to increase the public's misconception of what's happening?"

"I have to be honest. I have no idea," I said.

He waited before responding.

"Somebody better find out before more people die."

CHAPTER TWENTY-EIGHT

It was quarter to one when I pulled into the parking lot at Curran's. There were a few cars but no one in them and nothing that looked suspicious. My back was stiff from a long day in the Cadillac, but I didn't let it slow me down as I found myself running to get inside.

It was Friday night, so the music was up loud. The dance floor only had two participants, and the bar was only half full. Maureen was serving drinks, and the two dancers were Tinker and Kayla, and Stagger was on a stool cheering them on. They were dancing to Springsteen's hoot-a-nanny version of Buffalo Gals. Tinker was spinning Kayla around, letting her go, only to do that weird move where his knees go in and out with hands on top of them, creating the optical illusion. That made Stagger yell, "Yee Haw!"

Kayla laughed hysterically and moved around with just a little bit of a glassy look in her eye.

You put Tinker on assignment, and he comes through.

While the band was going into the big New Orleans horns finale, I got myself a Boomsauce and took the stool next to Stagger.

In between "Yee Haws!" Stagger looked at me.

"This one's a keeper, Tracy."

I nodded and lifted my beer. Stagger had a neat bourbon in

front of him.

"The coast is clear too." He said it low and flat. He wanted me to know without asking, and he didn't want to make a big deal about it.

The song ended with Tinker holding her hand like it was the end of some debutante dance and Kayla doing a sweet curtsy. Then they joined Stagger and me at the bar. She jumped into my arms when she saw me, and we kissed.

"I'm so glad to see you!" she said. "You have some fun friends!"

"We aim to please, ma'am. Son, you treat this lady right, or I'll take her away from you, you know." Tinker said.

"I'm not sure you haven't already," I said.

"Oh, I'd be worried if I were you, Tracy," Kayla said and looked down her nose at me.

"You know the older the dynamite, the more explosive it gets," Tinker said.

We all laughed and touched glasses.

"Not sure what that even means, but I think I'll get this little girl home before I lose her forever," I said. "You ready, li'l darlin'?" I said, paying homage to Tinker.

"Well, I guess..."

"Look, Tracy, before you go, let me have a word. He motioned his head over to the corner of the bar by the kitchen entrance where Rocky's bed was kept during the day.

"Thanks so much, Tink. I owe you big time. I—" He didn't let me finish.

"Untuck your shirt," he said.

"Huh?"

Quickly he pulled a revolver out from under his flannel shirt and put it in my hand. I froze.

"Put it in your belt, fast!" I did as I was told. "You should have that on you all the time now."

I nodded.

I was getting the feeling that my life was changing quickly.

I shook hands with Tinker and Stagger, and Kayla kissed them both goodbye. Kayla and I walked through the kitchen and up the steps to my apartment.

"Well, that was quite a night," Kayla said. "Tinker and Stagger have a way of making a girl feel safe, and they know how to have fun."

"That's for sure," I said.

I got us beers, and we sat at the kitchen table. Without saying anything, I took the gun Tinker gave me out of my pants and put it on the counter.

"What the hell..." Kayla said.

"Tinker just gave it to me," I tried to sell that it was no big deal. Probably unnecessary, but I didn't want to argue with him."

"I didn't think you were a gun guy." She frowned.

"I'm not a gun guy."

"Ever shoot one?"

"I went to a range once when I got hired to learn how. I know how to load it, clean it, and the basics of shooting. That's it. I'm not a gun guy at all." I did my best to infuse a no-big-deal feeling to it. I don't think it worked. Kayla was obviously uneasy at its presence, and I think it rekindled the fear she felt earlier in the evening.

She looked at me without saying anything.

"Tell me what happened." I handed her a Boomsauce.

She took a deep breath.

"Tinker did such a good job keeping me occupied and laughing, it doesn't seem as bad now. I went to the gym and noticed two guys in a car outside, you know, just sitting there drinking coffee. They were still there when I got out and when I headed toward my apartment, they followed me. They tried to stay back, but there wasn't much traffic. When I came out after showering and getting ready for school, they were across the street."

"You remember what they look like?"

"Late 20's, muscular types. The one on the passenger side had a tattooed neck, just like a single mark. He had a fade haircut, you know, with the exaggerated part. I remember a crooked nose too. The other guy was bald on top and very closely cropped hair on the side. He had on RayBans." I could tell she was doing her best to remember.

"License plate?"

"It was a Florida plate. I remember the first three letters, S-H-E, because it spells *she*. There were numbers after that."

"Probably a rental. That would explain the out-of-state car. What happened later on?"

"They were at school when I got out, and they followed me home again. That's when I got weirded out."

I gave it some thought. I didn't want to go to Jack. I could ask Tony about the plate and the guys' description. If he knew nothing, I could ask Ray. Not sure how much cooperation I'd get.

"Did they approach you? Say anything?" I asked.

"No." She hesitated. "I don't want to sound all victimy, but it was intrusive the way they looked at me. Like I was, I don't know, like prey." She shivered a bit.

"If they wanted to hurt you, they would've. I think they were looking for me."

"Why would someone be looking for you? Is there spy stuff you haven't told me about?" She looked at me hard, like she wanted an answer.

"I don't know, but there's been a series of odd things that I haven't connected."

"Like what?"

"The interview with my old supervisor. The meeting tonight with Eddie's cousin. A stilted conversation I had with my friend Ray...I don't know what it means."

"It creeps me out a little," Kayla said and looked away.

"Yeah, me too," I said. "It's why I called Tinker."

She looked up and smiled a little.

"What a couple of characters. You want to tell me how you know them again?"

I got two beers from the fridge and opened Kayla's for her.

"They've been coming to the bar since it has been open. When they came back from Vietnam, my dad let them drink free for a month. Some college kids started to harass them about the war one night, and my dad threw—physically threw—the punks out. The kids were the sons of local elected officials. Dad was loyal as hell, and he was standing up for the guys. Tinker and Stagger never forgot it."

She seemed to take it in.

"What was that about your father and the war that they were talking about?"

"I'm not sure. I asked Mom about it, and she didn't really answer. I've always thought that my father was a grunt in the Army. Sometimes Tinker and Stagger get a little weird."

She nodded and looked down for a second. She looked back up and looked me in the eye.

"Trace, what was George talking about when he mentioned that thing about getting back on the horse?" Her voice strained a little with the question.

I took a breath. I gave it some thought. Kayla and I were something new, but it was beginning to feel like, well, something. I think she deserved to hear about it.

"I was engaged. We met in grad school, and we were together for four years. We worked for the same psychology contract firm. The same day my dad died, I came home, and she was gone. She left a note."

Kayla didn't say anything. She kept looking at me as if she wanted me to keep going.

"Dad died, she left, and my agent killed himself and his family on the same day. I got a little fucked up, went into a psychiatric hospital, and took a leave from the job. It is why I'm in the honorable profession of barkeep," I mock toasted with my Boomsauce.

"Have you heard from her?" I could tell it wasn't easy for her to say.

"No." I broke eye contact. "I have no idea where she is."

"Have you tried?"

"At first, I did, but I quit. I figured if she wanted to get away from me so bad, what was the point of me pursuing her?"

"Get some closure?"

"For what? The honest closure is that she didn't love me anymore."

We both got quiet. I drank a little, and Kayla looked at me.

After a long moment, she spoke.

"Is there a chance for us?" she started to cry.

I walked over to her and extended my hand. She stood, and I looked into her eyes.

"Yes. I think there's more than a chance," I said. I kissed her, and she held me tight, and we kissed deeper. After a long moment, she broke free and held my hand.

"Let's go to bed," she said.

CHAPTER TWENTY-NINE

The next morning Kayla stayed for coffee, and I was glad for the caffeine time because I needed to wake up before I walked her home. Doing anything without at least two cups of coffee in my system was a real chore. There was also something exquisitely nice about seeing her in my oversized Notre Dame Hoodie, and nothing else, with her legs tucked up underneath her while she held a hot cup of coffee in two hands.

My iPhone's electronic ringer interrupted our morning's sleepy silence. It was Ray calling from Washington.

"What's up, Sugarman," I said.

"It is what it is, my man." Ray gave his usual greeting. There was a pause after our greetings.

"What's with the eight am wakeup call. Everything ok?" I said.

"I don't know, Trace. You sittin'?" The humor left his voice.

"I am," I said. "You're scaring me a little, brother. What's up?"

He took a breath and waited just a second. It was like he was deciding to talk or not.

"Look, I'm sticking my neck out here a bit, so this goes in the vault. Got it?" He said.

"Of course." All of a sudden, I could feel my heartbeat.

"I know I came down pretty hard on you last night about visiting his cousin. That's your business. I know how fucked up you got about Eddie and, uh, well, I came across some shit this morning that I wanted you to know about."

He paused. I didn't say anything. I had that feeling I get when I'm about to hear something difficult. I examined the feeling, took a breath, and focused.

Ray continued.

"I read Eddie's autopsy report from the coroner. It was in his file. I don't know how much you know about this sort of shit so stop me when I lose you."

"Go ahead," I said.

"Eddie killed his wife and two kids. He didn't use any of his service pieces to do that. Each victim took two to the head. That's a total of six shots. The forensics say the gun was fired 12 times."

"Meaning what?" I asked.

"Not sure, except they didn't recover the extra bullets at the scene. So, where did they go?"

"Okay..."

"They found Eddie hung, right?" He didn't wait for me to respond. "He used a regular rope you get at Home Depot or Ace or any of a million places. There was no other rope around in the house."

"So..."

"Have you ever used rope for a project and used the exact amount? Eddie either had to buy the rope for the express purpose of hanging himself, or he had it around the house. There are three places within 5 miles of his house, and none sold Eddie rope that day, or they don't remember a 6'3" Black guy buying rope."

"Yeah and..."

Ray exhaled.

"So, either someone would remember selling a guy like Eddie rope, or Eddie had rope in the house, but he had the exact amount needed to hang himself." Ray sounded a bit exasperated.

"Possible..." I said.

"Anything is. Let me move on. The scars on his neck were a long oblong shape, not a V-shape. That's consistent with ligature strangulation, not hanging. His entire neck was bruised and discolored. That doesn't happen with suicide. That happens with strangulation."

"Holy shit..."

"Yeah, and here's the kicker. You know Eddie to take tranquilizers? Some sort of Benzodiazepine, Valium, Xanax anything like that?"

"He never mentioned it," I said.

"Eddie strike you as the anxious type?" It was almost sarcastic.

"No."

"He had three times the normal dosage of a benzo in his system according to the toxicology report."

"Holy shit..." I thought about it. "Who knows, maybe he was hiding something. Maybe he liked to get high once in a while."

"C'mon Trace," Ray showed his frustration. "The biggest thing is, despite all of this, there is no mention on the comments of the report that this points to anything but a murder-suicide. Not even a question of it. It is like they wanted it to go unnoticed."

"But why? Who wanted Eddie dead?" I asked.

"You were the shrink? And what were you asking me about? The money? Could that have something to do with it?"

"My head is spinning, Ray. So, I found out that Eddie had a boatload of money that no one knows how he got, and then he winds up dead, and the coroner's report looks fucked up."

"That's about it," Ray said.

"Does that have to mean anything except bureaucratic government stuff? I mean, maybe Eddie had the right amount of rope around the house, or maybe he bought it twenty miles after a drive. Maybe he was good at investing. Maybe he had other guns; lots of guys do. Maybe—"

Ray cut me off.

"You do whatever you want with the information. I'm not coming to conclusions or trying to feed your apparent need for drama. I just thought you might be interested." He didn't hide annoyance well.

"Ray, I don't mean to discredit what you're saying. I just—"

"It's fine. It's fine. Look, I got to get to an appointment. You take care."

He hung up before I could say goodbye.

CHAPTER THIRTY

I walked Kayla home, waited for her to shower and dress, and then followed her to the university. She adamantly refused to have Tinker stay with her throughout the day, and after arguing for a while, I let it go.

I called Tinker and asked him to do it anyway, only in a way that Kayla couldn't detect it. He was thrilled.

I had an hour to kill before I was due at the bar. After the conversation with Ray, my uneasiness was heightened, and I felt like I needed to do something. I decided to take a chance at finding Kayla's followers. They had to be staying in a motel close by, and there weren't that many of them. A simple cruise around some parking lots looking for a Malibu would be easy enough.

The closest motels to Curran's, according to Google, were 3.9 miles, 4.2 miles, and 5.7 miles away. I decided to check them in that order.

The first one was a Motel 6, and there were no light blue Malibu's parked there. That meant that they weren't there, were already gone, were out for the day already, or parked away from the hotel. The second hotel was a Red Roof Inn. I prefer Red Roof when it comes to budget lodging, but that didn't mean that my new friends did. It was off Watervliet Boulevard by the old rail yards, next to nothing in particular but close to the entrance to 787, and that would get you anywhere in the area efficiently. A quick tool around the lot yielded nothing. I saw two Malibus, but they were the wrong color, and they were both older.

The next hotel was a Hampton Inn, and it was on Wolf Road, a whole different area of town, on the border of Colonie. It didn't feel like Albany, but it was closer to the airport, so it held, I guess, some promise. Nothing there, not even a Camry.

I now had half an hour before I was supposed to be at work, but I was close to the airport so decided to visit their rental car center. I parked in short-term parking and went to the airport's self-return section. It was on the opposite side of the parking garage, and it took me a good ten minutes to walk there. I felt a bit self-conscious because ever since 9-11, doing things without a good reason was kind of frowned upon at commercial airports.

The rental car return section was at the far northeast end of the garage, and Hertz, Dollar, and Budget were all in the same lot. I could see ahead of me travelers getting out and heading toward the airport without turning anything in at the kiosk. I wasn't quite sure how it worked, but the rental car industry had made it pretty damn easy to return a car.

I tried to walk with purpose, and it dawned on me that thinking about how I walked and appeared probably created the exact opposite appearance than the one I was trying for. I approached the cars looking at the plates but kept a steady pace. It looked like Hertz rented Chevrolets, Dollar rented Fords, and Budget rented Chryslers.

I passed Dollar and Budget first and felt my breath quicken just a bit when I get to Hertz. There were three Malibus in line, and I walked steady but with as much concentration as I could muster. The last two were light blue.

"Can I help you, sir?" The voice jarred me, and I turned around a bit too quickly to see a twenty-something guy with a Hertz uniform, a man bun, and khaki pants that were styled in that way so they hung off his ass.

"Maybe, man," I said. "I returned my car, and I think I left my phone in it, but I already locked it."

He looked a little annoyed, like this calorie expenditure was more than he had budgeted for today.

"Which one..." he said with a little more exasperation than I think my fabricated situation warranted.

"It was light blue. The plated started with S-H-E." I figured that might be something a renter would remember.

"There. You're standing next to it." He nodded to the third Malibu.

"You got ID?"

"No, it's with my wife at the gate. I was in a hurry..." I said it with as much frustration in my voice as possible.

"I'm not supposed to without your contract or at least ID."

"C'mon, man. My flight leaves in, like, 20 minutes."

He gave me a what-the-hell-I-hate-this-job anyway look and opened it up.

I did my best to rummage through the car as fast as I could, uttering the requisite amount of cursing as I looked through the McDonald's and Subway wrappers and under the seat. It looked like these people ate three meals a day of fast food. I sifted through the wrappers, through the onion and cold cut smell, and among all the crap, I found a handwritten note. I snatched it up before loudly admitting my fake missing phone wasn't there.

"Shit, it's not in there," I said, doing my best pissed-off act.

"That sucks, dude." Probably a lot of empathy for this guy.

"Thanks anyway," I said and headed toward the airport and back to short-term parking.

When I got far enough away from the rental car lot, I took the note out of my pocket and read it.

It is downtown, close to the river. Put it into your GPS. Find out who is in his life and what he's doing. Get a sense of what his day is like. Find out about the people in his life, anyone he might talk to, or who is important to him. Get info. Report back on Monday.

It was signed L.

L.

L. Like Lin.

Lin Williams.

It made me shiver.

CHAPTER THIRTY-ONE

When I got back to Dad's Cadillac, I called Ray. I filled him in on the two guys, Kayla, and the note. I was talking a mile a minute, and I wasn't sure if I was making any sense.

"Slow, the fuck down. Just take a breath, cowboy," Ray said. "Does the note mention your name?"

"No."

"Uh-huh"

"Does it mention where you work?"

"No."

"Does it say to hurt anyone?"

"No."

"Trace, man, don't let your mind run away with you. You think Dr. Williams is running a mob of some sort?" He was getting sarcastic, which was Ray's move.

"And she appeared at Eddie's cousin to question him. C'mon Ray."

"You don't know that for a fact and, and this is a big *and*, do you have any fucking motive for all of this super sleuth Tom Clancy bullshit?"

I didn't say anything. I was starting to feel stupid. I wasn't exactly known for steady rational thinking over the last couple of months.

"Ray, my apartment was ransacked, and Kayla was followed."

"Okay, I get that. You described the neighborhood you're in. About a block and a half from the 'hood, you said." He paused for effect. "You're a bartender. A guy who gets tipped and comes home after every shift with cash. Lots of one's and fives and an easy mark from some crackhead looking to fortify his resources."

"Uh..."

"Yeah, uh...and as for your girl. Did you see these guys who tailed her?"

"No, but Tinker did."

"That's the Vietnam whack job you've described to me. Collects guns, watches FOX News, and loves Nugent?" Ray said. I was beginning to feel foolish.

"Kayla's not a drama queen," I said, realizing I sounded defensive.

"Of course not. You've known her how long?"

"Almost a month," I said.

"Yeah, no one ever found out their new girl had issues after a month. No nuh-uh."

I didn't know what to say. Ray was always sarcastic and cynical, probably because of 15 years in law enforcement and dealing with people like me. I began to doubt my own story.

"Then Ray, what about the suicide that wasn't? What the hell is that all about?" I said, trying to sound calm.

"There are questions, no doubt. Something isn't right about that. Or, at least, something may not be right about it. It all doesn't come out crystal clear in an hour like an episode of NCIS, you know."

"Still..."

"Something's not right, but it is probably more along the lines of someone wanting to get a report done and off their desk or someone covering up that they cut some corners because they want to put this thing away. You know, let the family that was left get back to life and have some peace."

"Or it could be because having Eddie and his family around

made someone uncomfortable for some reason. That would be a reason to kill him," I said.

"Well..." Ray was getting to respond.

"And to make it like he did it himself would benefit, who?"

"How the hell do I know?"

"And what group of people do you know who would have the capability of manipulating a crime scene and knowing how to cover their DNA tracks and whatnot."

"C'mon Trace..."

"No, Ray, I'm sorry. I might still be crazy, but it doesn't mean I'm wrong." I said.

I hung up.

I was late, and I had to go to work. It didn't matter if I couldn't think straight and that I was distracted as hell, someone had to make sure George got his Coors Light and everyone else got what they needed.

George greeted me at the door, oblivious to my mental state. He asked if I watched the Irish on Saturday night. He wasn't pleased with the play calling and felt that the refs screwed ND because they always favored the Big Ten. I, of course, agreed, though I didn't watch the game or pay attention to the result.

Tony Crespo was also in this morning, this time without any other detectives, which wasn't all that unusual. I put a cold Lagunitas in front of him and asked him if he wanted to eat.

"Yeah, a cheeseburger and fries," he said. It was his go-to after a long shift.

"Long night?" I said to be saying something.

"Nah, not really." He took a sip. "I heard you had some excitement." He gave me a look and a wink. "There are no secrets at Curran's. You know that. Your girl ok?"

"Yeah, she's fine." I thought about something and decided what the hell. "Tony, is it hard to find out who rented a car if you know the company, the location, and half of the plate?"

"I thought you weren't in the spy business," He said with a laugh.

"I'd like to know who scared the hell out of this girl I like. That's all." I said it with a little more anger than I wanted to.

Tony didn't say anything. He drank his beer and looked at the TV for a minute, and then back at me. He took out a notepad.

"What company?" he asked.

"Hertz."

"At the airport?"

"Yeah."

"Make?"

"Malibu."

"Plate?"

"Started with S-H-E," I said.

He left his beer on the bar and went out the door, retrieving his cell phone as he walked. He was gone maybe three minutes. When he came back in, I gave him his cheeseburger without saying anything.

"Boy, the Giants have no damn defense this year, George," Tony said. He looked at me and frowned while he said it.

"Never recovered from Parcells leaving," George said with total confidence even though Parcells left in the late eighties.

Tony ate his cheeseburger without any rush and ordered a third beer. As he was halfway through it, Stagger came through the door. It was unusual to see him without his running buddy Tinker.

"How's it hangin' for all you homos." Once again, exceeding all expectations for inappropriate language and conduct for this millennium. He got my look.

"Sorry, kid."

I cracked open his Schaefer, and Stagger's first pull emptied half of the can. I stood in front of him, debating whether to engage him in conversation. I figured what the hell.

"Stags, what was that shit the other day about dad's military history, you know the spy stuff? That was just bullshit, right?"

He took another long pull of the Schaefer and appeared to be thinking about what to say, which was unusual for him. There didn't ever seem to be a barrier between his cognition and speech.

"Yeah, bullshit, kid. Fuckin' bullshit. Messin' with 'ya. You know how I get." He didn't look me in the eye, and he downed the rest of his beer. I got the impression he wanted to do something besides avoid eye contact. I looked at him for a little while longer and then let it go. Something was weird, but maybe this wasn't the time or the place.

When I turned around, Tony wasn't in his chair, but he had not finished his beer and he had a bite or two of his burger left. Less than a minute later, he came through the door, putting his phone into his suit jacket pocket. He put a note on the bar. It read:

Elliot Stanley, Rockville, Maryland. Former NSA, Marine, arrest for assault and menacing.

Tony raised his eyebrows and then nodded as if to say, "That's it, don't ask me again, and I don't ever want to hear about this."

I planned to honor that.

I went back to the business of bartending. Stagger, without permission, had gotten possession of the remote and had changed the channel to FOX News. It made me want to scream, but it just wasn't worth scolding Stagger.

"Look at this fuckin' guy. Fuckin' liberal homo!" I had to set a boundary.

"Stags!"

He looked away from the TV.

"Eww...sorry kid, I forgot," he said.

There was a story about a liberal politician's son taking money from a foreign country for his dubious role on a board of directors.

"That's it. Follow the money, motherfucker!"

"Stags! C'mon, man!" I raised my voice.

His face blanched like I startled him.

"Fuck! Sorry kid. I keep forgetting."

There was no use. I opened another Schaefer and put it on his coaster.

"On me," I said.

Stagger looked confused, but he smiled and took a Staggerian first sip.

I shook my head and smiled.

"What's so funny, kid?"

"Nothing, man, nothing," I said. "Just you with the 'Follow the money!' about every damn thing. Is there anything that isn't a 'Follow the money!'"

"Nope." He said it with complete confidence.

"Nothing?"

"Nope."

I chuckled to myself. I wish my mind were as free from complexity and ambivalence as Stagger's was.

"Take all this shit...politic equals money...war equals money...supreme court equals money...terrorisms equals money..." He drifted away from it.

The last one stuck with me.

Terrorism equals money.

Terrorism equals money.

As Stagger might say,

"Holy shit."

CHAPTER THIRTY-TWO

Follow the money...

Yeah, it sounded good, but what the hell did it mean in this case. Sure, I'm as much of a conspiracy fan as the next guy, and I've watched Jesse Ventura documentaries but besides the axiom, "Follow the Money," what did it mean here? Was it possible to somehow monetize terror? Was there a way to put real money in your pocket somehow from blowing things up? And who, exactly, would engineer such a thing? Who *could* engineer it?

I decided to call my old friend, Rick. We went to college together and, like Ray, was a guy I boxed with. He was a strange guy. All he ever cared about was the stock market and boxing. Maybe the competitiveness of both explained it.

I'd lost touch with him while I was in grad school, and he was on Wall Street, but we were the type of friends that could pick right up. We've talked about getting together for a sparring session at a New York gym like Gleason's, but we've never been able to make it work. He was married now with kids and worked a million hours a week. A man of extremes, he was either in fantastic shape or eating jars of peanut butter in one sitting.

I gave him a call.

"Rick, It's Trace," I said.

"Holy shit, are you kidding me?" He said with a laugh.

"Holy shit..."

"What's so funny?"

"Nothing, man, but it has been a while."

He was, of course, right.

"Last time I saw you was..."

I finished his sentence for him.

"Five years ago. We spoke once or twice since then," I added.

"You still goin' ahead with that whole marriage thing?" he said, keeping up the comedy routine. He had no idea of knowing.

"Uh, actually, no," I said. I didn't know how to make it not awkward. There wasn't a way to do that.

"Oh fuck. I'm sorry. Shit, I'm an asshole," he said.

"No, no, no," I said, trying to be as nonchalant about something was far from nonchalant. "You had no idea of knowing. She left. I'm not even sure where she is," I said.

There was no way to make it no big deal.

"That's crazy. Man, I'm sorry. What a kick in the balls that must've been." He said it without really looking for a response. I didn't give him one because I wanted to move along.

"Hey, I need your expertise," I said.

"Yeah, all of a sudden psychology start paying well?"

"No, that's not it. I still don't have two nickels to rub together. There's something that I want to know," I said.

He didn't say anything for a little while.

"Is this going to be creepy spy stuff? Am I going to bring down the Russians finally?"

"No, but you're not too far off," I took a breath. "Let me ask you some things and just do some brainstorming and free association. Does anyone benefit financially from terrorist acts?"

"You mean besides, like people getting paid to do it or putting some competition out of business?"

"Yeah, I mean the markets and stuff like that," I said.

"You kidding? Of course, people do!" he said.

"Walk me through it," I asked.

He laughed at me again.

"Dude, geezus, there's not one way. There are many ways to profit from terrorism."

"Fine, I got time. Go!" I said.

"Awright, get comfortable," he said. "School's in session. First of all, let's go simple and obvious. Ever hear of Larry Silverstein?"

"No," I said.

"When New York was struggling in the late 1980's he bought a 99-year lease on the World Trade Center for around 14 million. He turned around and insured it for 3.5 billion with that's with a 'B.' He also had a clause put in it that stipulated that he and only he would have the right to rebuild them if they were ever destroyed. I mean, Trace, my man, who thinks of shit like that?"

"Holy shit..."

"He sued the insurance company because he and his lawyers claimed that he should have received 7 billion because 9-11 was two separate attacks. He lost, but that's on appeal."

"Well, that takes some balls," I said.

"He then sued American Airlines for negligence."

"What?" I couldn't believe some of the shit I was processing.

"And only got $95 million in a negotiated settlement," Rick took a sip of something. If I remembered him right, it was Jameson.

"I guess that answers my question about whether anyone benefits from terrorism."

"Whoa, pardner. We're just getting started! Hang on, I need to fill my glass," I could hear him get up, pour the liquid over the ice. He returned.

"Still Jameson?"

"Yup, something works for you, why change?" He said with self-satisfaction. "Ok, next. Commodities."

"School's is in session," I said.

"People buy precious metals, Gold, Silver, and whatnot

when the markets are filled with uncertainty. Even you know that. They are safe and stable."

"Sure," I said. I wasn't all that sure, but I knew not to mess with Rick's roll.

"Like everything else, when the demand for something goes up, so does the price, especially when there's a limited supply of something. There's only so much gold going around, so when everyone wants it, it costs more."

"Gotcha," I said to keep the rhythm going.

"If you knew something was going to cause uncertainty, you could sell your stocks and load up on gold and watch its value increase while stocks plummeted. After 9-11, gold went way up," he said.

"So, right now, with all this Antifa shit, gold is a good investment?"

"Not so much now. If you got into it before the chaos started, you'd made a bundle. The key is timing. Getting in before people want to is where it's at. Same things when the Arabs start shit and blow up oil fields or piss off the US enough so that we blow up the oil fields. The price of a barrel goes up," he said.

"Makes sense," I said. "So, you could affect the markets by causing general instability or by targeting a specific commodity and investing ahead of time, right?" I said. I wanted to make sure I was getting it, and he knew it.

"Nice goin', Mr. Freud!" He said with a bad German accent. "You ready for some grad school diabolical shit?"

"Yeah, baby..." it was starting to get fun. It made my hair hurt thinking about it.

"Ever heard of a 'put' option?" He said with some apprehension in his voice.

"No..."

He exhaled.

"Okay, follow close. This gets weird. A put option is a bet that a stock price will fall. Say, you bought a single put option on American Airlines stock for $30 a share, and the stock fell to

$18 a share, one could then buy a hundred shares for $18 a share and immediately sell them for $30 you'd net a profit of $12 a share. Follow?"

"I think..."

"K, pay attention. This what happened with many companies around the world on 9-11. The put options purchased the week before 9-11 were something like six times higher than normal. Some estimate that profits from insider traders exceeded 15 billion," he said.

"What? Is this Jesse Ventura shit?"

"No, it is backed up with data from the finance world. It wasn't the usual put-option activity. Puts set to expire at the end of September that year were bought in August or earlier. For the month before 9-11, something like 30 put options were purchased on Morgan Stanley. On September 8, 9, and 10, there were over 2,500 puts purchased. The plane crash took out all of Morgan's headquarters," he said. His voice had lost its humor.

"Holy shit," I said.

"On September 10, there were 4,500 put options purchased on American Airlines and only 700 call options. Same with United but with no other airlines. Not only that, but these options were happening in markets all around the world on September 10."

"Are you shittin' me?"

"Nope. Look it up."

"Why isn't this common knowledge?" I asked.

"It sort of is. The 9-11 Commission ruled that people who made money on their puts were all coincident. Hell of a coincidence."

"Hell yeah."

"Now, because you're a CIA spy type guy, this next part might blow you away. At the time, the number-three at of the CIA, Buzz Krongaurd, headed a firm that handled many of these put stock options. He ran Bankers Trust, which merged with Deutsche Bank and handled American's stock until '98...that is...you ready...Before he came over to the CIA."

"What!"

"Facts. And, uh, Deutsche Bank is one of the banks the Bin Laden family uses. His family is in the Arab world construction biz."

"My hair is starting to hurt," I said.

"It should. Want me to stop?" he asked.

"You mean it keeps going?"

"Yup."

"Keep going," I said.

"Buzzy's successor, Mayo Shattock, a dude who helped mastermind Enron's loss coverup, is likely the guy who purchased the American put options. He resigned from Deutsche on September 12, 2001," he said. I heard him take another sip.

"You're shittin' me," I said.

"When 'W" got his wrist slapped for illegal insider trading when he was running a startup oil company in the 70's Deutsche Bank was at the center of the funding. Yet, after 9-11, when the US investigated all the banks that they suspected funded terrorism, Deutsche was left off the list."

"Oh my God..."

"Yeah, so who else benefits? 9-11 certainly meant the US was about to get involved militarily, so Allied and Northrup stock skyrocketed," he said. "The short answer to your original question is *yes, lots and lots of people can get rich off of terrorism*," he said.

"Why isn't this known?"

"Who says it isn't known? I may be a genius, but I'm not the only finance guy aware of this stuff. The press doesn't pick it up. It seems too dirty to be true, and most people's eyes glaze over when you mention the stock market," he said.

"So, let me ask you this. How can you know it is going on in real-time, in the present?"

"Ahh, yes, well, that isn't so easy. In retrospect, you can put the pieces of the puzzle together. You can hide what's going on when things are moving fast, and the bad guys are covering their tracks," he said.

"How can you tell how someone is invested?"

"You can't, at least not legally," he hesitated. "I mean, the SEC looks at patterns and great sums that come with shifts of money and stock."

"If you knew what you were doing, spread your money out, kept below a certain level, and maybe took a strategic loss now and then, you might be able to get away with it?" I was catching on.

"Yeah, and it goes on all the time. Goldman Sachs has been caught. They'll deny it, but they've facilitated some shady shit."

It sank in.

"So, there's no question you can profit from terrorism?"

He laughed.

"None at all."

CHAPTER THIRTY-THREE

I finished my shift and went upstairs. My head was spinning, and everything that had been running through it caused it to ache. I was overloaded, and I needed to slow everything down.

I called Kayla to invite her over, but she begged off because of a paper she had to get done. It was okay. I wanted to sit and just have a few Slanes by myself and hopefully fall asleep.

I said some prayers, talked to God about Mom and Molly and everything that was swirling around. It was hard to concentrate.

I was reading in bed with a few pillows propping me up so I could hold a book. Somewhere in the dead of night, the Slane paid off, and I fell asleep. The iPhone rang, and it woke me up. It was just after seven.

I didn't recognize the number.

"Trace, it's Aisha." I squinted my eyes and tried to clear my head. I dreaded whatever message was going to come from Dr. Williams. I usually did, but now, more than ever.

"The office number didn't come up. I didn't realize it was you," I said.

"I'm calling from my sister's phone. I don't want anyone to know I'm reaching out to you."

I was quiet for a moment. I didn't know what that was about, but I quickly imagined it wasn't going to be good news.

"Trace? Are you there?"

"Yeah, Eesh. I'm here."

"Trace, I wanted you to know that your friend Ray, the agent…he, uh…was killed last night."

My chest tightened, and I had that same unreal feeling I got six months ago. I didn't want to pass out. I didn't respond to Aisha.

I froze.

"I'm so sorry. I know you were close. He was shot in a robbery at a bodega in DC. It was totally random. He went to intervene, and he got shot in the chest. He died instantly."

Ray? Gone? The day after speaking to me? I kept silent. I didn't move and had to remind myself not to hold my breath. I couldn't keep track of my thoughts. I had to force myself to come out of it.

"Let me guess, they haven't found the shooter," I said.

"Well, they haven't…but why would you say that? This was a case of being in the wrong place at the wrong time. Horrible but…"

"But whoever did it got away, right?" I said.

"Trace…"

"Look Eesh, I don't know if it is even safe to be talking to you."

There was a pause. I heard her swallow back tears.

"What have I ever done for you to say that. I called *you*, didn't I?" she said.

"What's with your sister's phone? Why would you not be able to call me from your phone or from the office? My friend is dead. Why would that have to be something to conceal?"

She was quiet. She didn't say anything for a few long moments.

"Trace, you should be careful," she sniffed at her tears. "Dr. Williams is furious with you. I'm not sure what it is all about, but she won't even let your name be brought up. I don't know what that means."

"I think I do."

I didn't say anything for a while.

"Eesh, you need to give her a message for me. Let Dr. Williams know that I know what's happened. I know exactly what's happened. Let her know it is written down, and should anything happen to me, the world will know. You got that?"

"Trace, you're talking crazy. Are you okay? What the hell are you talking about?"

"I'm not crazy. Not this time. I'm totally not crazy." I gave it a second or so. I noticed I was breathing fast and heavy. "Make sure she gets my message."

I hung up and went to the *Washington Post*'s website.

Man Dies in Bodega Robbery

A good Samaritan who tried to stop a robbery at El Matador Bodega was shot and killed last evening. DC Metro police report that Raymond Brice, 34, of Landover, was shot twice in the chest from close range. He was attempting to stop the armed robbery of the store.

The clerk and owner, Miguel Berlanga, said

"It all happened so fast, and so it would be impossible to identify him except that he was male, about six feet, and with a muscular build.

Ray Brice worked for the US Department of the Interior as a senior auditor. He was single.

A sketch of the assailant accompanied the article, based on the artist's interpretation of the bodega owner's description. It was a generic mean white guy face. The nose was crooked.

Ray didn't deserve this. He warned me to mind my own business. He didn't know anything. He was a good honest agent, committed to his job. He was also a good friend.

My chest tightened, and I could feel panic coming on. I breathed through it, and I focused on my breathing. I chased it away, at least for now. I was still breathing hard and fast, and my vision was blurred while my thoughts raced.

Then all at once, it went away. In its place was a rage.

It was time. It was time for me to really get crazy. I was going to stop this.

PART THREE

CHAPTER THIRTY-FOUR

The next day I told Jessica I'd be out for a few days. She wasn't happy, but I didn't care. Tinker was put in charge of keeping an eye on Kayla, and it was time to get back to Delaware and find my friend Clayton.

My mind raced during the long drive, and several times I needed to reign my grief back in. Ray was gone, and I couldn't believe it, and I couldn't deal with it. I was going to do what I could to, if not make this right, to at least make sure no one got away with Ray's murder.

I got to Clayton's townhouse a little after seven, and he wasn't home, nor was his car in the driveway. I camped out in one of the parking spaces right out in front of his front door. It wasn't until 8:30 that he showed up.

"Clayton!" I yelled to him as he was getting out of his car.

I startled him, and he flinched. His eyes focused, and in a moment, he recognized me.

"Dr. Curran?"

"Yes, I'm sorry if I startled you."

"Damn well did. What are you doing here?" He sounded

annoyed.

"I need to know something about Eddie."

"You couldn't have called?"

"I plan on being down around here for a little while, and I thought it would be easier to see you in person," I said. I knew it wasn't entirely plausible, but it wasn't an out and out lie."

"What can I do for you that we didn't discuss the last time?"

"Eddie's investment guy. What's his name?"

"Why do you need to know that? What would that have to do with Eddie killing himself? His investment guy made him money," he said. He furrowed his brow and looked at me with disbelief.

"I think it might have to do with some of the problems Eddie might have had. It might..."

"Eddie didn't have no problems." Now he was just plain angry.

"Clayton, he had problems. You don't do what Eddie did without some problems. Look, I know you're dealing with a loss, but there's a lot at stake."

"What in God's name are you talking about? Does this have something to do with why that woman called me?"

"You got a call from a woman checking to see if you were okay?"

"She wanted to know if any more agents were seeking me out. I told them you came by," he had a confused look on his face.

"Who was the woman?"

"That woman who came by the other time. Dr...Dr..."

"Dr. Williams," I finished it for him.

"Yeah, that's it. This have to do with that?"

"I have no idea, Clayton. All I want to know is who handled Eddie's money. You gotta know he talked to you about his investments."

"He told me he was making money. He tried to tell me to invest, but I have a pension. I got what I need."

"What was his name?"

He shook his head in frustration and fatigue.

"Crowley and Vandenburgh. They're in DC. That's them."

"Who did Eddie work with?"

"Crowley. I'm pretty sure it was Crowley." He looked at me long and hard. "Now, can I go in my house? Now can you leave me alone?"

"Yeah, thank you."

It was now mid-afternoon. I had time to go speak to Mr. Crowley.

It was about an hour and forty-five minutes, which would get me there by the end of the workday. I could make a plan while I drove.

CHAPTER THIRTY-FIVE

I had to wait outside the office building for over an hour. It was your classic four-storey non-descript suburban brick structure that was home to investment companies, specialty medical offices, and some real estate companies. It was ten minutes to six when he emerged from the office looking not quite as handsome as he did on the company website.

"Excuse me, Mr. Crowley," I said. He was late forties-early fifties with wire-framed glasses, dark hair, an Irish complexion. He was heading toward his personalized parking space and his Mercedes Benz.

"Do I know—" He started to say. I had startled him. I ran to catch up with him.

"No, no, but I'm a big fan!" I said, doing my best to sound sincere.

He looked confused, but he stopped as I approached.

"Can I help you?" he said.

I pulled out the gun.

"Get in your car, behind the wheel." My heart was racing. This wasn't my world. I was acting off TV shows. It didn't matter. I was committed.

"Uh..."

"Now!" I said with emphasis.

He did as he was told and got in. I sat in the passenger seat.

"My wallet is in my suit jacket pocket. I only have about $300 in cash. You can take it and my credit cards. You can have the car." He was scared.

"Drive," I instructed. Remarkably, I was getting more comfortable.

"Where?" I could hear the tension in his voice.

"Go left and keep driving." It was a suburban neighborhood, and two men in a Mercedes would not draw any attention. I let him drive and didn't say anything for about five minutes. I kept the gun out and in my hand. We came to a professional building with only four cars scattered in the parking lot.

"Pull in there." I pointed to an empty section of the lot. "Keep the car running."

He exhaled hard.

"I'm going to ask you some questions, and you're going to answer me honestly. The first time you hesitate and don't give me an answer, I will shoot you in the foot. Then, I will do your next foot and then up your shin to your thigh...you get the theme?"

He shook his head.

"You handled Eddie Hutchins's finances."

He nodded.

"What was he invested in?"

He tried to act like it was a stupid question.

"He had a portfolio. He was diversified—"

I cocked the weapon and looked down at his foot.

"What do you mean what was he invested in?"

"You know what I mean." I looked him right in the eye.

"Mr. Hutchins was invested in defense contractors, pharmaceuticals, precious metals, the security industry—"

"He was making money on the terrorism. Yes or no?"

"Uh...I—"

I fired a shot into the floorboard by his foot.

"I missed on purpose. I won't the next time."

"Uhh...I don't know what you mean. He was—"

I fired a shot into his right foot. He screamed and grabbed

his shoe, which was spilling blood.

"Jesus Christ! Oh God! What did you do that for!" He was grimacing and doing his best to hold back a scream. He was terrified.

"Were you investing in the market based on the Antifa terrorist acts?"

He was crying and writhing in pain. I didn't care. They killed Ray. They probably killed Eddie.

I gestured to his left foot and cocked the gun.

He wet his pants.

"No, no, no, no! I'll tell you what you want. Jesus Christ!" I pointed the gun at his foot.

"Tell me!"

"It's not that simple—I can't say anything about—"

I shot his left foot.

"Oh God, he half screamed, half cried. The floor of the Benz was a puddle of blood. He was writhing in pain, and I thought he was going to vomit.

"Yes! Fucking Yes! He knew beforehand. We could time investments. We made money investing based on the Antifa shit. Don't shoot me again! Oh God!"

"Who else?" I said, aiming at his right shin.

"I can't. I swear they'll kill me. I can't!" I chambered a round and moved towards his shin.

"There were six of them. They made me do it. I couldn't refuse. It was their idea."

"Names." I was in a whole different state.

"Oh God, Oh God," his hands were covered in blood from rubbing his feet. I thought he might pass out.

I held the gun to the side of his head.

He threw up down his tie.

I smacked his head by the temple with the gun. I started to bleed.

"Williams, Michaelson, Colley, VanMeter, Taylor and Jordan..."

Marie's last name was Taylor.

My mind flooded with confusion and emotion.

"Drive me back to your office and get yourself to an emergency room," I said.

CHAPTER THIRTY-SIX

Think, goddamn it, think!

My mind raced. I felt panic coming on, and I did my best to breathe through it. It just came back and escalated. I was afraid I'd black out.

I barely paid attention to where and how I was driving. I set out to go straight to the CIA building and let people know what was going on. This had to be stopped even though I knew I was in way over my head. I don't know how I got to where I was, but I didn't see any way out.

I got stuck in the Beltway traffic, and it forced me to slow the car and myself just a bit.

I began to think, and I tried to let the gravity of everything sink in.

Just who the hell was I going to tell?

How would I tell them how I got the information?

Biggest question: what made me think there was anyone there I could trust?

That last one lingered and resonated with me. Six CIA employees and contractors were initiating terrorist acts to manipulate the stock market and get rich. That was six that I knew about. They already killed Eddie and his family and Ray, which meant they were coming for me. How could they not?

And why hadn't they come for me yet? Maybe they had and

were just trying to keep it neat and tidy, and I got lucky being out of town. Maybe they figured I was snooping around, and if I showed up dead, it would get people curious. I'm sure they could or would set me up for suicide. I had, after all, already been certifiable. They were capable. I already knew that.

Or, maybe I was just paranoid.

No, Crowley told me what they were doing. I knew that. *How*, I'm not so sure. There had to be a team, but who was the gang that showed up in the van with the black suits who painted the ANTIFA logo. Who were they?

I'm sure it wouldn't be hard for CIA types to find a group of mercenaries skilled in demolition and violence. Probably a whole slew of ex-soldiers or black ops types who would do anything for the right price. And with the backing of higher-ups, they could keep their anonymity. I was going off over-the-top thrillers I've read and movies I watched. This wasn't my life or my world. I was just guessing. Hell of a time to be guessing anything.

What made me think I was a match for any of this?

What made me think I wouldn't be eliminated?

Clearly, I was a threat.

Think! Think, goddamit.

I did my best to slow down. I looked at my thoughts. I said a short prayer asking for guidance.

I needed to make it against their interest to kill me. If killing me exposed them, then I had something on them. They could take their fortune and cut their losses and maybe get rid of me down the road when things got quieter. I could force a stalemate—I have something on them, and they could kill me. Hell of a stalemate. I could probably pause this damn thing in the short run, but for how long? And I'd always be a danger to keep alive.

What did I have? What did I know?

I had information. If I could get anyone to believe it, I had something on them. That information was the biggest chip in this poker game. Of course, I was just in a psychiatric hospital and on a mental health leave with plenty of reason to fabricate a story about my boss. There was a danger I wouldn't be believed.

Information was all I had. Crowley had the proof, but if you didn't shoot him, he wasn't forthcoming. He was far from an ally. If Williams and all of them knew I could let the world know, I had something on them.

Too good to be true, but, at the moment, I couldn't think of anything better.

I began to dictate into my phone:

To Whom It May Concern:

I, Dr. Trace Curran, a psychologist on leave from LW Psychometrics, a CIA contracted firm, have learned of corruption and terrorism within the CIA. Dr. Lin Williams, an expert on the dealings of Antifa-allied organizations, has worked with the investment broker Brian Crowley in Washington DC to devise a strategy that would manipulate the stock market so that they could reap the benefits of the unstable markets.

Crowley has admitted this to me. Probably working with mercenaries, they have been at the center of the "Antifa" terrorism. Each of the last six recent national domestic terrorist acts was followed by distinct stock market changes. After each, the portfolio of Dr. Williams and the others made gains that would be impossible to predict without advanced knowledge. This group also has the skill and ability to efficiently perpetrate these acts with expert precision and the ability to deflect public blame to the Antifa organizations. In addition to Williams, the others involved are Special Agent Brian VanMeter, Supervisor Colley, Analyst Keith Boggs, Counter-Terrorist Agent Jonathan Jordan, and contracted psychologist Marie Taylor.

I fully suspect that whoever reads this communication will believe it is the work of a paranoid mad man acting out in revenge because he was spurned from his job. I also fully suspect that the team involved will come after me to kill me and probably make it look like an accident or suicide. That is what I believe has happened to Agent Edwin Hutchins and Special Agent Ray Brice. Should I meet a similar fate, perhaps this communication will be taken seriously.

This communication has been sent to the Washington Post, the director's office of the CIA, each of those involved mentioned, "Danny O" of the Black Bloc Bros Antifa group, and it is in a safety deposit box. The executor of my will has instructions should I die.

Sincerely,

Trace Curran Ph.D.

I read it and reread it ten times. I felt sick to my stomach. I fashioned it into an email and did my best to find all the correct addresses. Took a deep breath, and not sure of anything, hit send.

Now, there was no turning back.

CHAPTER THIRTY-SEVEN

With nowhere else to go, I headed home. During the long drive, I tried to process the consequences of what I just did. I accused federal officials of what amounts to treason and terrorism. It wouldn't sit well even if it were dismissed as the rantings of a deranged and angry ex-employee.

I called Jessica from the road and let her know I'd be in the next morning for my shift and that I was sorry for leaving her high and dry. She was a little short with me but said she could cover the bar herself. That meant she worked a 16-hour day, on her feet, on top of having to handle the cash and deposits at the end of the day. I added her to the list of people I owed.

Next, I called Kayla.

"You left town with all that's been going on and didn't tell me?" was the first thing she said after "hello."

"There was stuff that came up that I had to, uh, address, and I didn't have time to talk to you," I said.

"Didn't have time?" I could feel the ice in her voice.

"You know what I mean, I—"

"Trace, what the hell are you in the middle of? What is going on? I don't live life this way."

I stayed quiet. She was right. I didn't know what to say.

"Maybe we can talk after work tomorrow?" I said. There was more desperation in my voice than I wanted.

Kayla gave a passive "Okay" and said "good night." I was afraid I just screwed up the only good thing in my life.

I was home just before midnight, opened a beer, and went to bed. I didn't expect to sleep, but I was exhausted and needed to lie down. My back was all knots from the time in the car, and my mind raced.

The vision of Crowley's bloody feet and his cries of agony raced through my mind. It was the cruelest thing I had ever done. It was the most pain I ever inflicted on someone. Despite the ends-justifying-the-means rationalization, I felt sick to my stomach.

Thoughts of Ray, dead because of being my friend, stirred. He didn't deserve to die, and it was my fault. I thought of his elderly parents, who had to process this. I thought of his friends and the people who loved Ray.

I got out of bed, went to the bathroom, and threw up.

I brought the bottle of Slane back to bed and sipped on it. I dozed on and off until the daylight coming through the window woke me.

I picked up Rocky at mom's, dodged her pointed questions about how I was doing—she always knew when something was wrong—and got to the bar on time to prep. CNN was on in the background, and I dutifully sliced lemons and limes and stocked the beer coolers. Tomorrow was kickball, so I made sure the Spaten was in supply.

George came in and gave me his "Top of the Mornin'," and I returned it. Rocky went and sat at his side. George was about to lapse into a Lou Holtz story when a CNN story caught my attention.

"Antifa leader speaks out on the rash of domestic terrorism, next."

My head snapped around.

"Excuse me, George." I turned up the volume and stopped prepping the bar.

A split-screen showed Jake Tapper and a darkened silhouette of a man. Underneath his image, it read *Antifa leader Danny O*.

Tapper introduced Danny as a leader of a domestic Antifa faction.

"Do you even know what that means?" Danny took over the interview from the beginning. It made me smile. "Antifa isn't the Mafia. It isn't a militia. It is a philosophy of being against fascism in all ways, by any means necessary."

"Yes, but you have to admit there has been violence and, often, irresponsible violence by members of Antifa over the last year in our society," Tapper said, trying to remain nonplussed.

"Violence has occurred during some protests that had an Antifa theme by some individuals. There is no single Antifa group to comment on this, accept responsibility, or decry it. It is a philosophy. The media, the Right, have formed the impression that the movement is an organization. It simply is no. This remains true despite how it is depicted."

"Why are you coming forward now?" Tapper went back to his script, probably knowing he couldn't match Danny O's sound bites.

"Because this rash of domestic terrorism attributed to ANTIFA is a false flag designed to promulgate anti-ANTIFA sentiment. Whoever is behind it, and I have a good idea who is profiting from this mischaracterization."

"How are they profiting?" Tapper did that facial expression that communicates disbelief.

"I'm not getting into that now. It was time to make the matter clear and to let the American public know that they are, once again being hoodwinked, bamboozled, and lead astray, to paraphrase Malcolm X."

Tapper abruptly said that was all the time they had. He raised his eyebrows and exhaled as if he had just heard a tall tale. They went on to the next story about flooding in Louisiana.

"...and that's why Holtz got the medal of honor from President Trump." Apparently, George hadn't stopped talking during the interview.

I guess Danny opened his email. Sounded like he was getting out in front of things. It wasn't like Antifa-affiliated individuals to talk to the media. It happened, but in doing it, they risked losing their anonymity, and that was disadvantageous to their goals. Danny seemed to give credence to what I had to say, but I'm not sure having him on my side was something I really wanted.

I went back to stocking the coolers.

"Momo! Give George a kiss!" George half yelled with enthusiasm.

I lifted my head out of the cooler and saw Molly hugging up on George. I said a quick prayer that she was sober.

"Hey, shithead!" She said. I looked in her eyes, and they seemed clear. She sensed the examination. "I'm fine. Thank you very much." She said it with annoyance.

"Good Morning. Why are you here and not at school?" I said.

"I got a break. Hey, can I bring the Rockstar into school? There's a kid I want to surprise. Kayla thinks Rocky could be therapeutic." Molly winked at me.

I didn't see why not. It would give Rocky a different experience.

"Better ask his drinkin' buddy before you take him." I nodded at George.

"He has my permission to go to school. I don't think he ever got his diploma." George said and flipped Rocky a Milk-Bone as Molly hooked up his leash. His tail went turbo at being in Molly's presence.

The lunch crowd was light. No cops and no nurses, just Ron the construction guy, by himself. He had his burger, waffle fries, and Diet Coke and didn't say a word after saying hello.

The bar was empty at two, and I was wiping things down and checking inventory when a guy in a suit came to the bar. He was a middle-aged, white guy with tortoiseshell glasses and a light grey suit. He had a conservative red tie with blue stripes, and it was tied up to the collar.

"Trace Curran?" he said. He flipped open a leather wallet.

"Brian Lashaway, special agent, CIA." He kept a flat facial expression. "You have time for some questions?"

"Sure," I said. I could feel my heart.

"Is there someplace we can go?" he said.

I called to Gus and asked him to watch the bar.

I motioned the agent out to the parking lot.

"Following up on the communication you sent to the Agency." He said without asking anything.

"Yeah, I figured."

"So, you did indeed send this email?" He unfolded a sheet of paper that he had retrieved from his inside jacket pocket.

I glanced at it.

"Yes," I said. I handed it back to him.

"Serious allegations." He said, again without an explanation.

"Yes."

He pursed his lips, looked down, and lightly kicked at some gravel.

"You got proof of the things you are accusing people of?" He looked at me and squinted.

"Proof, like actual documentation, video or audio of things transpiring? No, no, I don't."

He nodded.

"You make some pretty serious allegations in this." He tapped at his pocket.

"Yeah, I do."

He repeated the head-down-pursed-lips- kick-at-the-gravel routine. He paused for a second beat.

"You spent some time in a psychiatric hospital after leaving your position."

Again, not a question.

"That's right."

He nodded.

"And you were placed on a leave of absence?" He had a tone in his questioning that I was starting to not like.

"That's right."

"Was that leave at your request?" He raised his eyebrows.

"I agreed to it." I thought it over. "I didn't request it."

He nodded.

"How's your relationship with Dr. Williams?"

"I've worked with her for about four years," I said.

"How's your relationship?" He said with just a bit more grit in his voice.

"Employer to employee type relationship," I said.

"I was told you were angry when she brought up your negligence with the Agent Hutchins situation." He was baiting me.

"It wasn't a case of negligence," I said and looked straight at him.

He nodded and smiled a little. He didn't say anything else.

"Is that all?" I said. I didn't want to give him the satisfaction of being angry.

"Just one more thing," he rubbed his forehead. "You talk to Danny O?"

I looked at him. I gave it some thought.

"He called me the other night."

He nodded again.

"What did he have to say?" He put his hands on his hips.

"He told me he highly doubted that any of the recent attacks were legitimately Antifa related."

He nodded. He kicked some gravel.

"You doing any travel any time soon?" he said.

"No," I said.

"Ok, thank you for your time," he said and turned to walk away.

I watched him head for his Ford Taurus.

"Hey Lashaway!" I called to him. He stopped and turned my way.

"Go fuck yourself!" I said.

CHAPTER THIRTY-EIGHT

Great, I thought, my pleas to the powers-that-be were turned around on me. Instead of looking into the horrific corruption in their midst, they chose to question my sanity. As it sunk in, I wasn't surprised, but it created a rage. It felt more like they were checking on me and not anything that I brought their attention to. It fueled my suspicions about everything to do with the agency.

Back inside the bar, I noticed Tinker and Stagger had come in. Gus was standing vigil, and the requisite Schaefer's and bourbons were in front of the patrons.

"Everything all right, Tracy?" Tinker said. He looked at me hard, like he wanted an explanation.

"Yeah, yeah..."

"Who was your visitor in the cheap suit, driving the Ford Taurus?" He didn't have to say "Federal guy." The suit and car description did it for him. Tinker wanted me to know he was looking out for me, and he wasn't missing anything.

"Oh, a new friend from my old days." I knew it was evasive, and Tinker wouldn't let it go. I didn't make eye contact with him.

"The Agency?"

"Yeah." I decided to let Tinker know a little. "I sent a letter with some concerns. He was following up."

Tinker just kept looking at me. After a few beats, he spoke.

"In person? What office was he from?"

"Uh, I don't know where he came from," I said.

"Must've been a heck of a memo," Tinker said with just a touch of sarcasm.

"Probably not about the amount of toner needed in the printer," Stagger chimed in with his usual semi non-sequitur.

They waited. I didn't say anything. It probably wouldn't have been that big a deal if I did, but I just didn't want to deal with more people knowing about this than necessary. I didn't think it would turn out to be a shining moment for me. I wanted it to go away, but that wasn't going to happen. The situation called for action, whether I wanted to or not.

Tinker took a sip of beer and looked at me.

"You going to be okay?" He said.

"Yessir." I gave him a salute. He nodded but pursed his lips in annoyance.

After that, the questions stopped. Stagger asked for the remote and, even though I couldn't stand FOX News, I didn't have the energy to fight it. Instead, I wiped down the bar and cleaned already clean glasses. My thoughts were foggy, and I didn't have a sense of what would happen next. I presumed nothing. I figured that the parties who received my correspondence would dismiss it totally, or they did what the CIA always did and give it a perfunctory once-over. Either way, I felt screwed.

"Listen to this asshole…" Stagger offered commentary on the FOX guest.

"Stagger…" I half-heartedly corrected his language. I noticed Tinker was fixated on the television, something that was out of the ordinary for him. He and Stagger were fixated on the news.

I turned toward the screen, and it was Danny O, this time a guest of FOX's split-screen. I wondered if Danny had a PR firm that he used for press releases to get this kind of coverage. Twice in the same day—senators would envy that media response.

"I repeat, it is NOT true to Antifa philosophies or principles to commit violent acts without provocation, unless in self-defense or when it is deemed necessary to prevent fascist and fascist-like activities. You can try to put whatever words in my mouth that you want, but that is the truth," he said. Once again, he was shrouded in a camera shadow to hide his identity.

"Has the order gone out through the Antifa factions to be on heightened alert to meet with right-wing demonstrations?" the FOX talking head said. It was a stupid question.

"You're an idiot," Danny said. "There is no organized Antifa network. It is a way of thinking, not a mafia-type hierarchy, and no matter how many times that is said or how it is said, it doesn't seem to matter. These recent domestic terror events are not consistent with those philosophies."

"Are you aware of today's advisory from the National Terrorism Advisory System advising citizens to a heightened threat to faith-based organizations that oppose the pro-choice movements? Is this something your group is set to act on?" he said. That was the first time I heard of that advisory. They issue something almost every day.

"Uh, no. That's ridiculous. Though we support a woman's right to her body and would be philosophically opposed to anything that restricts that, this advisory is nothing more than an attempt to vilify what we are about," Danny said.

Anti-pro-choice. That was a new one. It wasn't in any of the Antifa research. On the other hand, there was evidence that anti-abortion extremists were part of the group that stormed the Capitol. Nothing was making any sense.

"Fucking snowflake probably lives in his mommy's basement," Stagger contributed.

I didn't have the energy to address it.

Thankfully, a blizzard in Colorado caused massive gridlock on the highways, and the FOX weather team was analyzing how much more snowfall the Rockies were likely to get in the coming days. Snow in November in the Rocky Mountains was evidently more newsworthy than I suspected. After that, there was coverage on a similar gridlock in the House and Senate over an aid package to the oil industry, and then the attention shifted to nuclear energy and the closing of New York's Indian Point and the ripple effect that closing would cause.

I yearned for a discussion of whether LeBron was the GOAT.

Then, abruptly, the rhythm of the news halted. The "Special Report" slide flashed. There was a helicopter view of a building, and the anchor was trying to take in information from his earpiece and translate it to the television audience.

We have just gotten word that a group has invaded a school in upstate New York. We are getting word that St Teresa's in Albany, New York, a K through eight Catholic school, has been taken over by a group dressed in black. The situation is unfolding as we speak. Speculation is that this might be consistent with the advisory issued earlier today about anti-pro-choice targets…

I just starred at the television.

CHAPTER THIRTY-NINE

Molly, Kayla, and Rocky were at St. Teresa's.

"Holy fuckin shit..." Stagger said. Tinker put a hand on his arm.

I called for Gus to take over. I headed through the kitchen and up the back stairs to get my gun. I didn't feel real. I didn't feel in touch. My thoughts raced, and I did my best to focus. I checked to see if the gun was loaded, and I opened the cylinder to see that I had four shots left.

I ran down the stairs as fast as I could and shouldered my way out the kitchen door to get the Cadillac.

Tinker was waiting for me.

"Tracy—"

"Tinker, get out of my way."

"Tracy—"

"Get the fuck out of my way!"

He blocked my way into the driver's door.

"You got a plan?" He was amazingly calm. "Law enforcement will have the place surrounded. You won't be able to get in even if you're stupid enough to try."

"I'm getting my sister, Rocky, and Kayla. That's my plan."

He put a hand gently on my chest.

"There's at least a half a dozen of them. They're pros. Paid soldiers. You're a shrink for fuck sake."

"I can't let it happen."

"Let law enforcement do it. They will be on it."

"Tinker, this is about me. They can't kill me because I know shit. I notified them yesterday. If I die, everything comes out. They're sending me a message to show what they're willing to do. They've gone after the people I care about the most, and they're doing it at a Catholic school. Just like Danny said."

"Danny a friend of yours or something?" Tinker gave me his look.

"Part of the research. He hasn't lied about anything yet."

I pushed him out of the way and headed to St. Teresa's.

It was less than a ten-minute drive, but I didn't want it to take that long. I cruised through lights and stop signs, doing my best to not end up in a crash but not wasting any time.

Tinker was right, of course. I had no business doing what I was about to do. My whole life, I had a bias toward acting before thinking, and when emotions ran high, that bias multiplied. I had to act. I simply had to. There was no way I could physically restrain myself.

I had spent years at St. Teresa's. I went to school there through eighth grade, played basketball after school, and did all the school kid stuff. Even in high school, there was pick-up hoop and meetings, so I knew the building better than any other building in my life. I knew the place, and I knew it well.

It was shaped like most middle schools built in the early sixties. There were offices when you came through the front door, a long corridor that turned off in two directions completing the T shape. Unfortunately, I knew Molly's class was all the way at the end of the building's right branch. That meant going through the entire building to get there.

I pulled into the parking lot, and Tinker was right. The media was all over the place, and there were at least 20 uniformed cops. The white van was parked in front of the principal's office. No way was I going in the front door.

But I was going in.

I drove back out to the street and around the block. I cut through the same yard and hopped the same fence my friends and I used to as a shortcut home from school at dismissal every day. I ran to the spot in short right field, and there it was just as I remembered it. It was the size of a manhole cover, and it looked like I always remembered it, except it had a Master Lock on it.

I pulled out my gun—Tinker's gun—like I knew what I was doing. I shielded my eyes, shot the shackle of the lock, and it broke open. The lid wasn't as heavy as I remembered, and I crawled down the short ladder. I turned on the flashlight on my iPhone and ran as fast as I could to the school entrance. The door at the end of the tunnel wouldn't budge, so I shot into the frame and it broke open.

I ran into the janitor's closet and out to the hallway by what used to be the cafeteria. I got into my best Danny Regan/Donnie Wahlberg gun pose, looked both ways, and ran down the main corridor to get to the T to make the right to my sister's room. The classroom doors were all shut, and it was clear that a "lockdown" had been called. One of those ridiculous drills that they put kids through once a month. Except now, they didn't seem so absurd.

I made the right, and there they were. Dressed in black, holding what had to be automatic weapons, each wearing body armor. There were three outside the door. I had no idea what I was doing, but in my rage, my panic, my lack of thought, kept me running toward them.

The first one turned. Steadied his weapon and called for me to halt. The other two aimed their guns at me. Reality hit me across the face, and I stopped.

A fourth came out of the classroom, a handgun at his side.

"Right there, right there!" he commanded.

He motioned to the others to stand down. They lowered their weapons.

"Drop the gun, Curran." He said. He was calm.

I held on to the gun. I held on to it way longer than I should have.

"Drop it." He said with an uptick of intensity.

I did as he said.

"Smart man," he said.

"Fuck you," I said. It was all I had.

"You should see this," he pointed into the room and motioned with the gun.

I walked slowly into the classroom.

In the corner, Kayla and Molly were bound to chairs, gagged with white cloths, and they had been crying. Their eyes lit up, and they screamed through their gags.

Outside the tall classroom windows were two more in the same garb holding weapons.

I looked into the eyes of the man who held the gun. The lower part of his face was covered, and he wore a plain baseball hat. I examined his eyes for familiarity.

"Why? Why them?" I said, almost demanded.

"Because you made it very difficult to kill you, frankly. You covered all those bases very, very well. We had to let you know the stakes. There's your sister, your girlfriend, and your dog—who, by the way, wouldn't shut up. After this, there's a mom and anyone else we can use to make you understand the seriousness of the situation. So, you'll get to feel some pain and the understanding that there's plenty more to come. You need to understand."

I could feel my heart pound.

"Where's Rocky?" I said.

He smirked, then laughed.

Something inside of me went bad.

I hit him with a left hand right at the point of the chin. It was a fast punch that I brought up from my waist, and I turned on it with all I had. He went down, and the three behind me aimed at me and looked at their fallen leader for the command. I knew what was about to come, and I was as good as dead.

And then all chaos reigned down.

CHAPTER FORTY

First, something exploded through the window, shattering the glass into thousands of pieces. An instant after that, a blinding flash of light seemed to bombard the room with a deafening series of bangs that knocked me off my feet.

I crawled along the linoleum, feeling my way through the smoke, unable to hear anything. I scurried on my belly, reaching for anything. I found a leg and could hear a faint cry and knew I had Kayla or my sister. I rose, pulled the two of them together, and instinctually covered them with as much of my body as I could.

"Now!" I heard a command come from outside.

An instant later, another series of glass crashing, ricocheting explosions, and falling glass blew into the room. It might have lasted 10 seconds or it might have lasted 30 seconds, but it was a storm of hell and death.

Then it was quiet.

The smoke in the room was wafting around us. Below me, I felt for my sister and my girlfriend. They were there. I rolled off them.

I prayed with everything I had that they were breathing.

I reached for the first body's gag and awkwardly pulled it down.

"Oh God, Oh my God..." It was Molly. She shrieked and

continued to cry an awful primal sound.

I reached for the other body and felt her move. I pulled the gag down, and Kayla just whimpered. She was traumatized, but she was okay. I did my best to unbind them.

In seconds, I looked around the room.

They were dead. They were all dead.

Their equipment was splayed out in front of them. They were in pools of blood, and they were dead.

I coughed hard as I stood. I looked out from where the windows had stood.

Three more dead bodies in the schoolyard.

My ears were ringing. Sound was coming back. I heard a high pitch cry and a scratch-scratch against the classroom closet door. I said a prayer as I ran to it.

I threw open the door, and Rocky jumped into my arms.

CHAPTER FORTY-ONE

Rocky seemed unharmed. Shook, scared, but unharmed.

In seconds, the sound of sirens was everywhere, and in minutes the room filled with law enforcement. Albany PD, guys in riot gear, state police, and soon after that, FBI, probably marshals. I couldn't keep track of it.

My ears were ringing, and my throat scratched from the smoke. By now, all of the students had been evacuated into the schoolyard. I couldn't even imagine being a parent.

"What the fuck were you thinking!" I recognized detective Tony Crespo come through the smoke and chaos.

"I don't think thinking had much to do about it," I said. "Tony, has anyone checked on my mom?"

"Yeah, she's fine. There're two cops in front of her house. She knows you're fine, and everyone's fine," he said.

Tony took a deep breath and exhaled slowly. He looked around, then back at me. He shook his head.

"Are you out of your fucking mind?"

"Probably. A lot of people seem to think so." I looked right at him. "Tony, why did the guys outside turn on the others. The two guys outside, why did they start shooting out the windows and firing on their own men?" I asked.

He looked at me without saying anything.

"What?" I said. His silence was making me uncomfortable.

He waited and then finally spoke.

"The guys outside with the automatic weapons? They're dead. Shot in the back of the head, both of them. They never saw it coming."

He just looked at me.

"What do you know about that?" There was just a slight hint of suspicion.

"Not a damn thing." I tried to think. "Who the hell…"

"That's what I'd like to know," Crespo said.

I stayed quiet. I had to ask, but it was hard to bring myself to do it. I made myself.

"Tony, uh, any kids?"

He shook his head.

"Not a single one. Not a teacher, not a cafeteria worker, not a janitor."

I felt tears pour down my face.

"Not sure how only the bad guys got killed but every now and then, I think God is looking over us."

"Amen," I said and said a quick thank-you prayer.

He got called over to a huddle of four men. Two had FBI jackets, and two were in street clothes with vests. They conferred for a moment or two, and then Tony came back.

"C'mere," he said.

I walked over to the circle they had formed. The body of one of the terrorists was behind them. It was the guy I punched. Tony knelt in front of the body, and half rolled him over. He had taken a shot to the top of his head, and there was part of it missing, but his face was intact.

Tony pulled down the mask.

"You recognize this guy?" he said. I could feel the other four look at me.

"Yeah, yeah, I do. He sat next to me on my flight to DC last week." It was the turtle neck guy with the broken nose.

"That was one of the guys following me." Kayla had come up behind me.

"I suspect his name is Elliot Stanley. He was the guy following your girl." Tony Crespo chimed in.

"Holy shit..." Things were moving fast, and the puzzle was coming together,

"Yeah..." Tony said and smirked.

One of the guys with the FBI jackets spoke up. He walked toward me, holding an iPhone.

"You recognize any of these numbers?" He had the recent call log opened. None had names attached. The first one on the list didn't need a name.

"Yeah, yeah, I do," I said.

The agent just looked at me.

"That first one belongs to my old boss. Dr. Lin Williams."

CHAPTER FORTY-TWO

The smoke began to clear. After they saw Dr. Williams's phone number, there was a flurry of activity. Agents leaving the room, agents coming into the room, huddles with various law enforcement, and the questioning. A lot of questioning.

Several different agents, cops, officers, detectives, whatever, talked to me. They interviewed Molly and Kayla. A couple of them even patted Rocky on the head. He hadn't left my side, and a couple of times, I heard low guttural growlings depending on my visitor questioner.

Tony Crespo kept checking on me.

"Still keepin' to the story about not being a big deal spy-type?" he asked with a smile.

I told him what I had found out, the conclusions I had reached, and whom I had shared them with.

He nodded quietly. He gave the whole idea some thought.

"So, this," he turned and looked at everything. "Was to get you. Your sister, your new girlfriend, and Rocky there—the things you cared about. They couldn't kill you, but they could kill them and let you know what you were up against."

I shrugged.

It was good as any other theory.

"And the guys outside. Shot with automatic weapons, probably from a distance. Headshots, efficient kill shots. Any idea about that? St Teresa's got a varsity rifle team?"

"It wasn't any law enforcement? There's enough of you guys around."

"Trust me," he smirked again. "Someone would take credit for it."

He looked at me just a little longer than usual.

"Hey, Tony. Can I go? I think Mom would probably like to see me. That, and I need a drink."

Tony checked with three or four guys.

"Yeah, kid, you can go. They want me to tell you not to leave town or anything."

"Yeah, try and stop me," I said. Tony laughed at that.

"You got the old man's Caddy? Let me call ahead, so the uniforms guarding mom don't greet you with too much, uh, enthusiasm."

I checked in with Kayla, who gave me a long hug. She promised that she was okay and said that I should go see my mother.

I headed over to the house I grew up in. I didn't drive quite as fast as my last ride in the Cadillac, but I didn't waste any time either. When I pulled into mom's driveway, the cops parked in front of the car got out.

They stopped Rocky and me before I went in to see mom. I showed ID to prove who I was, then they apologized.

"No need to apologize," I said. "Thank you for taking care of Mom."

They both nodded.

We headed up the steps to the porch when the older cop, a thirty-something black guy I'd seen at the bar once or twice, called to me.

"Hey, Trace!" he yelled. I turned to look at him. "Nice job."

I smiled and thanked him.

Mom threw open the door and ran into my arms. She had been crying for what looked like a long time.

"Mom, Mom, Mom…" I started to cry too.

"Tracy, I can't lose you. My God…" she held on tighter.

"Oh my God..."

Rocky jumped up and had a front paw on each of us. He was whimpering.

"Mom, Mom...I'm fine." I just held her. "Molly's fine. Kayla's fine. The bad guys are dead."

I held her for what seemed like a long time. Rocky sat and continued to whine.

"If we don't feed the beast, we'll be in real trouble," I said.

Mom finally laughed through the tears. She motioned us inside, filled Rocky's bowl, and asked me if I wanted a coffee.

"Mom, I could use a Slane," I said. She poured two. Neat.

"Tracy, I don't know what you did...but..." She started to cry again.

She had tears in her eyes, but she was smiling.

"I'll tell you what it was, and this is the truth. The leader had a gun in his hand, and there were two others with automatic-style machine guns. The leader had his gun at his side. I saw Molly and Kayla, and I knew I had to think and be careful."

Rocky was gulping down his food, and I had to speak up so Mom could hear me over his slobbering.

"Then the bastard said Rocky was making too much noise, and he had to take care of him. I lost it. It was stupid, but I flat out lost it. I drilled the guy in the jaw. I knocked him out cold. 'Cause of him" I pointed at Rocky with my rocks glass.

"I'll never tell you to stop boxing again." She sipped the whiskey.

"Then all hell broke loose..." I went on to tell her what happened and how only the bad guys got hurt. I told her it didn't make any sense.

The front door opened, and Molly came in. She had a beer in her hand.

"Don't think I'm cutting you any slack from now on because you saved my life and shit," Mom laughed at that. Molly hugged me, and Rocky jumped up on her. "If it wasn't for the Rockstar..." she didn't finish.

"So, I heard," mom said.

"That and my brother's anger management issues." She got up and got the Slane and a glass. She topped off our drinks and poured herself four fingers. "Here's to my favorite shithead."

We laughed for a while, a long while.

Deep inside, I knew this was going to take a whole lot of time to process. There was also a hint of satisfaction.

Just a hint.

We talked about it. We thanked God. We talked about how lucky we were. We talked about Dad and what he'd have to say about it. Mom told me he'd be proud.

That resonated.

After a couple of hours, Molly left for her apartment. Before leaving, she told me to call Kayla sooner rather than later. I promised.

Mom left the room for a moment and came back with an envelope.

"You take this with you. Open it up when you're alone."

I gave her a confused look.

"You heard me. Now go on home. Call that girl of yours."

CHAPTER FORTY-THREE

It had gotten dark. I was exhausted, and I had no idea what to do. All my psychology training left out directions about what to do on the evening of an afternoon mass killing. On my apartment door was a note from Kayla.

I'm at the bar with Tinker, K.

My new girl's new friendship with Tinker made me smile.

I went in to take a quick shower and change. I needed to get the smell of smoke, fire, and whatever out of me. Before that, I opened Mom's letter. It was a plain business size envelope, and inside it was a slightly smaller envelope.

It was formal stationery. The return address read:

General Daniel Szabo
Defense Intelligence Agency

The envelope was unsealed, and I unfolded the letter. It, too, was on the General's formal stationery. There was a yellow stickie on the letter in Mom's handwriting.

You asked about your father…

I began to read.

TOP SECRET
Dear Lieutenant Curran,

It has come to my attention through your commanding officer that you displayed remarkable courage, valor, and intelligence in recent events in which you put yourself in harm's way, with no concern for your own safety to save the lives of the men in your outfit and, particularly, soldiers in a most vulnerable position.

Your actions in uncovering a conspiracy within your outfit, following the situation through, and then intercepting a capture of men under your command demonstrated the highest commitment a soldier can make. It was noted that after identifying a conspiracy that would have endangered many men and the overall war effort, you pursued men who had been captured and held hostage. It was undoubtedly the plan of the kidnappers to execute American soldiers. Yet, you put your life in danger and, while outnumbered, rescued the men under your command, subdued the perpetrators, and single-handedly put them under arrest.

The men rescued, Corporal Edward Lee, Corporal Lawrence Tinker, Corporal Jeremy Berkshire, and Corporal Edward Graham, all owe their lives to you. You returned them safely and in good condition. Because of your assignment's nature, there will be no Silver Star awarded to you, but I am confident you are deserving. Let this memo show that your bravery, commitment, and selfless activity have been noted and recognized by myself, the Department of Defense Intelligence. The American people owe you a debt of gratitude.

It was signed by General Daniel Szabo.

I tried to let this sink in. The old man was involved in some sort of intelligence. He also uncovered some guys doing traitorous things, and he rescued some men held hostage.

I guess he wasn't just a bar owner.

I reread the names of the soldiers he saved. This was a little much to take in after today's events. Life doesn't always portion things out. You've got to deal with shit as it comes. It isn't always fair. I think I've learned that.

I decided to skip the shower. I headed down my stairs, through the kitchen, and into the bar. I carefully folded the letter in my back pocket.

I thought to myself, maybe Tinker and Stagger weren't full of shit and weren't crazy.

I gave it another thought.

Nah, they were still crazy.

Kayla jumped off her barstool at the sight of me and ran over to hug me. She held me as tight as my mother did. Over her shoulder, I could see Tinker had a broad smile.

"Well, well, well...I heard you had a busy day today, Tracy," he said.

"Yeah, something like that." I hadn't let go of Kayla yet. She was holding on so tight it was hard to breathe. I wasn't complaining. I could feel her crying. Meanwhile, Tinker kept up his one-sided conversation going.

"Your old man would be proud of you."

"Yeah, maybe," I said. I let that sink in. After reading the letter, it took on a different meaning.

"Tracy, This is some special girl you got here. I guess I might run into a burning building to save her too."

"Oh, you've been watching the news, huh?" I said. I realized it was a bit of an understatement.

"Hard to miss, my friend," Tinker said.

Kayla let go of me and kissed me on the lips.

"*Thank you* seems a tad inadequate," She said, looking me in the eyes.

"Yeah, kinda," I said. She punched me in the arm.

We took the seats next to Tinker. Maureen put a drink in front of me. She gave me a big smile. I had to ask Tinker something.

“Hey, Tinker. I got an odd question for you.” I sipped the Boomsauce Maureen placed in front of me. “Is your first name Lawrence?”

Tinker gave me a long look. Our eyes met, and it took him a couple of beats to respond. “Yeah. I used to go by Larry, but after a certain time in my life, I just became Tinker.”

“Yeah. Yeah, I get it,” I said. I knew he was suspicious, but I didn’t want to make a thing out of it. “Hey, Maureen. I don’t mean to be a pain, but I feel like drinking Schafer tonight. And can you set the three of us up with a Jim Beam?”

Maureen gave me a funny look but did as I requested. I felt Kayla’s hand on my shoulder. I looked over at her and smiled.

“Thank you,” she said again and smiled.

I smiled back at her.

“You’re welcome.” For some reason, she giggled.

“Tracy, I think it’s gonna take me a while to process this.”

I looked at her.

“You think?”

We had a little bit of a laugh at that. She called me “Tracy.” It felt good. Any concern about having an awkward intimate moment at Curran’s was interrupted when Stagger came through the front door.

“Stagger!” Tinker yelled without looking at him.

Stagger walked past Kayla and me, clapped us both on the back, and gave Tinker a fist bump. Right away, I noticed something. I couldn’t put my finger on it—something connected in my subconscious.

I decided to ask Stagger the same question I asked Tinker.

“Stags, I got an odd one for you. I realized today I don’t know you and Tinker’s full names. I learned Tinker is a Larry. What’s your first name?”

Stagger looked at me.

“I don’t tell people my real name.” Because it was Stagger, I couldn’t tell if he was serious, but I didn’t pursue it. Instead, I asked Maureen to set up Stagger with a Schaefer and a bourbon on me.

He smiled and came over to toast Kayla and me.

"Here's to good times," he said. "Oh, and nice work today." He gave me a big smile, and we touched glasses.

"You watch the news, huh?" I said.

"Yup. FOX." He said, emphasizing the "FOX."

I noticed something again. This time I could identify it. I motioned Kayla closer, and I whispered to her.

"Hey Kayla. Smell my shirt," I said.

She gave me a funny look.

"Oh, now you're gonna start getting kinky with me. Just because you saved my life—"

"No, seriously. Smell my shirt."

She took a big sniff. Let it register and looked at me.

"You smell like smoke, like the stuff from this afternoon."

"Yeah, that's what I thought. Do me a favor. Go over and make conversation with Stagger. Give him a sniff."

She tilted her head, looking kind of confused, but she went over to Stagger, kissed him on the cheek, and toasted him again. Stagger kissed her on the cheek, and they giggled. She came back, and I looked at her.

"Yeah. He smells like smoke." I look directly at her.

"Does it smell just like my smoke?"

Her jaw went slack.

"You mean..."

"It would be a funny coincidence, wouldn't it be?" I said. It started to sink in. Kayla looked like she had seen a ghost.

"The two of them? Today? How?"

I put my finger to my lips to silence her. Her eyes went wide. I guessed Tinker had the sense to go home and shower first. Stagger? Sense? I didn't assume anything.

I asked Maureen to set us all up with another round. I quietly let her know that I would pick up Tinker and Stagger's tab for the rest of the night. I gave Kayla a nod to tell her I wanted to go. I stood up with my glass again.

"Folks. Here's to friends you can count on." I looked directly at Tinker and Stagger. "And thank you."

Tinker and Stagger looked at each other. Tinker smirked. They both shared a laugh. I told them we were going to head out and that Kayla and I had some talking to do. Before I left, Tinker turned and looked at me.

"Hey, Tracy, I'll say it again. Your dad would be very proud of you." I gave him a nod, and we headed out.

CHAPTER FORTY-FOUR

We headed upstairs to my apartment. We passed Gus in the kitchen on the way.

"There he is! The hero!" Gus raised his fist. I smiled back, and kind of waved off the hero stuff. "Nice going, my man!" he shouted.

Kayla and I headed up the steps.

I got a couple of beers, and we threw ourselves on the couch.

"So, you're not going to come out and ask them?" she said.

"Nah, they won't admit it anyway," I said. Kayla was leaning into me, and I had my arm around her.

"And they're capable of, of...that?"

"They were military. They were in intelligence. They're gun nuts. Probably have all the crazy shit they needed. Probably not a single way to trace any of it."

She scrunched up her face.

"And they'd do it for you?"

I reached into my pocket and showed her the letter my mom gave me.

Kayla read it. She handed it back to me and took a second or two to think.

"Edward Lee & Lawrence Tinker...Your dad saved their lives." She looked at me. "Today was paying back a favor."

"Pretty big one, too," I said.

"Life doesn't give you that opportunity often," she said quietly.

She was right.

We were like that for a long time. Kayla broke the silence.

"Why did your boss do it?"

"I don't know if I have the answers." I gave it some thought. "Maybe greed, maybe power. Maybe it was about payback to Antifa for the loss of her college partner. Maybe it was not getting the CIA job. Maybe it was about getting abandoned by her GI father in Cambodia...I don't know."

"Some fancy psychology there," Kayla said.

"For whatever that's worth," I said.

Kayla, Rocky, and I were strolling down Champlain Avenue in Burlington, looking at the hipsters and occasionally going into a boutique or antique shop. Vermont was so woke that they didn't think twice about allowing a canine brother access, and Rocky loved all the attention he received. The shopping was okay, the hand-in-hand strolling even better, but I really liked it when we stopped for a craft brew at a place called "Champs." It was named after the Loch Ness-style monster believed to inhabit Lake Champlain.

Vermont was home to Boomsauce, and they didn't have any Schaefer stocked. The pint came with a perfect amount of head and a tv commercial-worthy condensation rolling down the side of the glass.

My phone rang. I recognized the area code. It sent a chill through me.

"Trace, it is Dr. Purcell at the agency."

My throat went dry.

"Yes, Doctor?"

"We, of course, know of the events from last week. I wanted to tell you personally that the six involved are in custody. There will be little, if any, media involved. It will be kept confidential, as you might guess. I wanted to thank you for what you did.

Words aren't enough but—"

"That's fine, Doctor. I appreciate the call."

He paused.

"Trace, uh..." I could sense him searching for words.

"Yes?"

It took him a while to say anything. Finally, he did.

"Would you consider coming back?"

I wasn't sure I heard what he had to say correctly. I didn't respond.

"Trace? Are you there?"

"Yes, yes I am."

"You don't have to tell me now. Please give it some thought."

We bumbled through some more conversation and eventually agreed to talk again soon.

I hung up and stared straight ahead.

"Is everything okay?" Kayla asked. She was petting Rocky's head with her right hand.

"They want me at the CIA," I said.

Kayla looked at me for a long moment.

"Do you want that?" she said.

I shrugged. She leaned over and kissed me.

"What do you want, Dr. Curran?" she smiled.

"I think I have just about everything I want right here, right now" I kissed her back.

"...only just about?" she said and gave me a coy look.

"Well, there's one thing..."

"And what would that be?"

"I'd like to get you in the ring one more time."

TOM SCHRECK is the author of Amazon's #1 hard-boiled mystery, *The Vegas Knockout*. He counts Robert B. Parker, John D. MacDonald, JA Konrath, Reed Farrel Coleman, Ken Bruen and Michael Connelly among his favorite crime fiction authors and his Duffy Dombrowski series has been referred to as "As good or better as the early Spenser." He is a columnist with Westchester Magazine and a frequent contributor to Crimespree Magazine, Referee, and other publications.

DOWN & OUT
BOOKS

More Groovy Gumshoes
Private Eyes in the Psychedelic Sixties
Michael Bracken, Editor

Down & Out Books
April 2023
978-1-64396-306-8

The Sixties were a time of great cultural upheaval, when long-established social norms were challenged and everything changed: from music to fashion to social mores. And the *Leave It to Beaver* households in Middle America didn't know what to make of it all.

From old-school private eyes with their flat-tops, off-the-rack suits, and well-worn brogues to the new breed of private eyes with their shoulder-length hair, bell-bottoms, and hemp sandals, the shamuses in *More Groovy Gumshoes*—a follow-up to the far-out original *Groovy Gumshoes*—take readers on another rollicking romp through the Sixties.

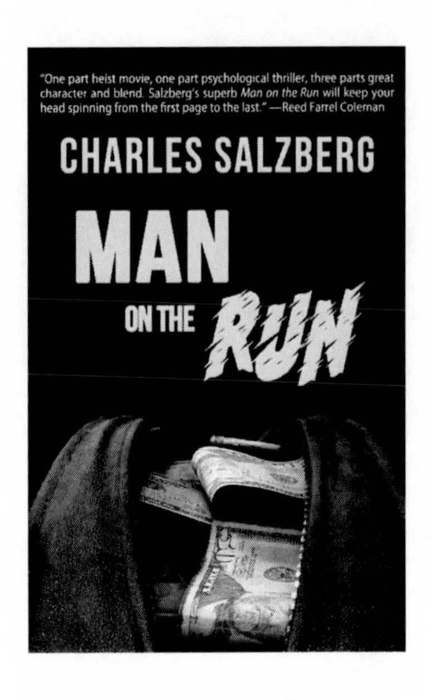

Man on the Run
Charles Salzberg

Down & Out Books
April 2023
978-1-64396-309-9

Master burglar Francis Hoyt is on the run. After walking away from his arraignment in a Connecticut courtroom, he's now a fugitive who has to figure out what he's going to do with the rest of his life.

And so, he heads west, to Los Angeles, where he meets Dakota, a young true crime podcaster who happens to be doing a series on Hoyt. At the same time, he's approached by a mysterious attorney who makes Hoyt an offer he can't refuse: break into a "mob bank," and liberate the contents.

Double Exposure
A Grant & McNulty Thriller
Colin Campbell

Down & Out Books
April 2023
978-1-64396-309-9

Titanic Productions is filming on a movie ranch near Los Angeles when Jim Grant pays a visit. A drug cartel that both Grant and McNulty have crossed paths with has tried to kill Grant's brother in Shelter Cove and is now after McNulty's sister. And her daughter. After a shootout at Nantasket Peninsula, Grant and McNulty decide to take the fight to the cartel. Their tactics include a pizza truck, a prison break and the FBI. And one last chance to print the legend.

"No one writes better action sequences than Campbell." —Dana King, author of the Penns River and Shamus-nominated Nick Forte novels

Splintered Loyalty
An Ava Rome Mystery
Mark Troy

Down & Out Books
May 2023
978-1-64396-311-2

A World War II cold case and a domestic violence case combine to pit Honolulu private eye Ava Rome in a dangerous struggle against a powerful, violent organization that wants the past to remain secret.

Ava's quest takes her to the remains of the Tule Lake internment camp on a dangerous mission to find the killer of a Buddhist priest and a Japanese-American teenager.

"Ava Rome, is tough, talented and tenacious and riveting to watch! Bravo!" —Matt Coyle, author of the Shamus, Anthony and Lefty Award-winning Rick Cahill crime series

Made in United States
North Haven, CT
25 May 2023